But as it is written, Eye hath not seen, nor ear heard,
neither have entered into the heart of man, the things
which God hath prepared for them that love him.

—1 CORINTHIANS 2: 9 (KJV)

Love's a Mystery

LOVE'S A MYSTERY

in

LAST
CHANCE
IA

PATRICIA JOHNS &
SANDRA ORCHARD

Guideposts

Love's a Mystery is a trademark of Guideposts.

Published by Guideposts
100 Reserve Road, Suite E200
Danbury, CT 06810
Guideposts.org

Cover and interior design by Müllerhaus
Cover illustration by Dan Burr at Illustration Online LLC.
Typeset by Aptara, Inc.

ISBN 978-1-961441-50-7 (hardcover)
ISBN 978-1-961441-51-4 (softcover)
ISBN 978-1-959634-05-8 (epub)

Printed and bound in the United States of America

Love's Vow

by

Patricia Johns

Single women have a dreadful propensity for being poor—which is one very strong argument in favour of matrimony.

—JANE AUSTEN, IN A LETTER TO FANNY KNIGHT,
13 MARCH 1817

CHAPTER ONE

Last Chance, Iowa
May 1905

Last Chance's only church smelled comfortingly of polish, dust, and the faint pine scent of some towering trees outside. There were only a few guests, this not being a big, fancy wedding. There would be no wedding lunch, and only a few of the faithful from the congregation had come to witness the event. Anne York sucked in a breath, her chest rising above her corset. She tried her best to keep her mother's advice to not lock her knees lest she faint away in the middle of the service. There would be nothing quite so undignified as crumpling into a heap at Reverend Bogg's feet.

"Dearly beloved, we are gathered here together to witness the union of this man and this woman in holy matrimony...," the reverend intoned.

Anne wore her best sheer cotton shirtwaist and light blue linen skirt. Her finely woven straw hat was a little too broad to be fashionable this year, but she'd trimmed it with some new turkey feathers, a brand-new piece of cream-colored ribbon, and a bit of lace that she'd bought at Wheaton's Millinery Shop where she worked three afternoons a week. It had cost her two days' pay, even with the discount Mr. Wheaton gave her on account of her being a hardworking employee, but it was worth the expense. She'd done her best on short notice for her wedding day.

Benjamin Huntington stood opposite her, his dark beard neatly trimmed and his slate-gray gaze locked on the ground a few inches from Anne's black leather boots. She wished he would look up, reassure her somehow, but he didn't. His expression remained solemn, and he stood with his broad, calloused hands folded in front of him.

This man would be her husband. Benjamin, the father of a five-year-old daughter who needed a mother. He had broad shoulders and the strong hands of a man who did physical work. And yet he looked refined too, for a woodworker.

That was one thing she liked about him. He'd moved to Last Chance a little over a year ago, and he'd set up shop right away. His work spoke for itself, and word spread. He made everything from furniture to wood paneling for a couple of wealthier patrons. With the railroad so close, he could ship his work all the way to Des Moines, if he could get the customers.

He had explained all of that when he proposed. At first, Anne thought he was offering her a job—maybe as his secretary. But no, he suggested something more permanent, and Anne's parents were already on board with the idea. Besides, Anne had been helping her mother care for Molly the last few months, and she'd grown fond of the girl. She was sweet, polite, well-mannered, and truly eager to please. With her little rosebud mouth and her dark glossy hair that curled on its own, she would grow into a beauty one day too.

"Therefore, if any man can shew any just cause why they may not lawfully be joined together, let him now speak or else hereafter forever hold his peace." Reverend Bogg paused and looked up.

The scent of talcum powder and lavender water lingered in the silence among the dancing dust motes that shone in the rays of sunlight slanting down through bright stained glass. The church was furnished with row upon row of fine wooden pews, all polished to a glow and smelling faintly of lemon. The reverend's wife, Eleanor, polished those pews herself every Monday morning to give the wood time to absorb the waxy substance lest it rub off on the back of a man's trousers or a lady's Sunday-best dress during the Wednesday evening prayer service. This being Tuesday, there was a small risk taken in sitting on those pews, and Anne's mother had brought handkerchiefs for her and Anne's father to put beneath them, just to be on the safe side.

"Who gives this woman?" Reverend Bogg lifted his head from the worn, leather-bound book of common prayer and looked expectantly toward the front pew.

Anne's mother, dressed in a long, gray, puff-sleeved dress with a spattering of lace over her chest that spoke of an earlier time, hooked a gloved hand under her husband's arm and helped him rise a few inches off the seat.

"I do," Father said, his voice quavering. The words slurred past the sagging side of his mouth. Then he slid back down into the pew. The apoplexy had ravaged her father, and Anne looked at him with a wash of love.

Her father might be the one giving her to Ben in marriage, but he was also the reason she'd agreed to this hasty union to begin with. He needed someone to care for him in his declining state, and she didn't have the means without a husband.

The sound of a distant clanging rang softly through the air, and the reverend frowned slightly. The old ladies murmured and looked toward the windows, even though they couldn't see past the colored glass.

"Benjamin, repeat after me," Reverend Bogg said, turning to Benjamin.

Benjamin took a gold ring from the minister's hand. This would be the ring she wore for the rest of her life. Her stomach fluttered nervously at the thought. A marriage either made or broke a woman, and she could only pray that this hasty choice was the right one.

The wedding service continued. They repeated their vows—until death did they part—and they exchanged rings and plighted their troth. All the while, the clanging bell from town grew louder. Anne's gaze flickered toward the doors of the church. It sounded like a fire alarm. Fires did happen from time to time, the town consisting entirely of wooden structures, and that, combined with pipe smoking, cooking stoves, and inebriated farmers come to town, resulted in some tragic fires. The sound of the insistent bell was enough to tighten every one of her nerves. If only it would stop—the sign of a false alarm.

If a rainy day was considered good fortune for a wedding—a sign of showers of blessings to come—then what did a fire alarm mean?

But the wedding plunged forward, and Reverend Bogg read the final section of the service, his voice sonorous and echoing through the high-raftered building. "Those whom God hath joined together, let no man put asunder. Let us pray."

That was it. The ceremony was done. She and Benjamin Huntington were legally wed. Anne bowed her head, trying to focus on the reverend's words, but her heart had a prayer of its own today.

God, give us happiness. Please, give us happiness. Bless this marriage, and show us how to love each other truly.

Because right now, all Anne really knew of her new husband was that he was a talented woodworker, he was a widower, and he had a five-year-old daughter in need of a mother. She knew that Ben could afford to help her parents where she could not and that other single young women in this congregation would have jumped at this opportunity to become Mrs. Huntington. But they were not Benjamin's choice. Anne was, and her heart pattered at the thought. Ben was strong, handsome, and solemn, and she'd developed some hopeful feelings for him over the last year of helping care for his daughter. But what did he feel for her, beyond gratitude that he'd have a stepmother for Molly?

She wasn't sure. Benjamin Huntington was the beginning of a whole new life…and a mystery.

Ben lifted his head as the reverend's prayer ended, and he met Anne's gaze for the first time as her husband. One thing he'd learned in his eventful life thus far was that a man needed to appear calmer than he felt—always—but looking into Anne's brown eyes, he felt a wave of uncertainty.

He'd been focused on getting to this point, the wedding, but now it was over. They were married, and he'd have to bring his new wife home and start life as a married man all over again.

What was Anne expecting? He wished he knew. The only thing he was certain of was that she didn't love him. Not yet. He was halfway in love with her from the start, watching her so kindly care for his little girl. But she hardly knew him, and he wouldn't push that.

The thunder of hooves sounded outside, and the front door to the church swung inward and banged against the wall. Joss Musgrave stumbled inside, with no hat on his head and his white shirt smeared with dirt and soot.

"Fire!" Joss gasped. Everyone exclaimed and rose to their feet. "Ben—your shop! It's burning down!"

Ben's heart hammered to a stop. His woodworking shop—the business he'd poured his last few dollars into, and his very livelihood.

"Molly, stay with Anne!" Ben yelled, bolting for the open church doors.

"Mama, can you keep Molly with you?" Anne's voice echoed behind him. He didn't notice that she'd run after him until he got out to his own horse and buggy and she clambered into the seat next to him.

"This might be dangerous," he said. "You'll want to stay here."

"Nonsense." She turned forward and braced herself in the seat.

"I can't take you into danger, Anne! I only just married you!"

Did he need another family blaming him for something outside of his control? Could his heart take losing another wife?

"And marry me, you did!" Anne retorted. "This is my future at stake too. Stop wasting time!"

Right. Her comfort was at stake as much as his. Ben opened his mouth to retort then shook his head and whipped the reins. He looked back only once as his buggy lurched forward. The few witnesses to the wedding had come running outside, shading their eyes and staring in the direction of town. His father-in-law, Thomas, was just now coming out the church door, leaning heavily on a cane and his wife at his side. Joss wiped his forehead with a handkerchief, talking animatedly to the pastor and his wife. Standing on the church steps, a little bit apart from everyone else, was Molly in her green cotton dress. She shaded her eyes against the bright spring sunlight, and he felt his heart tug.

Molly...his reason for all of this. The reason he'd seen more in Anne York and had begun to look closer.

"My mama will take care of her," Anne said, as if reading his mind.

Abigail York, who'd been caring for his daughter the last several months during the day while he worked, would be Molly's new grandmother. Molly would be safe. He was confident of that.

The horse sped up from a walk to a brisk trot just short of a gallop as they headed out of the church lot and down the gravel drive that led to the town of Last Chance. Of all the names for a place... But it had seemed oddly appropriate when Ben was choosing a new home to melt into and disappear with his daughter. This little town had felt like his last chance too.

Smoke hung in the air as they rattled onto the main street. Wooden walkways lined both sides of the dirt road. Women with baskets on their arms, skirts swirling around their ankles, and men pushing their hats back as they tried to get a better look, all gawked in the same direction he was headed—toward his shop where the last year of hard work, dedication, acquired wood, purchased tools, and a small loan still owing on the place was going up in a billow of gray, choking smoke.

He passed the first intersection with Maynard's Drugstore on one side and Wheaton's Millinery on the other. Then there was Abner's Saddle and Tack, the feed and supply shop, Eaton Café, Saul's shoe repair shop...all his neighbors. The air was thick and heavy with the smell of smoke.

Ben's prayer was a short one—*God, save my shop!*

The fire bells clanged, and he glimpsed a traffic jam of two automobiles with drivers shouting at each other and a farm wagon with a pair of horses rearing up and pawing the air at the scent of smoke and the sound of the honking horns. The horses were going to bolt—even Ben could see that, but there was no help he could offer as he kept a firm hand on his own reins, holding his horse back. Just beyond the melee, Huntington Woodworking stood between a bakery and the street, a fire wagon parked in front of it and water pouring from hoses into shattered windows.

The horses pulling the farm wagon took off when one of the cars backed up, providing an opening, and the wagon clattered over a pothole, the driver seeming to hold on only by some miracle as the horses galloped down a side street. His shouts of "whoa!" faded, and the crowd's attention was now split between the runaway wagon and the fire. There was no possibility for Ben's buggy to get any closer, so he tied off his reins and jumped to the ground. He reached up to catch Anne around her small, corseted waist and lifted her to the ground. This was the closest he'd ever been to her, and his breath caught as her feet touched the dirt and her worried gaze met his.

But there was no time for anything more, and she brushed his hands away from her. Ben turned and led the way through the throng of neighbors, pushing his way to the front, where the volunteer firefighters pumped the last of their water into a broken window.

There were no flames left that Ben could see, and a wave of relief surged over him. He looked back over his shoulder and saw Anne struggling behind him, people blocking her path.

"Let my wife through!" he barked, and surprised men stepped aside to let Anne pass. Ben shot out a hand, caught her gloved fingers, and tugged her up next to him.

"Is the fire out?" he asked.

The volunteer firefighters were men Ben recognized. Henry Ager, both a deacon in the church and the postmaster, stood nearest him with a soot-smeared, sweaty face. Next to him stood the sheriff—Wyatt Miller—a tall man with a hooked beak of a nose and eyes that didn't miss much. He wore a cowboy hat and had a toothpick sticking out underneath his mustache.

"Ben," Henry said, "I'm sorry this happened, today of all days. You just got married, didn't you?"

"I did," Ben replied. Anne slipped her hand out of his grasp, and he exhaled a shaky breath. "What happened? I know I banked the fire. I double-checked."

"I think I know what happened," Sheriff Miller said. "I'll show you."

The big man led the way to the front door, and Ben pulled out a key. He unlocked the door, swung it open, and they all filed inside.

His dripping shop looked like it was only half burned—the wooden floors marred with black scorch marks and the legs of his worktable charred too. His precious store of cherry wood that he'd acquired for a special commission was burned beyond hope, and his heart sank. But his tools on the walls were untouched by the flames, although smoke had smudged the whitewashed walls and ceiling. His desk at the far side of the room with his locked filing cabinet and wooden swivel chair were unharmed.

"I saw this through the window," Sheriff Miller said, nudging a broken liquor bottle with his boot. There were three in total, lying across the floor with burn marks surrounding them. "You don't drink, do you?"

"Not a drop. Those aren't mine."

"It's an arson tactic," Henry said. "An oiled or tarred rag is shoved inside a half-filled liquor bottle with part of it hanging out. You light the rag on fire and throw the bottle through a window."

Ben's stomach tightened. "Who would do that to me?" He glanced over at Anne. She looked like she was going to be sick.

"Do you have any enemies?" Sheriff Miller asked.

"I don't think so."

Except there were a few men who might not like him. Was there an actual enemy who would try to burn down his shop and his home over mild dislike?

"Wyatt would know more than me," Henry said. "I see fires, though, and one thing occurred to me."

"Oh?" Ben met the other man's gaze.

"We all agree that this fire was deliberately set, and whoever did it waited until they were sure you would be gone." Henry shrugged. "And what better assurance that you would be away than when you're getting married?"

Ben glanced at Anne again, his heart sinking. She looked so fresh and neat in the middle of this smoky mess. She stood with her feet together and one white gloved hand covering her throat as she surveyed the workshop. Just as she married him, someone tried to burn down his shop and their home. Anger simmered inside of him.

Whoever did this might very well be targeting him, but they were ruining Anne's future too.

Ben ran a hand through his hair, and he looked toward the staircase that led up to the bedrooms. He could thank God that it appeared to be unharmed, and at least there would be a safe place to sleep tonight. He headed past the workshop and looked into the kitchen beyond.

The kitchen was small, but functional, with a medium-sized woodstove, some counter space, white wooden cupboards, and a small table. Nothing was burned here, although the scent of smoke lingered. A second set of stairs, narrower than the first, ran to the upper floor so that the bedrooms could be accessed from the workroom or from the kitchen.

Ben returned to where Anne stood motionless.

"This could have been far worse," he said to Henry. "There is damage, yes, but I can clean this up. The kitchen is unharmed. If you and the fire brigade had not gotten here when you did, we might have lost everything."

"God is merciful," Henry replied. "I'll go gather up some wood to nail over your broken windows for today, at least."

"Thank you," Ben said, and he meant it.

"Think on who might have had reason to do this to you," Sheriff Miller said. "In my experience, this sort of thing is never random. Someone did it for their own reasons, and when we figure that out, we can press charges."

What would a man do without friends?

Ben watched as Anne plucked something off her skirt, leaving a black mark on her white glove. She looked down at the smudged fabric, tears welling in her eyes.

"I'm sorry, Anne," Ben said. He was sorry for all of this—that his promise to provide for her parents, for her, for her future, had all been threatened with someone's hatred. He did not know who had done this, who he'd offended so badly that they would stoop to this kind of violence.

"It's not your fault," she said, but he saw the look in her eye as she surveyed the room once more. She was deeply worried, and she had every right to be.

But today, of all days, he needed his wife to feel safe with him. And he could not blame her if she didn't.

CHAPTER TWO

Henry was true to his word, and neighbors brought wood to hammer over the two windows. When that was done, Ben walked around the outside of his shop, searching for any sort of clue as to who might have done this. Besides a tar tin lying next to the building, he did not see much that stood out as a clue. The rear of his shop opened onto a vacant lot, and he stood there looking over the clumps of tough grass, a few bottles tossed by vagrants, and some paper candy wrappers.

Beyond the lot was a house with a large yard and a wood-framed swing outside for ladies to enjoy. A chicken coop, a dog-house, and a generous garden were farther back on the property, and a wooden rail fence separated that yard from the scrub and debris of the vacant lot. The family who lived there consisted of the two Bertrand sisters, who'd commissioned him to make the cherry wood pulpit for the church. The curtains were all tightly shut over the windows that faced his shop.

Henry was right. Whoever did this had to wait until Ben was gone, or else they might have gotten caught. Besides that, the fire would have been extinguished much faster and done less damage if Ben had been there to snuff out the flames immediately. If the goal was to burn down his building, then Ben being away from home for an extended period was absolutely necessary. And whoever did this had chosen his wedding day. That cruel fact sent a chill up his spine.

Ben went back around to the front of the building. Its charm was marred by the planks of wood nailed over the front windows. He went in the front door and saw that Anne had changed her clothes. She now wore a gray skirt and a plain gray blouse, her sleeves pushed up to her elbows. She had a thick apron tied around her waist, and she stood on tiptoe, looking into an open cabinet.

"You changed from your wedding dress," he said.

"It is also my church dress," she replied. "And sometimes my work dress at the milliner. I couldn't ruin it, could I?"

"No, I imagine not," he said. "That was a short span to be a bride in all her finery though."

"It was not much finery." She took a step back from the cabinet. "And this is a pragmatic marriage, is it not?"

He swallowed. Yes, that was what they'd agreed upon, although he did hope more would grow between them.

"I still do not want to take away your happy day," he said.

"You haven't," she replied. "But someone did. Besides, this is your wedding day as well as mine."

It was, and some small part of him was glad for the distraction that this catastrophe had brought with it, because at least now he wouldn't be forced to sit and stare at his wife, wondering how to act.

"What do you need?" he asked, nodding toward the open cupboard.

"A brush and dustpan."

Ben went to the last cabinet on the wall, opened it, and pulled down the required instruments. She nodded her thanks and accepted them.

"Might as well begin cleaning," she said. "I won't sleep tonight knowing this mess remains."

"It will go faster with both of us," Ben said. "Let me change my clothes too."

He went upstairs into the bedroom he would share with his wife. Her trunk sat on one side of the bed—there wasn't much space. Her soiled white gloves lay on the bed, and her skirt and shirtwaist were hung in the wardrobe. He pulled out his work trousers and an old shirt, quickly changed, and hung his good church suit next to her clothes. They were married, but she didn't love him. He had begun with more emotional attachment, although he didn't know how to tell her that. Still, he saw potential here. He would not pressure her for more. He was a Christian man, and she'd already offered a great deal in agreeing to be a loving stepmother to his only child. It was enough for now.

When Ben returned to the workshop, he found Anne crouched on the ground sweeping up ash and broken glass. She looked up as he came into the room.

"Who could have done this?" he asked, more to himself. "I promise you, Anne, I would not have married you and brought you into danger if I thought this would happen."

"Is it *because* you married me?" she asked.

Ben sighed. "I don't know. I only have one man who openly dislikes me, and that's Cyril Welch, but to burn down my home and place of business?"

"He is your competition," Anne said. "I remember when Cyril's cabinets and chairs were the only ones to be found for miles. Then you came."

And he'd drawn business away from Cyril. Cyril's furniture was plain and functional. Ben, on the other hand, carved roses into sideboards and used different woods for inlays that mimicked the English furniture across the ocean. He used thick, ornate fabric to add cushions to chairs and armrests. His pieces cost more, but the housewives of Last Chance loved the opportunity to have beautiful furniture like that enjoyed in the big cities.

So Cyril's business had suffered.

"He was not pleased to see me come and set up shop in competition with him, but he has never shown himself to be violent or crude," Ben said. "Besides, he has expanded his business to include fencing and some roofing too. He is more successful now than he was when I arrived. He has a head for business. It makes no sense that he would suddenly lash out."

"Not to me either," she agreed. "Cyril made every single pew in our church. He has been a good friend to my father too. His wife is a dear soul who has gone out of her way to collect used clothing for the less fortunate, and she puts together hampers each Christmas to help poor families in our community."

That hardly seemed like the kind of man to burn down a building.

"He is the only one who has made me feel unwelcome since I arrived in Last Chance," Ben said. "Besides a few farmers who thought I put on airs."

"Yes. A few." Some color touched her cheeks. Something had sparked feeling in her. "One of those farmers—Jessop Guthrie— asked me several times to be his wife. He even sent his brother to plead his case. But he is a bully and a drunk. I would not have married him if he were the last man on earth."

"I did hear about that," Ben admitted. It was the talk of the town the spring he'd arrived, back before Ben knew who either Anne or

Jessop were. He'd seen Jessop Guthrie around sometimes—a big man with mean little eyes. He ran a hog farm a few miles away. "Has Jessop bothered you recently?"

"He has glared at me some," she replied. "And he spat on the ground once when I passed him in the street. I looked the other way and pretended not to see."

A loathsome man, to be sure.

"Is he the type to commit arson?"

Anne shook her head. "I do not know. I hope not. He is not exactly an upstanding man in this town."

"Did he love you?" Ben asked, almost hesitant to use the word. Love could inspire many rash actions.

"Love?" She smiled faintly. "What has that to do with marriage? He wanted a wife to give him sons, clean his house, and cook his meals. I did not want to do any of those things for him."

And yet, she'd agreed to marry Ben...to help her father. She'd made that clear when she accepted.

"Might he do it to make a point?" Ben asked.

"Burning down a woman's new home is not a way to impress upon her that she made the wrong choice."

"No, it is not." But Ben had to wonder if he'd have to worry about Jessop in the future. "All the same, unless you can think of anyone else who might have reason to harm either of us, those are our two suspects."

In a town full of people whose families had known each other for generations. He was the new man in town, and a year was hardly any time at all to truly become one of the townspeople of Last Chance.

"But we have no proof," Anne said. "We can't go around accusing people who dislike us. That isn't fair. And it is bound to cause some feud that will be Molly's problem when she is grown and married."

"And it does not hold up under the law," he agreed. "The sheriff needs a place to start though. I know I will not feel safe until whoever did this has been caught."

Would they find out who had wielded those bottles? Maybe someone would brag about it in the bar. But would the culprit's friends and fellow townspeople turn him in? Ben was still very much an outsider around here. They might side with the man they knew.

"Do you want to go to your parents' home until this is resolved?" Ben asked. "Just for a week or two?"

"A newly married woman going back to her father's house?" Anne raised her eyebrows. "People would talk."

"People might understand," he replied.

"No." Anne rose to her feet and carried the filled dustpan to a metal waste bin sitting next to his worktable. "We are married now, and I do not wish to go back to my parents. That would be"—she dumped the debris—"cowardly."

"The problem I see is I can't leave the shop," he said. "Whoever did this might return and finish the job. It was my absence that made it possible today."

Anne nodded. "I agree. Your shop is safer if we stay, and we cannot support ourselves without your business. We cannot pay for a nurse for my father without it either. That is just a plain truth. We must protect this shop at all costs."

This was part of why he'd chosen Anne. She was logical. She did not waste good time bemoaning how things were, and she faced facts.

"So we stay?" he asked.

"We stay."

Ben couldn't help but smile at his new wife. She was a brave woman, and she thought pragmatically—something he could appreciate. In New York City, he would expect a woman to swoon over this, to cry, and to complain, at the very least. But the women on the American prairies were different. Anne was different. She was stronger, more resilient, and she had earned his respect today. He was glad that Molly would have Anne's example instead of the society circles she would have had in New York City.

Without an inheritance, Ben had determined to raise his daughter with her feet on the ground, but it wasn't until he had gotten to Last Chance that he realized city life had buffered them both from a lot of difficulty.

The front door pushed open, and Ben glanced up to see Molly and Abigail standing in the sunlit doorway.

"Molly," Ben said, "we've had an accident."

Abigail gasped, looking around in dismay. "The fire was indeed right here! My word!"

"Where is Father?" Anne rose to her feet.

"I left him at home to have a rest," Abigail said. "And I am glad I did, because it looks like we have our work cut out for us today."

"Mama, your dress—"

"—will survive under a sturdy apron," Abigail retorted. "Do you have an extra?"

The women hurried up the creaking old staircase, and Ben held a hand out to his daughter.

"Molly, I am sorry I had to rush off like that," he said. "But Mrs. York is now your grandmother."

"I know," Molly said. She looked over the burned room, her lips pressed together in a thin line. "Who did this?"

"I don't know."

"Does someone hate us, Papa?"

"Hate is a very strong word," Ben said. "We will sort it out. This mess is all easy enough to fix. Upstairs is just fine. It will need a little airing out, but your bedroom is in perfect condition."

"Will you be sending me away?" Molly asked, her chin trembling.

"Where to?" Ben asked.

"Back to New York, where we came from."

It wasn't even an option anymore. "No, Molly. You will stay with me."

Molly nodded. "Good."

Looking at his dark-haired little girl with her solemn dark eyes, he was reminded of her mother. In the influenza pandemic, he couldn't bring himself to send Eliza away. Not when she didn't want to go. And she had died because of his soft heart toward her. Molly shared that soft place in his heart, and he worried at times that he would be her undoing as well.

It would seem that Last Chance was not the idyllic rural town he'd thought it was.

"You should come back to our house." Mama tied the apron around her waist with a smart tug. "It isn't safe to stay here!"

She and Anne stood in the upstairs hallway outside the bedrooms. There was no rug up here, no runner, no softening of the space. But it was clean and only had a little bit of dust and ash on the floor. Everything smelled of smoke, even though they'd opened the windows upstairs and down. The curtains in Molly's window fluttered in the cool May breeze, and light from her bedroom spilled into the hallway. Anne had shut Ben's bedroom door.

And it was *Ben's* bedroom. It did not feel like hers in the least.

"It isn't safe to leave, Mama," Anne replied. "They waited until Ben was sure to be gone and the shop was empty. If someone would try to burn it down in the light of day, we dare not leave it overnight."

"I see your reasoning, my dear," Mama said. "But what a terrible start to things."

"I don't mind," Anne said. "I think working together is as good a way to start as any. There would not be a honeymoon tour of the coast or anything so fancy as that anyway. We might as well get to the business that brought us together."

Mama met Anne's gaze with a sad smile. "It could be much more."

Anne didn't know how to answer that, because what could be and what was didn't often meet. When she agreed to marry Ben, he'd given her his solemn promise that he would not pressure her for more than she felt comfortable with. And she'd been grateful.

"I will do what I can to help you clean up, and then I will leave." Mama touched Anne's arm. "I said it before, and I will offer it again—I could take Molly home with me and give you and Ben some privacy on your first night as husband and wife."

"No, Mama." Anne shook her head. "You know why we married. He wanted a wife to take care of his daughter, and he offered to pay for Father's nurse. That is all this is. I know that."

"But you're *married*," Mama whispered.

"He made it very clear," Anne whispered back. "We all know that I am not a beauty. But I can raise Molly, and I can cook and clean. And Ben is providing for you and Father. I am not about to get my hopes up and my heart broken this early in my marriage."

"All the same," Mama said, "we will clean up quickly, and I will take my leave. Even if the privacy afforded is for the three of you as a little family, it is only right and necessary that you get that."

With her mother's help, Anne and Ben cleaned the smoky, burned workshop. Molly took a mop and a bucket with vinegar and water and mopped the upstairs to help rid the place of the bothersome smell. Mama took her leave just as soon as the downstairs was in order, and Anne was left in the quiet of a newly cleaned home.

Their dinner that night was simple. Ben had bought a piece of mutton, and Anne busied herself in the kitchen chopping potatoes, onion, and carrots for the cast-iron pot. Ben stayed out in his workroom, sorting through the charred and damaged wood that had been set aside for carpentry projects.

Molly stood in the doorway between the two rooms, watching Anne, with a wary look on her face.

"It is still me, Molly," Anne said. "I am the same Miss York you cooked with and talked to and took long walks with these last several months. I am just the same."

"But I cannot call you Miss York anymore," Molly said.

"No…" Anne smiled at the girl, and her heart swelled. Molly was the reason for all of this—on her father's side at least—and Anne had so been looking forward to being Molly's mother. "One day, Molly, I hope you will call me Mama."

"Oh…" Molly swallowed. "I don't remember my mama."

"I know." Anne turned and continued chopping. "And I am sorry about that. All I can say is that I will do my best and we can still take those long walks together." She shot the girl a hopeful look.

"One day, Papa might take me back to New York. That is where we are from."

Ben had assured Anne he would never do that, but telling Molly that did not seem like it would comfort the girl. This was a big change for her. Molly still clung to a memory of a city that was probably just a foggy wisp in her mind at this point. But she lived right here in Last Chance. This was where she would put down roots once she felt safe enough.

"Do you know the story of Lafayette Sherwood?" Anne asked. Molly always loved stories.

"No." Molly came a little closer.

"Well, a long time ago, there was no town here, just some spread-out farms. And there were some migrants traveling through the area with some teams of oxen. There was an accident, and a man named Lafayette Sherwood was killed. So his companions buried him in the middle of a field near an oak sapling that they probably didn't even notice."

"A tree?" Molly's eyes lit up. "Like the big one in the graveyard?"

"Exactly." Anne reached for another potato, continuing to work while she talked. "The farmers in these parts are very practical people, and they figured that was as good a place for a graveyard as any, so they started to bury their departed loved ones there with the stranger. Eventually, someone made a proper headstone for poor Lafayette, and a graveyard was born."

"That tree is really big now. Is it the same one?"

"It is the same one. That oak tree is at least sixty years old. But that was the beginning of this town. One little graveyard with one little tree. And see how it has grown!" She cast the girl a fond look. "This is our town, Molly. We are all a part of it. We are part of the story of the place, and you are a part of Last Chance too. In this place we can make much out of very little."

Molly stayed silent. Did she understand that they had gotten married for her? That Anne had accepted a man she hardly knew in order to be Molly's stepmother? Yes, she had agreed in order to help her parents, but she also cherished an image in her heart of being Molly's mother.

Later, the Huntington family ate dinner. They had worship together around the kitchen table after the dishes were done. Ben read a psalm from the big Bible, and then it was time for Molly to go to bed.

"Why doesn't Anne help you get into bed?" Ben said to his daughter. "She is your mother now. We had best start, I think."

Anne was grateful for the chance, and she followed her new stepdaughter up the stairs to Molly's bedroom. It was a small room with a double bed in the center.

Molly's nightgown waited under her pillow, and while the girl quickly changed, Anne set the oil lamp on her dresser and scanned the small room. An exquisite dollhouse sat on a small table underneath the window. The front had a wide front porch supported by white columns. The house was painted a lovely blue, with tiny painted ivy crawling up the sides. She knelt to get a closer look.

There were eight rooms inside, all outfitted with tiny furniture. The walls had real wallpaper on them, and the rugs were made of thick cloth. The floors, which were made to look like hardwood, were polished to a gleaming shine. Each tiny piece of furniture, from sideboards to couches to plant stands and four-poster beds, was carved meticulously by hand. Tiny cushions were attached to the Victorian couches and chairs. This dollhouse had the most luxury that Anne had ever seen in her life.

"I have dolls for the house," Molly said. "There is an old man and an old woman."

"Really?"

"They are on my shelf."

Anne rose to her feet and surveyed the shelf of toys. Most were carved from wood, and she spotted two jointed dolls. The old woman stood upright and had arms that moved. Her carved long dress kept her on her feet. The old man also had arms that moved and legs that bent at the hips so he could sit. The joints appeared to made by strings pulled through tiny holes bored into the wood. The figures were delicately carved so that even their faces seemed to have the lines and sags of age.

"My papa made all of it for me." Molly pulled back her covers and crawled into bed.

"They are beautiful," Anne murmured. "I have never seen anything like them."

"He made all the furniture," Molly said. "And all the clocks say the same time in every room so that it matches."

"That's wonderful." Anne smiled and scanned the kitchen. Hanging tin pots were fashioned by hand, and a pile of coal dust sat in a coal caddy next to the cast-iron stove. "Such detail. Has he made any other dollhouses?"

There was a squeak from the bottom of the staircase, and Anne straightened.

"Yes, he has made a few." Molly pulled her sheet up under her arms, and she scooted to one side of the bed. "Some girls wanted dollhouses too, so my papa made them. He sold them in New York City."

Would exquisite dollhouses like this one sell out here in Iowa? Maybe in the city where a family might be able to afford such extravagance. This dollhouse could not have been cheap to make, and considering the time Ben would have put into it, it would be more costly still. But he had obviously found wealthy customers, and she felt the rise of hope that he might do it again. She had never seen such workmanship in her life.

"My dollhouse is the nicest one Papa ever made though," Molly added.

There was a cleared throat at the doorway, and Anne glanced up to see Ben standing there. His beard hid the subtleties of his expression, but his eyes were softened with tenderness when he looked at his daughter.

"Ben, this is truly wonderful," Anne said. "It is like a tiny mansion. I cannot even imagine…"

A life like the one the dollhouse presented was out of reach for people like them. Wouldn't it be wiser to give Molly a dollhouse more suited to her station in life? Maybe a dollhouse like a fine farmhouse, or like one of the little houses around town?

"It was a labor of love." Ben smoothed his hand over his beard.

"Papa likes to whittle," Molly supplied.

"It uses up the quiet of an evening," he said.

Anne met Ben's gaze. Yes, she could well understand what he meant. How many evenings had she spent knitting scarves for the underprivileged, just to pass those lonely hours?

"Well," Ben said, "I will say good night then."

"Good night, Papa," Molly said.

Ben turned and left the room, and Anne went over to Molly's bedside. She sank down onto the edge of the bed.

"Will the bad people come back?" Molly asked.

"Not with your father here," Anne replied.

"Are you sure?"

"Yes. Very sure. They will not want to face his fisticuffs." She hoped against hope that she wasn't telling a lie. "You are very safe."

Molly tugged her blankets up higher. "I'm scared to sleep alone."

She was just one small girl in the middle of a very big bed. Anne glanced toward the hallway and imagined the bedroom opposite.

"What if I slept here with you?" Anne asked. "The bed is plenty big enough for both of us."

"Are you allowed?" Molly whispered. "You are not a nanny. Papa told me that."

"Of course I am allowed," Anne replied. It was an ideal reason to stay here in Molly's bedroom for a few nights, and she would have a chance to catch her breath. She had two roles here, wife and mother. Perhaps she could begin with motherhood.

"What if I lie next to you until you go to sleep?" Anne asked.

"Yes, please." Molly smiled and scooted over to make room.

"Shall we say your prayers?"

They bowed their heads, and Molly said her simple prayer. Then she closed her eyes, and Anne did as she'd promised. She turned out the light and lay down on the bed next to Molly. She could hear Ben's footsteps on the floor below, the squeak of the woodstove's door, and then the *thunk* of wood as he added another log to the fire.

Then she closed her eyes and listened as Molly's breathing grew slower and steadier until the young girl drifted off to sleep.

CHAPTER THREE

Ben looked through the singed planks of cherry wood. He pulled one out that was almost untouched by the fire, but that was the only one. Everything else was unusable. The wood had been sent by train from a mill near the Canadian border, and Cyril Welch had bought the remainder of the shipment. So there was some cherry hardwood to be had, but it was owned by Ben's direct competition.

Had that been the reason for this fire? Was Cyril trying to stop him from completing the new pulpit for the church?

He heard the stairs creak and looked over to see Anne coming back downstairs. Her dress was creased, and she seemed to notice at the same time, because she gathered up a handful of fabric and shook it out.

"She's sleeping," Anne said.

Ben smiled and suddenly felt a little bashful. He put the piece of cherry wood onto his worktable. He wasn't quite sure what to say, but then Anne broke the silence.

"Molly has a rather large bed," she said. "And she's afraid of sleeping alone. I think that is understandable considering"—she glanced around the room—"all of this."

"She said she didn't want to sleep alone?" Ben asked.

"She did." Anne straightened her shoulders. "And I think I should sleep with her in her bedroom for the next little while, until she's more comfortable, and…"

She did not complete her sentence, but he thought he understood. His last marriage was a happy enough union, but he and his wife had separate bedrooms as many people did who lived with comfortable enough means to have a home with servants. He was raised with the expectation that women would want their own space and privacy. There was not much room for that here.

"If you would like to be there…for Molly, I mean, then I think it is a very good idea," he said. Until she loved him. That might take time.

Anne came into the room and stood next to the woodstove. She held her hands out toward the warmth, and she looked so gentle and soft standing there. He had to do better by Anne than he'd done in his first marriage.

When Eliza died during the flu epidemic, his father-in-law, Ike Rumsfeld, had blamed Ben. And what defense did Ben have?

None, it turned out. Ben had offended his own father and been cut out of the will. In Eliza's panic about their fall from society, she had refused to leave New York and go to cleaner air in the country. Eliza's death was Ben's fault—in the eyes of her father, at least.

Now Ben was in Last Chance with only his talent and a few dollars to his name. And he had Anne now. A woman who needed his protection as much as he needed her support. But he had no privilege or position to offer her. Just his willingness to work as hard as he had to in order to provide for both her and her parents.

"I truly am amazed at the quality of your work with the dollhouse," Anne said. "For a humble carpenter to be able to create such a luxurious setting—you have vision."

Ben smiled faintly. It wasn't vision, it was memory. "It is easier to afford a dollhouse than the full-sized version, is it not?"

Anne returned his smile. "I fully agree. People like us will never live that way."

"No, I am afraid not." Those days were in the past for Ben, and his life of affluence was over.

"You have told me a little bit about your family," she said.

"Yes, my father disowned me, I told you that," he said. "He did not agree with my plans to work with wood. He wanted me to join the family business, and I balked. He did not expect to die when he did. He was strong as a horse until that heart attack. I think he tried to rattle me out of my stubbornness by taking me out of the will, but he never had a chance to put me back in."

"That is very sad," she said. "I doubt he wanted to leave this earth on those terms."

"Who is ever truly ready?" Ben asked.

"What was the family business?"

"He worked on the railroads." How much should he say? He didn't like to think about the life he'd left behind. It was no use having regrets. "We were...comfortable in our lifestyle. I feel I should tell you that."

"Oh." She was silent for a moment. "Well, we can become comfortable here too, if we work hard, and if I am thrifty with a penny. I can cook and make the groceries stretch. And I can sew. If I can get the patterns and the fabric, Molly will have all the styles coming from New England, sometimes only a year or two old."

He smiled. There was no possible way they would rise to the level at which he'd been raised, but he didn't care a whit. An honest life with honest work was better for his soul than the money-gouging business practices his father had been involved in. And Anne's frugal example would be good for Molly too.

"We will be very comfortable," he said. His desires were not too elevated. He wanted to have hot meals, a solid roof over their heads, and meaningful work to employ him.

"I am sorry you and your father did not reconcile before he passed," Anne added. "That must be painful."

"It is," he agreed. "My father would not accept me unless I did things his way. And I could not do it. I don't like to talk about him."

Could she understand?

She nodded. "My father is a dear man. I think you will find him very approachable and generous if you get to know him better."

"A father figure?" he asked with a rueful smile.

"Perhaps." Color touched her cheeks. "Maybe that is too forward for me to suggest just yet."

"It is kind of you," he said. "And I am glad to have you and your family. I appreciate that very much after all I have lost. Truly, your family will be my family."

Anne smiled. "Good."

There was a loud bang against the door, and both Ben and Anne startled. Anne's hand shot out and caught his sleeve. He put his hand over hers for a moment to reassure himself as much as her, then he strode over to the heavy wooden door and opened it a crack.

Outside was dark, a cloudy night with no moon, and he looked up the street then down the other way. A shadow disappeared around the corner. Ben started after whoever it was and then realized that with no lantern, he would not see much. A cool breeze coiled around him, and he returned to the front door that hung open and spilled light from inside onto the front step. Anne stood there, her arms crossed across her narrow waist, as she peered out after him. He spotted what had hit the door—a brick with a dirty piece of string tied around it to keep a fluttering piece of paper in place.

"Did you see who it was?" Anne asked.

"No." He bent down and picked up the brick. It had left a gouge in the wooden door, and he ran his thumb over the mark before he went back inside. He locked the door behind him and then pulled out his pocketknife to cut the string. The piece of paper fell away, and he unfolded it.

Watch yourself. Worse is to come.

Short and to the point.

"What does it say?" Anne asked.

He passed the page over, and her face paled.

"What could be worse than this?" she breathed.

Ben put his arm around her and tugged her against him. It was an instinctive gesture and, for a moment, he stood paralyzed with Anne's head against his shoulder. She smelled of soft soap and talcum powder.

"A brick against the door is not that bad," he said.

"It is a warning though." She pulled away from him. "Does someone really hate us this much?"

It would seem someone did.

"Anne, we will figure this out," he said earnestly. "This is one of our neighbors, and people can be very brave when they have not shown their faces. I want to face whoever is doing this and have them tell me straight why they feel this way."

"And if we cannot figure it out?" she said. "How far will they go?"

That was Ben's worry too. How far would this angry person go to get rid of him and his family?

"Let's go up to bed," he said. "I will stay awake for a little while and read my Bible. If there is any more mischief, I will hear it."

He picked up the piece of paper and brought it closer to his face, squinting as he looked at it. He knew this stationery. It was similar to the cheap paper that sat on the counter at the post office for people to write down their messages before the letters were counted up and a telegraph was sent.

But it was not the paper itself that caught his notice. In fact, with the faint smell of smoke still lingering in the room, he almost didn't notice at all.

But the paper smelled ever so faintly of roses.

"What is the matter?" Anne asked.

"Smell this." He held it out to her. Anne bent over the page and inhaled. Her eyes widened.

"That's perfume. They sell it at the drugstore. It's called rose water." Anne shook her head slowly. "This was written by a woman!"

He'd assumed he was the target, being the newest man in town who had ruffled some feathers when he opened a new business on

Main Street, but maybe the person doing this was not coming after him at all.

Maybe someone was coming after Anne.

The next morning, Anne fixed breakfast—cream of wheat and brown sugar—and then cleaned up the kitchen. Ben went into his workroom to restain a bed frame he had been working on in order to take away the smell of smoke. Even with all the windows open, the smell of solvent wafted through the kitchen.

"Molly, I have some errands to run. Would you like to come with me?" Anne asked.

Molly, who'd been helping dry dishes, gladly hung up her towel. "What will we do?" Molly asked.

"We will go mail this letter to my aunt first," Anne replied. "I am telling her I got married. That is very big news."

"And then?"

"And then to the grocery, and I will get us a few things for the pantry. We need sugar, flour, and some corn syrup."

They went out through the workroom, and Ben, seated on an upturned pail with a brush in his hand, looked up from his work.

"We are doing errands," Molly announced.

Ben smiled. "Very good."

"I am going to the grocery and the post office," Anne said. "Do we have a tab that you pay off each month?"

"We do have a tab at both places," Ben said. "But we need to be care-ful. Because of the fire, I am going to be set back on that cherry wood."

"I will be thrifty," Anne said.

She had plans to bake bread that afternoon and perhaps make some biscuits for supper, and she felt cheery already at the thought of filling her home with good food for her new family. This was what a wife and mother did. She brought cheer, love, and good cooking into a house and turned it into a home. It would be a start, at least.

Anne and Molly headed out the front door, and Anne couldn't help but look at those ugly, boarded front windows as she passed them. They would be fixed, of course, but they sent a shiver down her spine all the same.

The street was busy this time of day.

"Wait, Molly!" Anne put a hand out to stop the girl from stepping into the street as an automobile honked its horn and swept past in a billow of exhaust. A heavily loaded wagon pulled by a team of four horses came from the other direction, and they waited until the street was clear before they hurried across the gravel road to the wooden walkway on the other side. A man in overalls and a small wagon shoveled dirt and fresh gravel into the pothole that had caused the upset with the wagon the day before. He nodded at Anne as she hurried past.

"Good morning, Amos," she said brightly.

"Morning, Mrs. Huntington." He shot her a grin. "Congratulations on your nuptials."

"Thank you, Amos."

"Morning, Molly," he added, tipping his dirt-streaked fedora.

Amos was a few years younger than Anne, and he was married already with two small children. It felt nice to have some equal footing now with a stepdaughter of her own, and she returned his grin with a smile that she hoped retained some of her dignity.

The post office had a false front that made the building look bigger than it was. Theirs was not the main post office. The big one that had letters sent directly on the rail was in Derby, eight miles away. But every two days, their postmaster, Henry Ager, took the white canvas bag of mail—sometimes with only a few letters in it—up to Derby so that the letters could be sent, and returned with the mail from Derby to be put in the postboxes in Last Chance.

A little bell tinkled overhead as Anne pulled the door open, and she stepped into the post office that always seemed to smell of new paper and wood polish. Ernestine Mabry, the postal assistant, stood behind the high counter. Beyond her was a large wooden crate that drew Anne's eye. Something so interesting seldom came to Last Chance.

"Anne," Ernestine said, "how wonderful to see you. What a day, yesterday! I hear congratulations are in order, and then that dreadful fire!"

"Yes, but congratulate me first, then you can sympathize," Anne said, and she held the door open for Molly to come inside too. "I would especially like you to meet my stepdaughter. This is Molly."

For a few minutes Anne chatted with her friend about her wedding, about the fire, and how thankful they were that there was not more damage done. Then Anne bought a stamp and handed her letter over to be put into the canvas bag destined for Derby.

"I see a very large parcel behind you," Anne said. It would be wrong to ask particulars, but she was curious all the same.

"That came with only half an address attached and without a return address," Ernestine said. "It would be a terrible shame if we had to send it to the dead-letter office."

"What will you do?" Anne asked.

"Mr. Ager says we will hold on to it for a while. He is going to search the mail wagon from Derby to see if the label might have torn off there. There is always a hope. And maybe someone will send a telegram, checking to see if it was received."

Anne looked over the counter at the big wooden box, and she wondered what it might be. Had someone ordered an item from the city? And if so, what was it?

"Aren't you curious?" Anne asked.

"I am dying of curiosity," Ernestine replied. "I will tell you what happens with it. But you know how it is—people will talk about it, and word will spread. If someone is expecting a large package, they will know it arrived."

Anne and Molly took their leave, and Anne looked down at the girl with a smile.

"Should we guess what is inside?" she asked.

"We used to get packages like that in New York," Molly said. "It was never toys or dolls or anything interesting. The last time we got a package like that, it was a sink to put into the kitchen."

"A sink? That is more interesting than you think, to a grown-up lady," Anne said.

Molly didn't look convinced, though, and when Anne asked more about what she thought might be in the crate, Molly only shrugged.

The next stop was the grocer. The grocer's shop was larger than most on the street. There were two large show windows, and there was a set of dishes on display in one window—real china with little flowers around the edges. Behind the glass on the other side of the door was a selection of tea cakes. The tea leaves, pressed into a rockhard rectangle, could be chipped off and put into a teapot for some proper tea. The tea set and the tea came all the way from England.

The bell tinkled over their heads as they went inside. The aromas of cured meats mingled with pungent spices. The walls were lined with shelves, all stacked full of boxes, cans, jars, and bags. A line of people stood waiting to be served by Mrs. Reese, who was speaking with Bernadette Sisk.

Bernadette was the wife of Verne Sisk, who was the schoolteacher. The Sisks had previously owned the shop and the attached apartment that now belonged to Ben. That was back when it was a bookshop. Verne had both a fancy education and an inheritance from his grandfather, which gave him the ability to open the bookshop. Verne had encouraged the citizens of Last Chance to better themselves and buy books. But farmers had little need for stories of fiction or pictures of architecture from cities they would never visit. Anne had enjoyed browsing in the shop, and she had even bought a small book of poetry once, but when Bernadette and Verne started hovering too much and asking her to buy what she was looking at, she'd stopped frequenting the shop. She could not afford more books, and she hated to disappoint them. Within a year, Sisk Bookshop had gone under.

Bernadette counted her coins in her purse and watched with an eagle eye as Mrs. Reese put shaved ham on the scale one sliver at a time.

Anne bent down and whispered to Molly, "You may choose one sweet, if you like."

"May I?" Molly brightened.

Anne nodded, and while Molly hurried over to the jars of stick candy to look at all the flavors, Anne spotted her mother on the far side of the shop. She went to her mother's side and smiled at her.

"How are you, Anne?" Mama asked, squeezing her hand. "Is everything put together again?"

"Yes, things are fine. Ben is working on a bed frame today, and I'm taking Molly on some errands."

"A real little mother."

"I hope so."

Two women chatted to the side, and Anne watched as Mrs. Reese took a piece of ham off the scale, her expression grim.

"One moment, dear," Mama said. She slipped to Bernadette's side and leaned forward to say something to Mrs. Reese. There was a quiet conversation, Mama opened her own purse and counted several coins and one bill out onto the counter, and Mrs. Reese took the entire ham, wrapped it in paper, and handed it to Bernadette.

Bernadette's mouth worked, but nothing seemed to come out. Her face flushed red, and she looked miserably toward Anne. Anne could read the humiliation, gratitude, and conflicted emotion in her teary gaze. For a moment, Anne's breath stopped in her chest, then Mama hooked an arm around Bernadette's shoulders and hustled her to the door. The bell overhead tinkled a farewell, and Mama ducked her head and slipped around the side of the shop to where Anne waited. All eyes were on her, though, even if she tried to escape notice.

"Mama, can you afford that?" Anne whispered.

"I'll make do," Mama said softly. "The Sisks have been struggling the last year, and there are the little ones at home who need food in their bellies."

The bank had taken the shop, and the Sisks had moved to a small house just on the edge of town, within walking distance of the school where Verne taught first through eighth grade.

"How bad has it been?" Anne murmured.

"Bad."

Was it bad enough that Verne might be filled with anger at the man who'd taken over his shop after his inheritance was eaten up?

"Are they angry?" Anne whispered. "I mean, do they have hard feelings, or bitterness, toward Ben?"

"I think not," Mama said. "Those are good Christian people, Anne."

And yet suffering could change people. For one man to succeed, another had to make room for him. And in this case, the Sisk bookstore had failed in order for Ben to buy the foreclosed property at a steep discount.

Next, it was Mama's turn, and Anne watched as her mother ordered her groceries. When Mrs. Reese reached for a cake of tea, Mama shook her head. There would be sacrifices so that the little Sisk children could have their ham, but Mama and Father would make them willingly.

How much had the Sisks suffered? Anne wondered. Enough to lash out?

CHAPTER FOUR

Ben put down his paintbrush and plucked a stray bristle off the bed frame. He'd thought this brush would last a little longer, but it was coming apart in his hands. He'd need to pick up a new brush or two so he'd have one in reserve. There was no way around it. It seemed that every time he tried to be thrifty, something else needed replacing.

The door rattled, then opened, and he looked up as Anne and Molly came inside. Anne lifted her rose-colored skirt, the toes of her black boots peeping out from under the layers of fabric. The lace detailing on the dress was a little worn and discolored. She'd need enough fabric to make herself a new dress.

If only he hadn't lost that cherry wood. It still grated at him. It was a large expense, and he did not want to have to return the money already given to him by Emily and Elizabeth Bertrand, who'd commissioned the pulpit.

Anne carried a brown paper package in one arm, and Molly had a stick of candy in her hand, licking it carefully—a rare treat.

"I didn't think you would mind," Anne said when she saw the direction of his attention. "I got a little less bacon to make up the difference, and I wanted her to have something special."

"I don't mind at all," Ben said.

"I am glad." Anne and Molly disappeared into the kitchen together, and Anne emerged alone a couple of minutes later without the package. She took her hat off and revealed her hair piled high underneath it.

He liked her hair. It was glossy and full, and it made him want to touch it. He pulled his gaze away. It still felt too familiar, especially for a wife who preferred to sleep in Molly's room.

"Molly went upstairs to play with her dollhouse," Anne said. "Do you know the family that used to own this shop before you bought it, the Sisks?"

"The schoolteacher?" Ben asked.

"Yes. I saw his wife, Bernadette, in the grocer's today." She told the story quickly, and he felt a wave of pity at the thought of that family's hard times.

"I have done the same for them before," Ben said. "I put their groceries on my tab a couple of months ago. I feel badly for them. Verne Sisk is an educated man and a skilled teacher. He will be teaching Molly when we send her. Maybe in a bigger town a bookstore might succeed, but out here..."

He shook his head, going over the mental estimates for the cost of opening such a business. It would require high overhead and small returns over a long period of time. It was the kind of business his father would have shot down immediately with a quick tally of numbers.

"I saw her face when my mother paid for the ham," Anne said. "Bernadette was torn apart. You can tell how much she hates the charity. Are you...friendly with Verne?"

"I wouldn't say friendly," Ben said, thinking back to his interactions with the man. They acknowledged each other. They knew each other's names. But there was a certain reticence between them.

"It occurred to me that we might have another suspect for our list."

Ben weighed her words. "You may be right."

"I do hate what this is doing to me," Anne said. "Here I am, suspecting all my neighbors of the worst behavior! I have no evidence, and yet I think about the possibility of each one of them lighting that fire."

"Because one of them likely did," he replied.

Anne dropped her gaze.

"I understand," he added. "Too many times in my life, I saw things the way I wanted to see them instead of as they really were. I never wanted to believe that my own father would disown me over a disagreement, but he did. Or that my wife would be in danger in the influenza pandemic, but she died of it. Or that my father-in-law would blame me for his daughter's death, but he did. Seeing the best in others is a good thing unless it blinds you to things you need to see."

"Your father-in-law blamed you?" she asked.

He hadn't meant to bring it up, but here he had. "He did. He said if I had sent her to the country, regardless of her feelings on the matter, she would have lived. And he was right."

Add to that, if he had just pleased his own father and kept his inheritance, Eliza would never have been so determined to maintain her place in her social circles by staying in the city. She had married him for richer.

"I am sorry to speak of her," he added.

"It's all right," she replied. "She is Molly's mother. She should be spoken of."

"My point is that there are very real dangers we need to see in order to protect our new family," Ben said. "There is someone in this community who wants to run us out. That is the plain fact. We have to face it. It might be more pleasant to believe that everyone here is filled with goodness, but they aren't. And it is not a failure in character to face it. It is a necessity."

Ben watched her face as she thought over his words.

"Your father-in-law would not forgive you," she said at last. "Do you forgive yourself?"

Ben hadn't expected that question, and he turned back toward his work to shield his face.

"I suppose so. I was a different man then. It is not a mistake I would make again."

"How are you different now?" she asked.

He faced her again. "I am not so naïve."

He'd chosen a different sort of woman this time—one who didn't have her eye set on their joint inheritances, a woman who wasn't a social climber. The problem was, Anne had all the characteristics he needed in a wife, but he did not have her heart yet. He must do better this time. While a young man's disastrous errors might be forgiven him, an experienced man repeating those mistakes did not deserve to be let off the hook.

"I am not the same man I used to be," he said, softening his tone. "And you should be glad of that. I am older now, and wiser, I hope. It is because I am looking at things differently that I saw the potential between us. You are mature, strong, levelheaded. I was... drawn to that in you."

Could she see what he meant? He needed her to continue to be logical and practical. It helped him to stay on the right path. And his attraction to her was different—deeper, even. He did not see a beautiful girl who made him feel lightheaded. He saw a beautiful woman who made him want to be a better man. This was part of his struggle to improve himself.

"Well, I am all of those things. I am glad to have my strengths appreciated."

"I truly do."

Ben flexed his hand, tempted to reach out and touch her, but she didn't move toward him, so he didn't. She was silent for a moment and then she said, "I had intended to make bread today."

"Fresh bread," he said, and couldn't help but smile. "I would like that very much."

She returned his smile. "Then I will go get started."

Anne turned and disappeared into the kitchen. Ben could not articulate everything inside of him. In fact, he'd failed in that respect, but he'd spoken the truth. He'd married her because she would make a good wife and mother. But he had not been following some sweeping emotions like he had in the immaturity of his first marriage. He would not do that again.

The hardware store wasn't far from his shop. Just a couple of stores up on the same side of the street. There was a bakery and a tack shop between them. When he stepped into the hardware store, he noticed a couple of customers browsing among the items. An older woman compared two different garden rakes, and two young men considered some saw blades.

Ben went over to the paintbrushes, and he felt the bristles of three different ones, looking for the best quality for staining wood, when he heard his name.

"Hey, Huntington!"

Ben turned to see Jessop Guthrie heading in his direction. The farmer was frowning fiercely, and he crossed his beefy arms over his worn shirt.

"I hear you married Anne York," Jessop said, his lips turning down in distaste.

"I did," Ben said. He straightened his shoulders. Jessop was now dealing with Anne's husband, and Ben would not have this man giving her trouble or speaking ill of her.

"And your shop caught fire at roughly the same time." A smile flicked at the corners of the big man's lips.

"Yes, it did." Ben met Jessop's gaze, refusing to be cowed. "Do you know anything about that?"

"Just that it happened."

"Did you have anything to do with it?"

"Trying to get me to confess?" Jessop barked out a laugh, looking around at the other customers who'd stopped to stare. "How stupid do you think I am?"

Had he just admitted to it? Ben's heart hammered hard in his throat. But it was hardly a confession. Jessop might look dull-witted, but he was far from it.

"It makes me wonder," Jessop said, lowering his voice, "if Anne is regretting marrying you yet. If you ask me, you come with bad luck."

But Ben didn't believe in luck. He believed in blessing, although this fire seemed like the opposite.

"Hey, hey!" Isaiah Kompf, the owner of the store, came bustling in their direction. "I don't want any fighting in here!"

"There is no fight," Ben said. "I've come for brushes."

"I will put them on your tab," Isaiah said. "I want both of you to leave."

The man had a store to protect, and Ben could appreciate what Isaiah had to do. It was best to leave anyway, and stay away from a man who obviously wanted a fight.

"I'm still shopping, Kompf!" Jessop retorted.

Ben took the opportunity to exit the shop, the belligerent bellowing of Jessop left behind him. Jessop was just being rude, as he always was, but there was something in his insulting words that had struck a nerve for Ben.

Did Anne regret marrying him? It was too late to back out. The wedding was done. But what did she feel about all of this? Not only had their marriage come with a fire to his shop, but someone in her own dear community had turned against them.

This was supposed to be a practical marriage. It was supposed to benefit her. Anne's life should be brighter because of her vows to him...and so far, she'd only been met with disaster.

That afternoon, Anne was due to work at Wheaton's Millinery. She changed into a work skirt and a durable shirtwaist. She ran her hands over her hips and noticed the soft shine of gold on her hand. This was the first time she'd work in the store as a married woman. She had intended to give her notice before the wedding, but she'd held back because part of her had been afraid that Ben would change his mind about marrying her. It had all happened so quickly and was such a joyful opportunity to have a family of her own after she became convinced it would never happen. She'd been afraid to give up everything, just in case she'd have to return to Mr. Wheaton and beg for her job back in humiliation.

And now that she was married and there was the financial strain of the fire, she hardly thought that quitting a proper place of employment was wise.

She looked at herself in the mirror, adjusted her small, feathered hat just so, and pushed the hatpin through to keep it in place. Traditionally, married women did not work in shops unless they owned the place, but then, many things were untraditional in this union.

Anne took her gloves and headed down the stairs. The saw swished, and the scent of cut wood floated through the air.

"I'm going to take Molly to my mother and then go to work," Anne said.

Ben stopped and brushed his hand over his forehead.

"To work?" he said.

"Yes. I have not given my notice yet."

"Then give it now. Gabe Wheaton will understand, I am sure. You are a wife now. Wives need not go to a job. Your job is here at home."

Was that part of why she married him? And yet now, staying here with Ben all day, every day, was starting to make her feel panicky. He was a nice man, a good man, even, but she realized now how very little she knew him, and this little home was feeling pinched.

"I thought that with the fire, the extra money might help us," she said.

Ben put the saw down, his mouth pressed in a tight line. She'd offended him—she could see it all over his face.

"I mean," she blundered on, "maybe it will help with paying for the wood you need."

"You need not worry about that," he said. "I will take care of it."

"I don't have to worry about such things," she retorted. "I know that. I know that you will sort things out and you will provide for me. I am not worried, Ben. But this marriage of ours is a different sort of arrangement, is it not? And this is something I can do that will make things easier for all of us."

She might as well just say it. They weren't husband and wife in every way. And they hardly knew each other. But if she wasn't going to be his wife after dark, then she could bring him some income to ease the burden.

"And what will people say?" he asked. "That I am not able to provide for you?"

Anne stood still, her gloves clutched in one hand. Her breath came quick, and she licked her lips.

"Are you forbidding me?"

Ben blinked. "What? No."

"I will bring my pay to you, and you can use it to make up for the lost wood," she said.

"All right," Ben said curtly. "If that is what you want."

She could hear plainly in his tone that this was not what he wanted. But what did he expect? He came to this marriage with a heart that was, if not still broken, severely scarred. He did not seem to want tenderness between them. He had not yet even so much as kissed her cheek. Should her life consist of endless hours in the kitchen and upstairs, cooking, cleaning, and fixing her mind on all she did not have? Or should she be grateful for the little things that added up to one beautiful life? And one of those little things was her employment at Wheaton's.

"Molly!" Anne called. "It is time to go to your grandmother's house."

Molly appeared at the top of the stairs. "Today?"

"Yes, today. I will be at Wheaton's this afternoon, and your father needs to work."

Ben gave his daughter a nod, and Molly came down the stairs. How much had the girl overheard, she wondered? And what must Molly think of her?

Anne took Molly to her mother's house, and Mama was delighted to have her new granddaughter come spend a few hours with her. When Anne left them, Molly was being led inside for a piece of sugar pie.

Wheaton's was quiet when Anne arrived. The millinery shop was really more than a women's hat shop. Mr. Wheaton sold hats and all the trappings that came with them as well as other women's accessories. There were gloves sold here, some intricately worked shawls, and even some brooches and pins that were made of glass instead of precious stones. A display cabinet ran through the center of the store with hat stands and different styles of hats on them. The walls were lined with more cabinets filled with ribbon, lace, feathers, and other baubles to decorate a fine woman's hat.

Mary Nelson sat on the stool behind the counter. She was at work on a hat, a length of pink ribbon in one hand and a needle and thread in the other. She looked up as Anne came inside.

"Anne!" Mary shot her a smile. "I owe you congratulations!"

"Thank you."

"Are you here to buy something?"

"I am here to work."

Mary blinked. "Still?"

"Yes, still. I have not given my notice, and I won't leave Mr. Wheaton in a bind." Anne walked briskly across the shop, took off her gloves, and tucked them under the counter. She would not have her position given to someone else because of an assumption.

"Shouldn't you be off on some fine holiday to Des Moines or something?" Mary asked. "I thought Mr. Huntington could afford to do that much." Already, there was a sound of judgment in Mary's tone. Then she sighed and nodded. "But the fire. Of course. You know, I knew something was wrong when I heard the glass break. I was just coming outside at the end of my workday, and I saw him."

Anne shot her friend a wide-eyed look. "Saw who?"

"I don't know who it was, but it was a man running away from the shop. He ducked his head and headed around the far side of the building, so I couldn't see who it was."

But the letter had perfume on it...

"Are you sure it was a man?" Anne asked. "Is there any possibility it was a woman?"

"A woman?" Mary's eyebrows went up. "I hardly see a woman starting fires. It is not the feminine thing to do. Sheriff Miller came by and asked if we had seen anything, and I told him exactly what I saw—a man running away. He wrote it in his little notebook and thanked me kindly for being so observant."

"A woman sent us a threatening note," Anne replied. "She didn't think of her perfume—it was all over the paper."

Mary blinked, and some color rose in her cheeks. "Oh..."

What did that reaction mean? Had she really seen a man running away? Or was it guilt? But what reason would Mary have to want to set fire to Ben's shop? What could she gain?

"So what will you do?" Mary asked after a moment. "Will you leave Last Chance? Move somewhere else?"

"Why would we move away?" Anne asked. "This is my home. Our home, I should say. I was born here. My parents were born here. Why should we be pushed out?"

"If someone has it in for you," Mary replied, "it might be the only thing to do."

"There is another option. We could catch them at it." Anne met her gaze.

Mary's cheeks pinked again. "Or that."

Did Mary want Anne and Ben to leave town? And if so, was she lying about seeing a man fleeing the scene? Or was she telling the truth? Was a man trying to make his threat seem like it came from someone else? Or were there a man and a woman working together? A married couple, perhaps?

"Anne, what is that look on your face?" Mary asked, turning to the hat in front of her.

"Something just occurred to me," Anne said.

"What's that?" Mary's gaze flickered back up.

"That someone might truly want to chase us out of town," she said.

It had only occurred to her now that that might be the effort—to be rid of them completely. Her home, her parents, her extended family, her memories, even the old churchyard where her grandparents and other relatives were buried... Someone wanted them to leave this place. And as horrible a thought as that was, something else brought a mist of tears to her eyes. She would have to leave Last Chance with her new husband. Go somewhere else where she would live alone with a man who did not love her, and be a mother to a child who would grow up and leave as children did.

If they were chased out, Anne would eventually lose everything that gave her life meaning.

The front door opened, and Mr. Wheaton came inside. He was dressed smartly, as he always was—his hat set at a fashionable angle on his head and a walking stick in his hand.

"Anne," he said, stopping short. "I had assumed you would be at home with your husband."

"Mr. Wheaton, I do not wish to give up my position here," Anne said, folding her hands in front of her. "My husband knows I am here, and he gives his support." If only barely. "And I want to continue working here, if you will have me."

"I am certainly not dismissing you," Mr. Wheaton said. "But it is not ordinary at all."

"No, not ordinary," Anne agreed. "But I will work hard, as I have done all this time, and I will bring no trouble to you."

Mr. Wheaton lifted his shoulders. "If Ben has no issue with it, I don't see why I should."

Anne nodded. "Thank you."

When Anne looked over at Mary, she saw her lips pressed together in disapproval. Why would Mary care so deeply whether Anne continued in her job or not? She'd thought her friend would be happy that their afternoons together wouldn't end. Mary didn't have some hidden grievance, did she? She wasn't the woman throwing bricks at their door…was she?

One thing was certain. If they didn't find out who had set fire to Ben's shop soon, Anne would be second-guessing every single neighbor and friend for the rest of her life, and she could not live that way. They needed to know the truth.

CHAPTER FIVE

Prayer meeting night was an important evening for the faithful attendees of Last Chance's only church. Ben had been attending church ever since he arrived in Last Chance—a tradesman with a little bit of money in his pocket and a prayer in his heart that God would grant him a new life out here with real, hardworking people in Iowa. And every week, he'd seen Anne sitting in the front row of the church next to her parents, and she seemed so innocent, so good, and so much better than he deserved.

This evening, in the periwinkle twilight, Ben parked his buggy between a farmer's wagon and an automobile belonging to the two Misses Bertrand. He let his gaze roam over the Packard Model C in the light that spilled from the open church doors. It looked like a horseless carriage—no windshield and a waterproof leather roof that could be removed in pleasant weather. The chrome and shining black paint were muted by dust from the road. He knew the car—New York City had more automobiles than rural communities did. He had wanted a Packard Model C of his own not so long ago, but he had made an effort to stop dreaming of such things. The things a man hoped for in New York City felt possible, just with the hustle and bustle of businesses and people going about their affairs. But here in Last Chance, he had to be more realistic.

His father had always said that New York City was the kind of place where a man could climb, if he was just determined enough. Ben had been a disappointment. He was not the man building the mansion, he was the one designing and carving the wooden railings. He was not the man investing in the railroad company, he was the one loading up crates of his work onto a train car to send to customers in another city. But Jake Huntington's dreams for his son had been more aggressive than Ben wanted for himself. His father's words when he'd told him he was cut out of the will still stung. *I am not leaving you a penny. You cannot be trusted to keep building what I have started. If you shape up, I will reconsider. But as for now...*

Anne didn't wait for Ben to come around and give her a hand. She gathered up her gray skirt and climbed to the ground. When he got to her side of the buggy, she gave her skirt a shake with gloved hands. Molly reached for Ben, and he lifted his daughter down. Anne had helped her to dress tonight—one of Molly's regular dresses of pink cotton, but Anne had added a new pink ribbon as a belt and a little feathered clip in her hair. Her dress looked almost new, and Molly took some extra care with adjusting her own skirt, watching how Anne smoothed hers.

Molly was learning from a woman who knew how to look elegant with very little, and he felt a burst of pride. Any woman could stand still and have servants dress her or go into a city shop and have a skilled dressmaker put something together for her that made her look her best. But it took a special quality of woman to use the few things at her disposal and come out with such results.

Together—a new family of three—they walked into the softly glowing church. Familiar voices murmured, and the tap of heels resounded upon the wooden floorboards. People milled around in the foyer, greeting each other and sharing the latest news from their lives, but there wasn't much room in the entrance, so some spilled outside to talk in the cool evening air. Others moved inward to the pews, where a more hushed whispering and greeting filled the atmosphere.

Ben glanced into the sanctuary, and he spotted Abigail and Thomas York in their usual spot in the front row. Abigail always had a peppermint candy in her handbag for Molly—one tiny luxury that had won his daughter's heart. Molly looked up hopefully at Ben for permission.

"Go on," he whispered, and Molly headed into the church and slipped into a spot next to Abigail. It warmed his heart when he saw Abigail's smile as she leaned over to whisper something to Molly. It had been a long time since Molly was in the presence of a grandparent who loved her for who she was instead of looking down on her disapprovingly because of Ben's choices. Molly had lost just as much as Ben had—maybe even more, because she had no choice in the matter. But Molly would have a true family here. One where time together and peppermints mattered more than money and control.

Ben was about to see if Anne was ready to go sit down too, when Reverend Bogg came over to shake his hand and give Anne a smile.

"The Huntingtons," the reverend said with a satisfied smile. "A family who prays together stays together. This is a wonderful start to your marriage."

"Thank you," Anne murmured.

"Where is your daughter?" Reverend Bogg looked around.

"With her grandparents inside," Ben said. That felt good to say out loud.

"I am so sorry about the fire," the reverend said, keeping his voice low. "That was a terrible thing. I have been praying for you, that God will pour out His blessings on your new marriage. This kind of start can be disheartening."

"It is," Ben agreed. "But it is not so bad as it seemed. The fire brigade managed to get the fire out quite quickly, and the damage was limited to my workroom."

"Praise God."

"Yes, I have been thanking Him for that mercy," Ben replied. "I have to get things sorted out with my projects, but I can do that."

"I had heard that you are leaving town," the reverend said. "It sounds like maybe you will stay?"

Ben felt Anne stiffen, even without looking at her. He was tempted to reach out and touch her arm, reassure her somehow, but he didn't. He had promised her that they would stay, and he wasn't about to break his word.

"Leaving?" Ben shook his head. "We are not going anywhere."

"When I heard that, I was disappointed, to be sure," Reverend Bogg said. "But I would have understood. To be targeted like that… Has the sheriff come up with anything?"

"Not yet," Ben said. "We have to give it some time. He is an insightful man, and I have full faith in his ability to suss out who did this."

But now that the reverend brought up the likelihood of moving from here, Ben had to admit that it was tempting. Last Chance might be a perfect place to hide from the world, but it was a difficult place to grow.

"Well, I am sorry I spoke out of turn," Reverend Bogg said.

"May I ask who told you that we were leaving town?" Ben asked. That detail might matter, because it wasn't true.

"I was visiting the Nelson home. Old Reverend Nelson has taken ill, and I had gone to pray for him."

Ben looked at Anne. Her gaze was fixed on the reverend's face, her lips parted. He could almost feel her bated breath.

"Reverend Nelson said this?" Ben clarified.

"No, I believe it was his granddaughter, Mary. You know her, Anne, don't you?"

"I work with her at the millinery, but I told her nothing of the sort," Anne replied.

"Oh. I see. I misinterpreted what she said, then. I thought she spoke seriously, when perhaps it was just idle conjecture. I don't mean to cause problems." Reverend Bogg looked distressed. "I should not have said anything. I know how gossip can get out of hand, and I never want to be a part of it. I do humbly apologize to you, Mrs. Huntington, and to you too, Ben. From my heart."

"It is forgotten," Ben replied.

"Thank you," Reverend Bogg said. "Don't let this ugliness take your attention off of each other. I say this as your pastor. Life will have many ups and downs, but a man and wife can find comfort and constancy in one another. That is my advice to you today, mere days into your marriage."

"We appreciate it, Reverend," Ben said.

As the reverend moved on to shake someone else's hand, Ben looked down at his wife. Constancy. Would he be able to provide that for his wife? He no longer had the financial position to give her a life free of worry in that respect.

"What did you say to Mary?" he asked softly.

Anne looked up at him, her expression grim. "I told her plainly that we were going to find out who did this. She was the one who suggested to me that we leave town. I told her we would not."

She pressed her lips together, and she looked as unsettled as he felt.

"It will be well," Ben said. "Don't worry yourself over it. It is gossip. These things happen in any community. Maybe she just wanted to feel important, having a connection to you."

"Mary also said she saw a man running from the shop when the fire started," she whispered. "I did not know if I believed her, though, because she seemed quite interested in us leaving town, and disapproving of..." Anne stopped then lifted her chin. "Disapproving of me keeping my position at the shop as a married woman."

"Do you think she lied to you about seeing a man run from the scene?" Ben asked.

"If she knew who did it, maybe so," she replied. "Because the letter had perfume on it, remember? A woman wrote that."

Ben nodded slowly. "Maybe Mary did."

Anne didn't answer, but her eyes misted with tears. The truth was painful, and these were people she had relied on all her life. Here he was, in the foyer of the church, wanting to go inside and find some spiritual comfort in the midst of this storm but at the same time looking around at the people he'd worshiped with the last year, wondering if one of them had torched his shop.

"I don't know if Mary started that rumor, or someone else," Anne whispered. "But it sounds to me like someone is trying to plant the idea that we would be better off leaving."

Ben wished he knew who had done this. An enemy he could name could be dealt with—faced, challenged, reported, even. But a faceless threat? It was as insidious as a rumor.

"I saw Jessop Guthrie yesterday," Ben said. "I did not want to upset you, so I did not say anything, but he seemed gleeful about the fire. He asked if you regretted marrying me yet."

Anne pursed her lips. "He is a distasteful man."

"I agree," Ben said. "But I wonder if he is the one who wants to be rid of us. Or more accurately, perhaps he wants to be rid of me."

Anne shook her head. "The letter. That was a woman. Women are often underestimated in their intelligence and their abilities."

"But the fire could have been a man," Ben countered. "And the letter could have been a woman. Maybe the two know each other. Maybe one is helping the other. It might not be so easy."

"Maybe they are a couple," she murmured.

That was a striking thought. A couple who'd pitted themselves against him and his new wife? But she was right. There were many powerful women in New York City who had wielded more power in drawing rooms than their husbands had managed out in the workforce. How many business deals were concluded because wives decided they liked each other? A powerful man chose his wife carefully. She could truly make him or break him.

He heard noisy boots on the church steps, and he turned at the same time Anne did. It was Jessop Guthrie. His loud voice reverberated through the foyer. His shirt had an oily stain on the front, and his boots left deposits of dried mud behind them on the floor.

"Good evening, Reverend," Jessop's voice boomed. "I have decided to take my soul more seriously."

This time, Ben did reach out and place his hand protectively on his wife's back.

"What is he doing here?" Anne breathed.

"We should be glad if he truly is taking his soul more seriously," Ben murmured wryly.

The man had not attended church once in the time that Ben had been in Last Chance. But then Jessop's glittering gaze swung around the foyer and landed on Anne. His lips curved into a dangerous smile. He was here to mock them—Ben could feel it in his bones. The man had come to church in order to make them tremble, and Ben trembled for no man.

"I'm surprised they left that shop unattended." Jessop's voice carried strong and sharp.

Was that a threat? Ben wouldn't cause a scene, but he suddenly wondered if he should be heading back. For how long would he have to keep watch over his shop lest it go up in flames and be lost completely?

"Ben, he cannot go on like this," Anne whispered fiercely.

"Let him be," Ben said. "If he is here, he's not setting fire to anything, is he?"

Anne looked up at Ben, her gaze glittering in anger.

"He does not own me. I am not his to fight over," she whispered. "And the sooner he accepts that fact, the better."

She slipped away from Ben's touch and marched directly toward Jessop Guthrie.

Apparently, Anne trembled for no man either.

Anne's heart hammered hard in her chest, and inside the sanctuary, the first hymn, "There Shall Be Showers of Blessing," began. Right now, she would be grateful for a few drops. She would not cower before Jessop Guthrie again.

"Do you have something to say to me?" Anne demanded. "Because if you do, I suggest you say it now with witnesses present. Say your piece and have it out. I am tired of your glares and your comments behind my back. What have you to say to me, Jessop Guthrie?"

The foyer stilled, and she could feel all eyes locking on to her, sending a shiver up her neck. Ben touched her arm, and she shook his fingers off.

"Well?" she pressed.

Jessop stared at her in momentary shock. He'd obviously expected a gentle woman to simply quell under his bullying, but Jessop Guthrie was another man who needed to learn not to underestimate a woman.

"I'm surprised you married this man, is all," Jessop said. "He's as mild as a bowl of milk."

"You insult my husband now?" she snapped.

"You could have been mistress of my entire hog farm!" Jessop's tone darkened. "And you chose him?"

"Jessop, hear me clearly." Her voice shook. "I did not wish to be mistress of your farm, or wife to you. Find a woman who will value what you offer. I am not that woman."

Jessop's lips turned up in an ugly snarl. She'd succeeded in angering him, although with Ben behind her and the rest of the church at her back, she was safe enough. But anger and liquor had several things in common—the most important of which was that they loosened lips.

"Now what have you to say about our home?" she asked. "Did you set that fire to teach me a lesson?"

"Me?" Jessop's confidence started to falter.

"Admit it!" she spat. "You wanted revenge because a paltry woman defied you! You wanted to show me that you were a man and I was nothing."

Jessop's face paled, and he tore his gaze off of Anne and looked at the people behind her. Anne refused to turn. She could feel them there, hear their shuffling feet and their intakes of breath. She was giving them something to talk about for the next year at least, but she didn't care. If Jessop Guthrie had tried to burn down their home, then she wanted to know it. And she wanted the whole community to know it too.

"I did not set that fire!" Jessop said, raising his voice. "That would be against the law, and I am a law-abiding citizen."

The singing in the sanctuary cut off, one voice lingering longer than the rest, and then falling quiet.

"I did not set it!" Jessop repeated, his voice echoing. "Do I think this woman is too headstrong and needs to be tamed? I do! But she is not my problem, is she?"

Jessop took a step away, and Anne felt Ben's steadying hand on her back once more. She longed to lean into his touch, but she didn't dare show weakness or a faltering nature in front of this bully.

"I will leave you be, Mrs. Huntington." He put stress on her new name. "You and your precious church."

"You are welcome here," Ben said. "But you are not welcome to let my wife's name pass your lips again."

"I won't trouble you further," Jessop said, and he stomped out of the church.

Anne stood with her breath trapped in her chest and her heart pattering in her throat. That had been a very public display, and she felt heat creeping into her face. A quality woman did not raise her voice, let alone have a shouting match with a farmer! What had she done?

Except she regretted nothing. She'd had her say, and she had pushed Jessop to the brink. And he had backed off. Would he leave her alone now?

Outside, the thunder of hooves and the rattle of Jessop's wagon faded into the distance. Anne slowly turned, and the people remaining in the foyer—people she had known all her life—stared at her like she was a stranger.

The door of the sanctuary opened, and Reverend Bogg looked out at them, eyebrows high.

"Come outside," Ben said in her ear, and he nudged her with a hand on her waist toward the door.

The singing in the sanctuary began again. Anne allowed Ben to usher her out the front door and down the steps, his hand firm. She started to feel foolish for her outburst, but if Ben thought he was going to reprimand her—

"Anne…" He stopped just outside the pool of light from the front doors, and he bent his head a little to make eye contact. "You are quite extraordinary."

Anne blinked at him, and then laughter started to bubble up inside of her. It was not because she found the moment humorous, but she was so filled with relief at his concern that she could not help herself.

"Anne?" He looked perplexed.

"I am sorry, Ben," she said. "I thought you would be furious."

"I am not. I may be surprised, but I am not angry," he said. "Why did you do that?"

"I will not live my life cowering before a bully," she said. "If he set that fire, I wanted him to say it in front of people. I thought he might say it if he was angry enough." The foolhardiness of it all started to occur to her, and she smiled weakly. "It made more sense five minutes ago."

"Please don't poke a bull." Ben smiled back though. "I would have had to defend you, and he would have crushed me."

Anne laughed softly. "In the church? No, he would not have done that. But he didn't confess, either, did he?"

"You were certain it was him?" Ben asked.

"I thought so." Anne exhaled a slow breath. "Maybe he didn't do it. Or maybe he is a good liar. I can hardly expect an arsonist to tell the truth about it, can I?"

"Let's walk that way a little," he said quietly.

A few minutes in the quiet of the evening would be helpful in getting her equilibrium back again. Light from the church's stained-glass window shone cozily into the near darkness. A few stars had appeared in the sky, and a half-moon hung low over the black hills in the distance. The light washed over the gravestones above them on the hill, and the big oak tree stretched its branches over the graves like a mother hen might gather her chicks.

It was a peaceful scene, the singing from the church melting into the velvet night—songs of hope and purpose. The air was brisk and cool, and Ben's arm was warm next to hers.

"Would you really have defended me?" she asked quietly.

"You are my wife. Of course."

She smiled wanly. "I did not expect this kind of reaction to our marriage."

"Our home to be set on fire?" His voice was low and deep.

"That, and some people are truly happy for us. Others… You can tell they are not."

"Perhaps a little jealousy?" he asked.

"To be expected, isn't it? But somehow, I didn't. I did not think anything would change, least of all my relationships with other women."

"Are you talking about Mary?" he asked.

She nodded. "I thought we were friends. I told her I had decided to marry you, and she helped me choose some items to dress up my outfit for the day. I thought…"

She sighed. That her friend would react this way, and pass along gossip that was so untrue, had stabbed deeper than she had let anyone see.

"Marriage changes more than we think," Ben said.

"What about you?" she asked. "Is it different for you being married?"

Ben nodded. "Yes, it is. I have a wife to provide for now, as well as my daughter. And I want to do well by you. I want you to have everything that pleases you."

She smiled. "I am happy, Ben."

"I detest telling you to be careful in how you spend. I want to simply pay our tabs and let you enjoy life."

"That would not be realistic though." She shot him a quizzical look. "Who can live that way?"

She didn't know anyone who did not have to count their coins and be careful about them.

"We might live that way, if I grew my business more." Ben met her gaze meaningfully. "If we moved away…"

Anne's breath caught. There it was again—the suggestion that they leave. "When we agreed to marry, you told me—"

"I know, I know. I told you we would stay here with your family. We wouldn't go away."

"You promised me." Her throat felt tight.

"I did. But you could change your mind about that," he said. "I will be able to grow my business and our financial position a little bit here in Last Chance, but I will never be able to make enough that money wouldn't be a worry ever again. We would have to watch our spending, be thrifty… But truly, I want to do more for you. It can't happen right away, but in a bigger place, with a little time, you could be a wealthy woman."

"Me? Wealthy?" Anne started to laugh, but when he didn't even break a smile, it evaporated. "I have never seriously thought about that, Ben. I do not come from wealthy people."

"Would you like to be a woman with an automobile?" he asked. "Or have a maid in your house who cleans? A cook who prepares meals for you? A grand house where you can have guests and big dinners and invite your family to come see you?"

"And live…where?"

"I have heard that Duluth has many opportunities. It's on Lake Superior. There is a port, and a lot of shipping is done there." Ben reached out and touched her hand. His finger moved down hers, and she felt a shiver go up her arm. "Would you be willing to move away from here…with me?" Ben asked softly. "With me and Molly?"

Anne's heart galloped in her chest, and she turned away from him, pulling her hand back. Was he changing his mind so quickly? Were the promises he made only to convince her to marry, and then to evaporate? She'd believed him.

"Anne?"

She swallowed. "My grandparents are buried in the Last Chance graveyard. And three uncles, two cousins, and an infant sister who died when she was only a few months old."

Ben was silent.

"I sat under the shade of that oak tree during the burial service for my grandmother when I was ten. I come see the graves sometimes, to remember the people we lost. This is my home. I do not want wealth or a maid or a fancy automobile. I want family and roots and people who know me. I hardly know you, Ben. That is just the truth. We married for the benefits to each of us. I will raise your daughter and love her. I will show her how to be a good woman. But I cannot show her the ways of city people. I don't know them. I know how to live well here, not in some fine mansion where I won't know how to teach Molly how to drink her tea, let alone how to dress. To move away from everything I do know, to go to some big city... It is too much to ask. I do not need wealth. I need you to keep your promise."

Ben sighed, and she could see disappointment in his dark eyes. "I understand."

But what did that mean? He understood how she felt, but would he still insist upon moving away? And if he did, would she be willing to go with him? Because she *would* have a choice.

"Ben, we do not know each other very well."

She needed time. But would she get it? The singing had stopped inside the church, and Ben nodded in the direction of the glowing stained-glass windows.

"I know," he said. "I am sorry I upset you. I just wanted to see what you thought. Let's go inside."

She wordlessly angled her steps with his as they walked back toward the church. For better or for worse, in sickness and in health... She'd given him her vow.

But he'd *promised*.

CHAPTER SIX

Ben and Anne slipped into the church as Reverend Bogg began to preach. They slid into the front row next to Molly, who smelled of peppermint. The sermon was a sober one about the true meaning of church—not a building, but a community of people. It was timely, and while the reverend didn't mention the fire, it was clear what was on his mind.

"Can you truly, with a peaceful conscience, claim to be a part of the church if you are not your brother's keeper?" the reverend asked. "We must take care of each other and side ourselves with truth and justice. We are responsible for one another!"

Ben appreciated the message, and it did make him feel a little safer. Reverend Bogg was right. In a church of true believers, no one was ever alone. When the sermon was over, they sang another hymn, and then everyone gathered their things and headed out of the sanctuary to go home.

Outside in the chilly May breeze, Emily and Elizabeth Bertrand stopped to talk with Ben beside their car, and he stood at his horse's head. The Bertrand sisters were a strange mix of Old-World proper and American adventure. At church, their dress style was decidedly Victorian—twenty years out of date and filled with layers of fabric, whale bone stays, and lace. But Ben had spotted them dealing with a new horse behind their house, and he could have sworn he saw Elizabeth hoist her skirt up to her knees and climb over a fence!

"How bad was the fire, Ben?" Emily asked gently. "I mean, really."

Emily was a middle-aged woman with silver in her hair. She and Elizabeth had never married, and they still lived in the family home and ran the Bertrand estate. Ben wasn't fully sure how the inheritance had worked, but Elizabeth and Emily were known for their charitable donations and the good work they did for the community.

"It was bad enough," Ben said. "I must tell you that the cherry wood I bought for the pulpit was destroyed."

"Oh…" Elizabeth shook her head. "That came from the Canadian border, didn't it?"

"It did." He and Cyril Welch had gone together on the order. The larger order was cheaper for both of them if they shared it. Ben had thought that Cyril might be a friend at that point. Things had deteriorated since.

"Is there any way to get more black cherry wood?" Elizabeth asked. Her heart was set on black cherry.

"There is one way," Ben admitted. "I'll see what I can do. But if you want to find another carpenter to do this commission—"

"We do not want another carpenter," Emily interrupted. "We want you, Ben. Your skill is unmatched around these parts. That pulpit will be with our church for generations, and we want our gift to this church to be truly beautiful, not just functional. I don't know another carpenter who can do what you do."

Except the wood was gone. Should he ask the sisters for more money, or should he swallow the loss? The Bertrand sisters were generous, but they were exacting too. If anyone thought they could take advantage of the two middle-aged women, then they should think again. They'd already paid him and, if possible, Ben needed to deliver.

"I appreciate that," he said. "I do know of one place where I might be able to get that beautiful wood. I will try."

"We will say a prayer for your success." Emily smiled. "Thank you, Ben."

The women got into their automobile. Emily opened the hood to flood the engine, and Elizabeth put the various levers into position.

"Let me help you with that," Ben said as the hood slammed shut. He accepted the crank handle from Elizabeth, who sat in the driver's seat.

"Do you know how?" Elizabeth asked, leaning over to supervise him.

"I do, actually." He inserted the handle into the sprocket and gave it a hard turn. The engine rumbled to life like a large, satisfied cat. It was a beautiful sound.

"Good night," Ben said, passing the handle back to Elizabeth.

"Good night," Elizabeth replied, and she gave Ben a peculiar, evaluating look. "Keep us up to date on that commission, would you?"

"I will."

The Bertrand sisters drove out of the parking lot, and Ben pulled himself up into his buggy, where Anne and Molly waited for him.

"What will you do?" Anne asked.

He flicked the reins, and the buggy started forward. "I have to go talk to Cyril and see if he'll sell me his black cherry wood."

Anne didn't answer. She didn't have to. She was probably wondering the same thing he was. Was Cyril the one to start the fire? He'd have a better idea tomorrow after he talked to him.

The next morning, Ben woke up to hear Anne and Molly talking in Molly's bedroom as they chose Molly's dress for the day. Their voices were cheerful. He hadn't heard such happiness in his home in a long time.

He'd been thinking last night about their future in Last Chance. He'd promised Anne that they would stay right here in her home community, but what if there was no future possible here? What if this enemy just kept attacking them and there was no way to build themselves up here? What if moving to a bigger town was the only way forward?

Would Anne trust him enough to go with him?

And yet her argument that she could not raise a daughter to be a fine lady when she herself didn't know the social rules was a strong one. He had married Anne to be Molly's mother—her example, her guide. That was what he had told her. Was it fair to ask Anne to leave the place where she was equipped to do that job?

Anne had breakfast on the table when he got downstairs. Oatmeal, toasted bread, and some sausage she'd fried up. It was a delicious meal, and he realized that it was not only food that warmed him. It was the smiling woman across the table. And yet, when she smiled, she did not quite meet his gaze.

Welch's Carpentry was located down a side road at Cyril Welch's home. He had a big workshop in a building across a large yard. The house had a fresh coat of white paint, and the beginning of a garden that was large and free of weeds peeked from the backyard. The clothes that hung on the line looked bright and plentiful. A dog sat panting by the door, and it gave a big woof when Ben drove his buggy onto the property.

Gertie, Cyril's wife, poked her head out the front door.

"Hello, Ben." Her voice wasn't exactly warm.

"Gertie," Ben said, tipping his hat. "Good morning, ma'am."

"Good morning. I imagine you are here to see my husband, not me."

"Yes, ma'am, although it is a pleasure."

She angled her head toward the workshop and then disappeared back inside, the screen door clattering. She didn't call the dog in.

Ben got out of the buggy, and the dog barked a few times but didn't come any closer. Cyril appeared in the doorway of his workshop, his expression wary.

"Good morning, Cyril."

"Good morning. What brings you here?" Cyril's tone was on the edge of warm, but not quite.

"Well, as you know, my workshop suffered a fire," Ben said.

"I heard." Cyril crossed his arms. "Who did you upset?"

"I wish I knew." Ben met the other man's gaze frankly. "At one point, you and I got along. So I'm going to level with you. I lost that black cherry wood in the blaze. I needed it to complete an order, and I wondered if you might be willing to sell me your share of the order. For a fair price, of course."

"Why should I part with it?" Cyril asked. "Everyone knows what you were working on. It was the pulpit commission from the Bertrand spinsters."

That was a cruel name to call the Misses Bertrand, in Ben's humble opinion.

"Yes, that is the job I need to complete," he replied. He wouldn't be derailed.

"Even if I wanted to"—something in Cyril's tone suggested he didn't—"I've already taken an order for a kitchen hutch using that wood. I can't give it up."

"I understand," Ben said. "That is fair."

Cyril crossed his arms over his chest. "How bad was the fire? I heard they put it out pretty quickly."

"They did," Ben said, "but I will be honest and tell you that it worries me. I have a wife and a daughter in my home. To do that? It was cruel."

Cyril chewed the inside of his cheek.

"Do you know who did it?" Ben asked, meeting his gaze.

Cyril spat on the ground. "What makes you think I do?"

"Look, this is someone willing to impoverish a man for some grudge," Ben said. "I am pretty sure that if someone feels that strongly, he is going to talk about it. You might have heard something."

"Not me." But Cyril did look just a little bit smug.

"I have been fair and neighborly since I arrived. Are you so certain you have fewer enemies than I seem to? If someone can get away with this in Last Chance, what makes you so sure you will not be next?"

Cyril eyed him for a moment then spat on the ground again. "If I were in your boots, I'd move away. I would pack up and take that family of mine to some other city, and I'd never come back. Take that for a little piece of advice."

"Why?" Ben pressed.

"Because, like you said, you don't seem to think you've done anything! I'd be thinking of my family's safety, is all. What use is pride if the ones you love get hurt?"

"I agree with that," Ben said. "But my wife loves this place. I would like to stay for her, if I can."

Something in Cyril's gaze softened. "She is a good woman. Better than you deserve."

The jab was almost friendly, and Ben chuckled. "I know it. And I am grateful for her."

They were silent for a moment.

"I am sorry about the wood," Cyril said at last.

That was a farewell. Ben gave the other man a nod. "Thank you. I'll figure something out."

Cyril went back into his workshop and, when the door shut, the dog's lips curled with a low growl. A shiver slipped down Ben's spine. He walked briskly to his buggy, hoisted himself up, and flicked the reins.

Maybe it was time to pack and find another place to settle. If they left town, it would be because they had no other choice.

Anne cleaned up the breakfast dishes, and Molly sat at the table, a pencil and paper in front of her. She carefully wrote out the alphabet in neat printing. Anne peeked over at her work as she dried another dish.

"That is very good, Molly," Anne said.

"I can write all my letters. The big ones and the little ones," Molly said. "And I can write my name."

It was very impressive for a girl who had not gone to school yet. Children started school at seven years old in Last Chance. There were still another two years at home, but maybe Anne could start to teach her a few things. That was a pleasing thought. Something to work toward with her stepdaughter.

"Can you read a little bit?" Anne asked.

"Just some words."

"Would you like to learn to read more words?" Anne asked hopefully.

Molly nodded, still hunched over her sheet, her pencil gripped tightly as she outlined the curve of an *S*.

"Your father must be a very good teacher to have you know so much already." Anne put a bowl up into the cupboard.

"Papa didn't teach me. My nanny did."

Anne frowned. "Your nanny?"

"My nanny in New York."

Anne had heard of nannies, of course. She understood the idea of a woman paid to care for someone's children, but no families in these parts had nannies. None that she knew personally, at least. Mothers raised their children, and fathers worked hard to provide.

But Molly had lost her mother when she was very small. Was there a family member who'd stepped in, perhaps? Maybe Molly misunderstood. A nanny would be incredibly expensive. She could only imagine the cost.

"We had a big, lovely automobile in New York too," Molly said.

"You're teasing!" Anne said, because it was a much better option than Molly telling fibs.

"No, we had an automobile. We rode in the back, and a man with a hat drove it for us."

Anne licked her lips, sifting through these new stories. Was Molly misunderstanding something? Had she perhaps gotten a ride in an automobile once? But Anne was only realizing now how little she knew her husband's history. He'd come from New York, widowed with a child. He was a carpenter. She'd thought that covered it. But New York was a large and wonderful place. Maybe they could get rides in automobiles there like children rode ponies. Who knew?

"Your papa is a carpenter though," Anne said gently.

"Yes." Molly stuck out her tongue as she concentrated, forming her letters with much care.

"New York must be a very different place," Anne murmured.

"Yes. Very different. It is like my dollhouse in New York."

Ah, there it was. She was playing imagination, making up a wonderful place in her head.

"Wouldn't that be something?" Anne said. "But dear, if your dollhouse was a real, big house, it would be a mansion. It would be a house that very rich people lived in. People like us would never live in a house like that."

But Ben's words about moving away echoed through her mind. He'd asked if she'd like a maid and a cook and a big, grand house. She'd thought he'd been exaggerating, or dreaming out loud. Had he talked like that in front of Molly one too many times?

Molly looked up, confused. "But my dollhouse *is* like New York."

"Did you see houses like that when you drove by them?" Anne asked, silently wishing the girl would tell the truth. Fibs were wrong, and Anne didn't want to shame her, but she couldn't allow it to continue either. Or maybe she was just very young and didn't remember properly.

"It was our house."

"Molly…," Anne said gently. This was going too far.

"It was! We lived in a big house, and my nanny read books with me and took me for walks in the park. And Cook made my lunch and served it upstairs in the nursery. And Sally laid my clothes out on my bed."

"Molly, this is very naughty of you," Anne said. "I am sorry you have not stopped yourself already. You cannot tell lies. It is very important to tell the truth."

"I'm not lying!" Molly said. "I don't tell lies!"

Anne shut her eyes for a moment then opened them. "Dear, did you think I was your nanny before I married your father?"

Molly shook her head. "No. You weren't my nanny. Nannies live in your house. And Papa said you weren't a nanny and I should never call you anything but Miss York."

"Maybe your home in New York felt much bigger than this one," Anne suggested.

"It *was* much bigger," Molly insisted. "My grandpapa built it."

Anne put the last dish into the cupboard. Maybe it was best there was time before Molly was sent off to the schoolhouse with the other children, because they would need to work on her truthfulness. What an imagination she had though! Anne knew the girl had a good heart. This was why Ben had needed a mother for her. Some things could only be fixed by a loving, feminine hand.

There was a knock at the front door, and Anne exchanged a look with her stepdaughter. Ben had not returned yet from his errand to the Welches' house, and Anne would feel better if he were here.

All the same, she was the lady of this home now. She pulled off her apron, smoothed her skirt, and walked briskly out of the kitchen, through the workroom, and to the front door.

Normally, she'd look out the front window, but it hadn't been replaced yet and was still covered over with wood. So she straightened her spine and pulled open the door. Standing on the step was Henry Ager, the postmaster of Last Chance.

"Mr. Ager, hello," Anne said.

"Mrs. Huntington." Henry tipped his hat. "I have something for your husband."

He stepped away and gestured, and two young men pushed a dolly with a big wooden crate up over the step and into the shop. Anne had to step quickly back to give them space, and she looked at Mr. Ager with wide eyes.

"Is this that crate that didn't have a proper address?" she asked.

"The one and only," he replied. "I went all the way to Derby, and I searched through their mail wagon and found the missing piece of label." He held it out. Written in bold letters on a creased, beaten piece of paper was her husband's name and the first part of their address.

Anne shook her head in disbelief. "It is for Ben?"

"Yes. Appears to be," Mr. Ager replied. "Is your husband at home?"

"No, he's—" Suddenly she felt very vulnerable admitting she was here alone. "He's due back any minute though."

"If he were home, I'd be forward enough to ask to see what's inside," Mr. Ager said. "But it will have to wait. We have all been wondering what's in it, and we are awfully curious to know the truth. If it isn't a private matter, at least."

"I am sure Ben will be happy to talk to you about it," she said, looking the large crate over. "Thank you for bringing it, Mr. Ager."

"My pleasure."

Mr. Ager took his leave, and when the door was shut once more, Anne looked up to see Molly standing in the doorway to the kitchen.

"Do we have a present?" Molly asked.

Anne laughed softly. "I think this is a little too large for that, Molly. We shall have to wait for your father to find out."

"It might be a sink," Molly said soberly. "I remember last time there was a crate like that, it was a sink."

And maybe it was. What did Anne know? But she was still thoughtful about her stepdaughter's stories. Molly sounded like she was telling the truth, and she'd been so insistent that she didn't tell lies. Was there more to her husband's family than she'd realized?

Ben arrived home about an hour later. He came inside with a frown on his face, and he pulled off his hat and hung it on a peg before he even acknowledged their presence. Anne and Molly stood next to the crate.

"What is this?" Ben asked, looking at the crate in surprise.

"Henry Ager brought it over today," Anne said. "It was in the post office for a few days. They didn't have the complete label."

"Who is it for?" He picked up the crinkled piece of paper with his name and address on it. "Then who is it from?"

He looked around the box as if he might see another label.

"I have no idea," Anne said. "Did you order something from far away?"

"Nothing since the black cherry wood," he replied.

Anne didn't know what else to say, and she waited while Ben fetched a crowbar and began to pry the top boards loose, one creaking nail at a time. The slats came off the top of the crate, revealing crumpled paper and sawdust within. He pushed the packing material aside and pulled out a cloth-covered item. He slowly unwrapped it, and Anne gasped.

It was a china teapot with gold scrollwork over the entire surface. It shone in the light from one of the windows, and Anne's heartbeat sped up.

"Is it some sort of mistake?" she whispered.

Ben looked up, his face ashen. "I don't think so."

He put the teapot on his worktable and bent down to pull out another cloth-covered item. It was a cream pitcher, and then a sugar bowl, and a saucer, then another saucer… One by one he pulled the gold-worked tea set out of the crate. Teacups, a small, oval platter… Everything appeared to be undamaged except for one saucer that came out cracked in two.

"This must be a mistake," Anne said. "Who would send such an expensive item? I don't understand!"

Anne looked over at Molly. The girl's eyes had filled with tears.

"Molly?" Anne said, bending. "Dear, it's okay. Your papa will sort it all out."

"It's Mama's tea set!" Molly said, and a tear slipped down her cheek. "It's here!"

Anne's breath caught, and she glanced up at Ben to find him looking grim.

"Ben?"

He slowly nodded. "It is my late wife's tea set. Or…it belonged to her family, at least. It originally belonged to her great-grandmother, I believe, and when we married, it came to her. When she died—" His voice grew thick. "When she died, her father demanded it back and said that we would never see it again."

"Is it real gold?" Anne whispered.

Ben seemed to shake out of his reverie. "What? Yes, it is. It's gold plated. It is worth quite a bit."

"You say that so calmly," she said with a half laugh.

"It is—" Ben sighed. "I don't know why it was sent to me. That is what worries me. Did something happen to my father-in-law? You don't understand—this tea set has immense emotional value to my late wife's father. He was so angry with me when Eliza died. He blamed me for her passing, and he wouldn't let this tea set remain in my keeping."

"It should be locked in a safe," Anne murmured, her gaze locked on the swirls of gold.

Ben smiled faintly. "We used to drink out of it on special occasions."

Anne's throat closed. A house that looked like that dollhouse. A cook, a maid, and a nanny. An automobile and a gold-plated tea set… She felt a little faint, and she sank down onto a stool next to the worktable.

"It's Mama's tea set," Molly murmured, reaching out to run a finger over the delicate curve of the teapot's spout.

"Be careful, Molly," Ben said. "I don't know why this was sent to me."

"Ben," Anne said, her throat tight, "you said your family was comfortable in New York City."

"I did."

"How 'comfortable' were you?" she asked.

Ben rubbed a hand over his beard. "Very. My father owned a railway company and did some money lending too. As I told you, he wrote me out of his will when I decided to pursue a trade. Everything was left to my cousin."

"Who was your father, exactly?" she asked. She knew the man's name, and that was all.

"Jake Huntington," he replied. "Owner of Union Rail."

"So Molly's stories of a house that looked like her dollhouse?" she asked.

"I fashioned the dollhouse after my father's house," he said. "I grew up there, and Molly was born there. It was cathartic to make a little replica. I suppose I missed it."

It was true!

"And your wife's family?" she asked weakly.

"Eliza's father, Ike Rumsfeld, owned a shipping company with a fleet of seventy vessels."

Rich. All of them. Anne's heart thudded in her ears. "Oh no," she breathed.

"I am sorry, Anne," Ben said. "Comfortable is the polite word for, well, rich. I thought you understood that. Don't you see? When I wouldn't join my father in his business, I gave up everything. My wife was furious. My father-in-law was furious too. I was denying Eliza the life she was accustomed to, unless my father-in-law made it possible for her. I half expected Eliza to go back and live with him."

"Mama wouldn't go," Molly said.

"No, Molly, she wouldn't go," Ben said, softening his voice. "But she also wouldn't go to the country when influenza swept through New York. She didn't want to give up her place in the social circles she enjoyed. She thought if she just stayed…" He sighed. "So there was plenty of reason to resent me, you see. When I walked away from my rightful inheritance, I failed to protect Eliza. In every way."

Anne let out a shaky breath. "Then why did you marry me, Ben? I know nothing about raising a girl to be a fine lady. I can raise Molly to be a hardworking wife of a hardworking man, but that is all I know. I can show her how to read, how to add up a row of numbers… Why did you marry me, Ben?"

"Because all of that is behind me now!" he insisted.

But it wasn't quite, was it? Because Ben had asked her to move somewhere bigger where he could start to grow again, and buy a big house and hire a maid and cook… The money might not be in his hands, but his heart wasn't in an ordinary life in Last Chance either.

CHAPTER SEVEN

Ben's mind spun. Those gold-worked cups and saucers were dominant in his memories, but they felt so out of place in this humble home. They were part of an old life that no longer fit, and yet, that old life was Molly's heritage. Watching his daughter touch the familiar teapot, he felt a wave of sadness.

That teapot was part of her childhood—part of a life they'd never return to. And he couldn't imagine why his father-in-law would willingly send it to him.

"Anne…" Ben moved toward the kitchen where Molly wouldn't hear, and Anne followed him. "The tea set leaves me unsettled. I can think of only one reason why we would receive it."

"Why?" she asked.

"In the event of my father-in-law's death."

Anne's eyes widened. "Oh. Do you think?"

"I only guess. I do not know, obviously, but I suspect he probably died and the set was sent to me for my daughter. However, Ike Rumsfeld is a prominent enough man that if he'd passed away, it would be in the papers. The New York papers will have arrived on the train this morning. I'm going to go into Derby to buy a newspaper and see what I can find."

Anne nodded. "That makes sense. I hope it isn't the case though."

Her voice shook, and she wished that it didn't. But all of this was incredibly overwhelming.

"Anne, I left that life for a reason," he said. When she didn't say anything, he plunged on. "My father made a fortune, but it wasn't easy. It involved buying out smaller rail businesses, pushing them under, and then swooping in to take them over. And every smaller business he decimated, that was a family. I could not continue like that and take over from my father. I am not the man my father was. I needed a business I could grow on my own with a clear conscience. Do you understand?"

Anne met his gaze earnestly. "Ben, I don't want that money. Not a penny of it!"

He smiled faintly. "I don't think you understand how much there was…"

"I probably do not," she said. "But you promised me a life here in Last Chance, and this is the life I want. I want to live above your shop and raise Molly here. I want our neighbors in our lives, and I want to attend the church we got married in for the rest of my life. I want this life, not the wealth you came from."

Her gaze was so clear and steady that he knew she told the truth. A woman who truly wanted a simple life with a carpenter? Ben smiled down at her tenderly, took her face in his hands, and pressed a kiss on her forehead. He hadn't thought it through, and once he'd done it, he felt a little foolish. But she smiled up at him.

"I chose the right woman," he said, his voice gruff. He dropped his hands. "I will be back. I need that newspaper."

She nodded, and Ben headed out into the workshop.

Later that evening, Ben and Anne sat together at the kitchen table, newspaper spread out in front of each of them as they scanned the columns with the tiny, cramped print for any mention of Ike Rumsfeld's death. There was none.

Ben's eyes ached. He turned up the wick in the oil lamp to get a brighter flame, but he was tired. He rubbed his eyes.

He appreciated his wife's desire for a simple life with him, but he wasn't sure he could provide even that much for her here in Last Chance. Not with some hidden enemy.

"Wait…I see something," Anne said. "Not a death notice though. A robbery."

"A robbery?"

Anne put her finger on the small article and handed the newspaper to him. He angled it toward the light.

Ike Rumsfeld of Atlantic Shipping suffered a robbery at his personal abode in Manhattan two days ago. The sum of the items taken from his home are estimated to be over $30,000. The home was broken into when Mr. Rumsfeld was known to be away on a business trip. The household was under the control of his butler at the time, who has been charged as an accessory to a crime. He has yet to face his charges in court and until proven guilty, is presumed innocent.

"So he is in good health," Ben said. "I know he doesn't think much of me, but I thank God all the same."

Anne nodded toward the paper. "Did you notice that something happened when he was out of the house? The same as you. The shop was set on fire when you were known to be getting married."

"Rather on the nose, isn't it?" he murmured. Then a thought struck him. "What if this tea set was one of the items that went missing? It is worth a large amount of money. And it gets shipped to me, of all people. If this tea set has been listed as missing, and if word were to get back to the New York police that I had it, I could be charged as conspiring in a robbery."

"But you didn't do that, did you?" Her face paled.

"No, of course not," he said. "I'm not suggesting that I am actually involved. But I might very well be set up to look like it. Ike loathed me, Anne. I walked away from the one thing that mattered most to him—money. And not only did Eliza agree with her father that I was making a monumental mistake, but she was willing to do anything to maintain her position in New York's top social circles. Ike has a grudge, and I don't think it has diminished. This tea set? It is not for my betterment, I am sure."

Anne was silent for a moment. "Could he pay someone to burn down a shop?"

So she saw it now too. "He could. He's got the power and financial ability to buy anything he wants."

Anne deflated and leaned back in her chair. "Are we being targeted by one of the wealthiest men in New York?"

That was his fear, but Ben no longer had any money at his disposal to protect himself. His father's businesses and financial holdings were all with someone else now, and Ben had nothing with which to fight back. He was as ordinary as any citizen in this town.

"I don't know, my dear. But let us go to bed," Ben said. "We are in God's hands."

Because if Ike Rumsfeld had fixed his intent for revenge on Ben in Last Chance, then only God would be able to protect them. Powerful men with personal grudges were very dangerous indeed.

The next day, while her husband worked on the bed frame for his customer, Anne put the tea set back into the crate for safekeeping. She worked slowly and carefully. The crate seemed like the most protected place to keep the delicate china, and if anyone came to return the pieces to the Rumsfeld family, Anne would not stand in their way. This was the most expensive item she'd ever touched. She could not imagine sipping tea out of those gold-worked cups, but it would seem that Eliza's family in New York City had done just that.

Was it possible that the person intent on ruining all Ben had worked for was not someone from Last Chance, but someone from his past?

When the tea set was carefully stowed away, Anne took Molly along with her to see her parents. With all the uncertainty, Anne longed for a down-to-earth visit with her mother, with tea sipped out of regular china teacups that had already been chipped with no tears shed, and with honest advice coming from the heart.

Anne drove the buggy with her stepdaughter at her side toward the short gravel road where her parents lived. Her mother was outside gardening when they pulled up, her father on the porch with a blanket over his legs. Mama pulled off her gloves and shaded her eyes against the sun.

"What a lovely surprise!" Mama rose from her knees. "Molly, I happen to have made some cookies!"

Molly jumped down, running to first hug her grandmother and then clattering up the wooden steps to wrap her arms around Anne's father.

"Come inside, Anne, and you can bring some sweet tea for your dad," Mama said.

Anne paused at her father's side and squeezed his limp hand. "How are you doing, Father?"

"I'm blessed." He smiled his lopsided smile. "Still here."

"I am sorry I haven't been back to see you in a few days," Anne said.

"You are a married woman," Father replied. "I understand."

"A nurse came yesterday," Mama interjected. "She said her services were paid for her to come once a week and help your father exercise his arm and leg. She is showing me how to do it too. Ben kept his word."

"She came already?" Anne looked up in surprise. Even with the fire and Ben's worries about completing that commission, he'd paid for the nurse.

"You married a good man, dear," Mama said. "Come inside and help me carry things out."

It would seem Ben was as good a man as she had hoped—and he kept his word. Anne followed her mother inside, and as she passed through the sitting room, she cast her eyes around the familiar rooms that had been the only home she knew up until her marriage.

It made her feel a little misty-eyed, but then her gaze landed on a square, white piece of paper lying on a table. Anne glanced down at it. The handwriting was familiar.

Thank you for your kindness. I am dreadfully sorry I didn't express it properly. It is hard for me to accept charity, but the ham has fed my children for days, and I pray God's blessing upon you and your husband.

Anne brought the paper up to her nose. It smelled of rose water. Her heart hammered to a stop in her chest.

"Anne?" Mama turned back. "Oh yes. That came from Bernadette Sisk. I didn't mean to leave it lying around. She is a good woman. Honestly, Anne, she has done so much with so little this last year, and when I saw her trying to afford an extra shaving of ham, I couldn't let her take that paltry amount of meat home to her five children. God more than nudged me to do that. He knocked me hard! So she should be thanking the Lord, not me."

"We got a note written in this hand, on paper just like this, smelling of roses," Anne said.

"Don't judge her a small luxury," Mama said. "It was likely a gift—maybe from her husband. That man likes his books and beautiful things. You know that."

"I am not judging the scent on the paper," Anne said. "But that paper was tied around a brick and thrown at our door!"

Mama blinked. "What?"

Anne's mind spun. She and Ben had seen their home set on fire, and that very night the threatening note on the brick.

"What did it say?" her mother asked.

She remembered the words clearly. "It said, 'Watch yourself. Worse is to come.'"

Mama put a hand on her chest. "Bernadette and Verne? I never thought they would stoop to such ugliness. Anne, I want you to tell your father what you just told me."

"I do not like to worry him, Mama."

"He'll worry anyway. It was his body that was affected, not his mind. And he might have an idea. Your father is still the man of this house. Now go on out and tell him."

Her father looked up as Anne sat down on the porch swing next to him. He gave her a lopsided smile and patted her knee with his good hand. Keeping her voice low, Anne outlined for him what had happened since the fire. She told of the brick, of the threatening note written in a woman's hand, of the people who might have reason to dislike them and wish them ill, and of the strange reactions some of their neighbors had given them. Then she told of the tea set—worth a fortune and now sitting in a crate in her husband's workshop, and her husband's worry that his late wife's father might be the one behind this desire to drive them from town. Father listened in silence, his expression grim.

"I am going to talk to Bernadette Sisk," Anne concluded, "but Father, I don't know what to do. Ben is talking about us moving to Duluth, or some other city where he might be able to build himself up better. And I don't want to go. If this has shown me anything, it is that I hardly know the man I married. I might have nursed a silly softness for him, but mostly, I wanted to make sure that I could provide for you. I don't want to move off to some city where I will be

alone with a husband who is kind and dear and sweet but who is
almost a stranger to me." Her breath came in quick gasps. "And if I
went with him, how can I raise a little girl in a lifestyle I don't understand? He married me to raise his daughter, but I can't do it properly
away from the home I know."

Anne blinked back tears. It had all come tumbling out of her,
but she was glad to have someone to tell.

"If you can't find out who is behind all this, you have a choice,"
her father said slowly, his words slurred.

"I know. But can I send my husband away to another city?"
The thought of doing so nearly broke her heart. "Or could I leave
with him, and face all those unknowns, knowing that he never
would have married me if he knew he'd be living a higher life than
this one?"

"That isn't necessarily true," her father replied.

"Father, I am not a beauty," Anne said, tears choking her voice.
"I am a decent woman with a good heart, but I'm no society belle,
am I? He chose me because he thought I had the makings of a good
stepmother. That is all. And I don't think I can even be that much in
Duluth."

"You need to know who lit that fire."

"I know, but I don't see how we are going to find that out."

Father was silent for a moment. "People here will not rat each
other out. They will keep each other's secrets."

"And that is the problem."

"You can't chase a rat through your house and catch him,"
Father said, his good eye twinkling. "If you want to find the rat and
trap him, you have to lure him out of hiding."

"How do we do that?" she asked.

Father smiled that half smile of his, and he laughed softly. Then he outlined his plan. It was simple, but quite brilliant, and Anne had a feeling that her father was right. It would work. But she'd need to discuss this with her husband first, to make sure he agreed. Because there was a risk involved. When they lured out their rat, he might be more dangerous than they feared, especially if he ended up being a wealthy shipping mogul in New York City.

"Mama, I need you to keep things cheerful and happy for Molly for a little while. I need to drop by and speak with Bernadette myself, and then I need to talk this over with Ben."

"Are you sure it is wise to go to the Sisk place alone?" Mama asked.

"It is better than reporting it to the police right away if I am wrong," Anne said. "Bernadette won't hurt me, but if they tried to burn down our home, I want her to look me in the face and tell me why."

Molly sat with Father on the porch with a plate of cookies and two tall glasses of iced tea between them. Mama put her gardening gloves back on and continued weeding the flower garden, and Anne flicked the reins and wheeled the buggy around. If it was the Sisks who'd done this, then she needed to know. Great hardship sometimes changed people, but that didn't make them beyond redemption.

The Sisks lived on another gravel road near the one-room schoolhouse. Their house was small, with a roof that badly needed repair. It dipped slightly on one side and was propped up with some lengths of wood.

Bernadette stood outside hanging laundry on her clothesline, pinning children's trousers and dresses and moving the line along with a squeak. She looked over her shoulder as Anne's buggy pulled in. She startled then paled.

Anne was not a welcome sight, it would seem.

"Hello, Mrs. Sisk," Anne said, reining in the horse.

"Mrs. Huntington." Bernadette wiped her hands down the front of her wet apron. "You've caught me on washday."

"I see that," Anne said. "I won't take much of your time."

"Sally, Emma!" Bernadette called. Two girls appeared around the side of the house. "Carry on with hanging the laundry, please. But wash the dirt off your hands first."

The girls went to the pump to do as they were told, and Bernadette waited while Anne hopped down from the buggy seat.

"Mrs. Sisk…" Anne paused. Bernadette was ten years older than she was. She'd always been Mrs. Sisk to Anne since she married Verne. "I wanted to ask you about a letter that was…delivered to our door."

Bernadette's chin trembled.

"I know it came from you," Anne said, lowering her voice. "I saw a similar letter in my mother's home—although it wasn't similar in content at all."

Bernadette sighed. "I had to warn you."

Anne eyed her warily. "About what?"

Bernadette looked around then waggled a finger in the direction of the trees. "Aaron! Simon! Go find your little brother!"

Two boys climbed down from their perch where they had hitherto gone unnoticed, and Bernadette watched them until they were out of earshot.

"I couldn't come tell you myself," Bernadette said quietly, "because I overheard a conversation my husband had with another man. I don't know who—it was only overheard, but my husband said that as Christians we should help you and your husband in your time of need. And the man said…" She swallowed. "He said that fire wasn't the end of it! He said any help would be wasted."

"So it wasn't you or your husband who set the fire?" Anne asked.

"Us?" Bernadette's eyes widened, and she shook her head. "Why on earth would we do such a thing? We used to own that shop, and when the bank took it, it broke our hearts, but we would never take some petty, unchristian revenge on the new owners!"

"But the brick—"

"I had to make sure you got my warning, but I couldn't deliver it myself. I didn't want whoever my husband was talking to to take revenge on us next! I tied the note to a stone first, but it kept coming off. So I used a brick, and I threw it as gently as I could." Bernadette sighed. "I see now how it must have looked. I wasn't threatening you. I was trying to tell you to be careful."

"Then your husband knows who set fire to our shop," Anne said.

"He does, but he won't tell me." Bernadette lowered her voice. "He's afraid. He's not a street tough. He's a schoolteacher. And we've already lost everything trying to raise ourselves a bit higher. Someone has threatened him, and he won't say a word."

A threat by someone who scared the schoolteacher into silence. A man, it would seem. A tea set sent to their home with no return address, and a theft in New York City. Who was doing this to them?

Chapter Eight

That afternoon, Ben and Anne sat together on the back step overlooking the empty lot. He listened somberly as she told him about her visit to the Sisks, and while it was heartening to know that someone knew the identity of at least one person threatening him, Verne wouldn't talk. That was what his wife had said.

Verne was a gentle man, bookish, smart, and cautious. If there was a concerted effort to drive Ben out of town, Ben could understand a powerless man trying to stay out of it.

"My father had an idea," Anne said. "He says that chasing after the one who did this is like chasing a rat. They will always get away. We have to lure them out."

"How?" Ben asked.

"With our happiness."

Ben looked at his wife in surprise. "Our happiness?"

"Think about it," she said. "This person loathes us to their very core. They hate us so much that they tried to burn down both our home and your shop. They want us out of town. That is not a person who wants to see us do well, is it?"

"No, you are right," he agreed.

"And this person may have taken a payment in order to wreak havoc on our life here—that is a suspicion, at least," she went on. "So we need to show joyful happiness, as if something wonderful has happened. We need to celebrate."

"A party?" he guessed.

Anne shook her head. "A grand reopening of Huntington Carpentry. My father suggests that we spread the word to anyone who will listen that we are having a grand reopening and that all is going splendidly. Inside the shop, we will have barrels full of water, and we will be ready for any attempt to burn it down again. But if that isn't the cheese to lure out our rat, I don't know what is."

His wife was right. In the shadows, this person had too much power. They seemed bigger and scarier than they really were.

"That is a good plan," Ben said, sifting it through his mind. "But I have two things I insist upon."

"Oh?"

"First of all, you and Molly must be at your parents' house for this grand reopening night. I want you as far away from any danger as possible. I will not be able to confront this person if I am worrying about your safety."

"And the second thing?"

Ben met her gaze. "If this doesn't work, we move away from here."

"What? No!"

"Anne, it is the only way. Can we pay for the nurse your father needs with a floundering business? Not likely. Can I get ahead while someone is always watching for a way to undo any good fortune? If this does not work, I cannot keep my promise to you here."

"Last Chance is my life," she said. "You would want me to leave my parents behind?"

He could almost feel her trepidation. She'd have to trust him with her future in every way. But it might be too much to ask.

"I know you do not want to move, but I want you to think about it. It might be our only option if we can't flush out the one intent on ruining us." He paused. "I should not say they are intent on ruining *us*, Anne. They are intent on ruining *me*. You had no trouble until you married me. This has nothing to do with you besides the fact that you are now my wife."

This marriage was supposed to benefit them both, and he realized with a sinking feeling that Anne had yet to benefit. Except for the nurse coming to help her father, this marriage had brought nothing but trouble to her. And he had to wonder… If he did not manage to flush out the rat, would Anne come with them to Duluth, or would she stay here in Last Chance with her family, her friends, and the community she loved so well?

He wished he knew.

That evening, Molly begged for another doll for her dollhouse. Ben sat down in the quiet evening with his penknife and a piece of wood just the right size.

"She needs to be a mama doll," Molly said. "And she needs to have a kind smile and a baby she can hold."

With a baby to hold…that would be a little harder. He'd have to carve one bent arm so he could place a little infant in the crook. Yes, he could do this. It felt good to have something different to focus on for a little while.

"I will do the carving, and maybe Anne will make the clothes for us." Ben smiled at his daughter. "She is very good with a needle and thread."

Ben looked up to find Anne watching him carve, and he sent up a prayer that God would find a way to bind them together in this marriage. He worked the wood, little curls falling to his lap as Molly leaned forward to watch.

If only families were as easy to build as the ones he carved for his daughter's dollhouse.

The next day, Ben and Anne spread the word. Anne took Molly with her up and down the main street, telling each store owner that they were having a grand reopening the next evening. They encountered the Bertrand sisters outside the tack shop, and the women were most surprised.

"He must have gotten the wood he needed after all," Emily said.

"Did he?" Elizabeth asked, fixing Anne with a steely look.

"Uh—no," Anne said. "Not yet. But he might." She couldn't lie, so she added, "It is important for people to know and trust that we will be here for a long, long time."

They would not be chased out.

"I agree," Emily said. "He has a good mind for business, that husband of yours. But after that fire, I will not pretend to think you have no struggles, Mrs. Huntington. Please, let us provide some small cakes and pastries for the event."

"Are you sure?" Anne asked, guilt washing over her.

"Very. It is only right we celebrate your marriage and your grand reopening. Accept this as a wedding gift," the older woman said. "We insist."

This was meant to flush out their enemy, and she hadn't considered that it might also prove their true friends. Anne almost felt bad in accepting, but what could she do? Everyone must believe in their happiness.

Henry Ager at the post office was disappointed when Anne couldn't tell him the contents of the crate, but he said that he certainly wished them well and that his wife had been asking for a new cabinet for some time. He wanted to hire Ben for the job. Mr. Wheaton at the millinery shop promised to come and gave Molly a small clip for her hair with ribbons on it. Mrs. Reese at the grocery shop also said how pleased she was for them and insisted upon providing some sticks of candy for any children who might come by.

This sudden and joyful celebration was turning into the real thing, and Anne couldn't help but wonder which of their neighbors was behind the fire, because everyone smiled and said appropriate things.

Anne came upon Mrs. Welch on the street, and when she told her of the grand reopening, the woman said quietly, "I do wish you well. Congratulations on your marriage, Anne. Truly."

Before Anne took Molly back to her parents' home, she and Ben talked quietly at the workshop. Ben had had the broken windows repaired with bright new glass, and it was almost like the fire hadn't happened. Almost.

"If anyone is to be enraged by all of this celebration, I suspect they will come and try something tonight—before there are crowds of friends and family here to witness anything," Ben said.

Suddenly, this whole plan felt incredibly flimsy. Everything was based on jealousy and hatred wanting to vent itself. What if their enemy had more self-control? What if he was biding his time? What if he wasn't local and he knew nothing of this grand celebration?

"Be careful, Ben," she said quietly.

Her gaze moved over to his worktable, and she spotted the carved doll. It needed a proper dress still, but the carving was complete. She went over and picked it up. The mama doll was indeed beautiful. With curls close to her head and a round, cheerful face, she was lovely to behold. Her arms were carved so that one was held out and bent, as if carrying something. Anne's throat closed as she looked at it.

"It's for Molly," Ben said, coming up behind her. "She needs a dress though."

The mama doll did not resemble Anne in the least. The doll was short and plump where Anne was slim. Its face was round and pretty, while Anne's was narrow. Its arm was ready to cradle a baby, while Anne had no baby of her own.

The mama doll, carved to fill a dollhouse with love, was nothing at all like the stepmother Ben had brought into his own home, and she felt tears rising up inside of her.

Of course. He'd carved a mama for a big, grand house. And she was the stepmother for Last Chance. There would be no happy life for them in Duluth, would there? She was right that she would never know how to raise a girl in a big city, and she could never run a house like the one that Ben had left behind and seemed intent on earning again.

"It is beautifully carved," Anne said, her voice feeling tight.

"Have I done something?" Ben asked, frowning slightly.

She shook her head. "No. Not at all. I must be tired."

Because how could she explain to him that the perfect mama for Molly's dollhouse was the perfect wife for Ben too? And she was nothing like Anne.

That evening, Molly stood next to Mama in the kitchen, watching as she stirred up a batch of biscuits. Anne's mind was in turmoil. The sun had slipped below the horizon, and her father sat in the living room with two oil lamps burning, illuminating the house in a cozy glow.

She paced out of the kitchen and into the living room, and her father lifted a hand and beckoned to her.

"Yes, Father?" she said. "Do you need something?"

"You're worried," he said.

"I'm afraid I am." Anne sank onto the settee next to him. "If this plan doesn't work to bring out his enemy, Ben wants us to move away."

Her father was silent.

"I won't do it though," she said. "He married the right wife for a life here, Father. Not for a life of social climbing in a city. What does an up-and-coming businessman want with a plain wife at fancy parties?"

"You are not plain," her father said, frowning.

"I am not in the mode of the day either," she said. "I am…I am the woman God created. And I believe God made me the way I am for a reason and for a purpose. But I was too rushed in marrying Ben. I was excited at the chance to have a family, and perhaps I was a little overcome at the thought of a handsome husband. But I didn't think it through."

"You are his wife," her father said. "That is a fact."

"I will not bring him success in Duluth." That was a fact too.

Her father sighed. "Let us wait and see what happens. Maybe all will be well for a life right here."

But Ben had started to think bigger thoughts, and she doubted that he'd stay content here in Last Chance now. What could Last Chance give? A community, limited growth, Anne as his wife, and a one-room schoolhouse for his daughter. Perhaps Ben should have thought this through a little more too. She looked around at her parents' sitting room—with the upright piano that was never in tune because they couldn't afford a piano tuner and the worn rug in the center of the room with the little burned dots from popping logs in the fireplace in the wintertime. There was the couch where they sat for family worship and the picture on the wall of the family all together the one time they'd splurged on a portrait.

Would this dear old house be her home again when Ben and Molly left? It wouldn't really be so different than the spinster life that had been waiting for her.

God, protect Ben tonight, she prayed in her heart. Because whatever their future held, tonight Ben intended to face a very real threat—the pure hatred that had been dogging them since their wedding. And while she doubted she was enough for the rest of his life, those fledgling feelings she'd encountered before their wedding had blossomed into something much deeper. Anne had begun to truly care for her husband.

There was a knock at the front door, and Anne rose to her feet to go and see who it was. She already felt like this house was calling her back again.

She opened the door to find Bernadette Sisk standing there, twisting her gloves in her hands.

"Anne!" Bernadette gasped. "I am so glad you're here! I came here because it was closest... My husband just arrived home, and he was passing the saloon when some men came stumbling out. They were drunk, and they said someone inside was riling men up to go confront Ben!"

Anne gulped. "Confront him about what?"

"I don't know," Bernadette said. "But Verne said there's a whole group of them. And they're drunk and riled up and carrying sticks. They're going to drive Ben out, Anne!"

A whole group of them? They had anticipated one man, or perhaps a married couple, but not a mob of riled-up drunks. What had they done?

"I am going for the sheriff," Anne said. She looked over her shoulder. "Father, I will be back."

Her father had pushed himself to his feet and limped heavily forward a few steps. His face was drawn.

"Oh no. I never intended—"

"Father, your plan worked better than we thought. But if this coward is hiding behind a mob of drunks, Ben cannot face him alone. I will go get help." Anne turned back to Bernadette. "Thank you for coming to tell us. You may have saved my husband's life!"

CHAPTER NINE

Ben sat in front of the woodstove, a piece of carving in his hands. Outside, the wind had picked up, and he could hear its distant moan. Just wind—not rain yet. He had already gone out to check on the horse, and all was calm in the stable, but Ben could feel the gathering electricity in the air.

Spring storms were a matter of course, but tonight, the sound set his nerves on edge. He leaned over the piece of wood, his knife digging out bits that curled up at the blade then fell to his feet. This carving was not commissioned. It was not for sale. It was for him.

He had been this way since he was a boy, when he would sit out at the stables with his penknife and a piece of wood, creating something beautiful and letting the rest of the world around him melt away. And tonight, he needed comfort. He'd already prayed his heart out for protection and for illumination. He'd prayed for justice and for the people of Last Chance to see him as one of them. He'd prayed that God's will would be done.

Ben was in God's hands, and while he waited for things he could not control, he whittled the wood he held in his hands. It was funny how God taught him. He'd learned more about God by being a father himself than he'd ever learned before. And as a woodworker, he learned more still—about how God must work with the knots and distortions of Ben's own character that needed forming before it could be beautiful.

In each piece of wood, Ben could see what was possible and what was not. And as he carved, he began to see possibilities he hadn't seen before. The curve of the grain revealed a cheek. The sweep of wood bulging up over a hidden knot deep in the tree was at the perfect position for her hair. It was Anne's face he whittled, and it was thoughts of Anne that gave him some comfort right now. Her face came out of the wood without any effort from him at all. He'd make it into a little wooden cameo and give it to Anne. Or maybe he'd keep it in his pocket, a reminder of the woman he married.

Would she move away from here with him? Or would she be a memory?

God, I married her, and I know she doesn't love me yet...but would You open her to the possibility of loving me?

How did a man win his wife's heart after the marriage?

Outside, he heard the sound of distant voices. He listened for a moment then turned back to the whittling. It was just some drunkards shouting at each other. That and the disconcerting rumble of thunder. A couple of raindrops hit the new windowpane at the front of the store—fat plops of water. But the sound of drunk voices didn't follow the normal pattern. There was no laughter, no sudden anger, no singing or crying. It sounded more united...and it was moving in his direction.

Ben's stomach curdled, and he put the carving aside and rose to his feet. He'd been waiting for a broken window or a burning bottle, not a crowd.

He went to the window and shaded his eyes, looking out. It was hard to see, but a mob of about twenty men marched down the road, some carrying torches that made his breath lock into his chest. Anger. Belligerence. Fire.

"God, help me," he breathed. It was a short prayer, but it encompassed the rising fear inside him.

Had it been a mistake to push for a confrontation?

But then another thought struck him—what coward hid behind a mob of drunk men? The men milled around in the street in front of his shop, shouting, but they seemed more confused about what to do now. One voice shouted his name.

"Benjamin Huntington, you are not wanted here!"

The others took up the theme.

"Get out of town!"

"We don't need no lily-livered city boys here!"

So this was it—the plan had worked, but perhaps better than Ben had even hoped. He swung the front door open and stepped outside.

"Who put you up to this?" Ben shouted.

"We don't want you here!" a voice slurred.

Ben scanned the faces. "Jay Turner!" he yelled back. "What did I do to you?" The man fell silent. "And is that you, Red Smith? I see Nicholas Phipps there too. Do I have a quarrel with any of you?"

Their names said aloud seemed to break the mood, and the men muttered and sidled off with a few others following them. The numbers thinned.

"Who put you up to this?" Ben shouted. "I have done nothing to you! I have set up shop, worked honestly, and done my best to be a good neighbor. You've come out here with torches and threats as if I am some dangerous person? I am your neighbor!"

"You are no neighbor of ours!" From the back of the crowd, Cyril Welch marched forward, and the way the men looked at him, it was clear he was the leader.

"Cyril?" Somehow Ben wasn't entirely surprised. "Why are you doing this?"

"Why?" Cyril belted out a bitter laugh as if no explanation was needed.

"There is enough work for both of us!" Ben said. "We have different strengths. If we were friends, we could—"

"Do you think I fear your womanly carving of flowers and birds?" Cyril retorted. "I knew who you were the minute you arrived in town, Benjamin Huntington. But do you know who I am?"

Ben squinted at the man, dumbfounded.

"I tried to make my start in New York fifteen years ago," Cyril said. "You wouldn't know my name, would you? Your family has driven down countless honest men."

"Were you involved in the railroad?" Ben asked, confused.

"No. I was a carpenter, and your father lent me enough money to start a business. After the first two payments, which I met on time, he increased the interest rate until there was no way I could pay him back. Then he sent in his goons to beat me up and take my inventory. I came home with nothing to my name. Your father ruined me!"

"Do you know that I was cut out of the inheritance?" Ben shouted. "I didn't get a penny when my father died. I gave it up!"

"But you still came prancing into our town and took over my customers, didn't you?"

A crack of lightning flashed across the sky, a blinding jagged light coming earthward, and a few seconds later a thunderous boom rattled the new windowpanes. Rain started to fall then, and the torches hissed in the onslaught. A black automobile pulled up behind the crowd, and Ben felt a surge of relief when the sheriff got out. Anne got out of the passenger side. The wind whipped at her hat, and she put a hand on top of it, her panicked gaze locking onto him.

"So you burned down my shop?" Ben shouted, egging Cyril on.

"I'll burn it down properly tonight if you don't get your things together and get out of my town!" Cyril bellowed.

"What's going on here?" the sheriff called.

The drunken men panicked and started to melt away into the night. Cyril stiffened and looked like he wanted to do the same, but the sheriff was bearing down on him.

"He doesn't belong here!" Cyril shouted. "Ask anyone!"

But the sheriff wasn't listening. He pulled out a pair of handcuffs and grabbed Cyril by the arm. Cyril jerked back.

"Don't fight me, Cyril Welch," the sheriff warned. "It will go worse for you if you do."

Cyril deflated, and the cuffs snapped on his wrists.

"Do you know who he is?" Cyril protested.

"He is one of the citizens I've sworn to protect," the sheriff said curtly. "If you have an honest charge to press against Ben Huntington, you can do it the legal way. But seeing as you came in the night with torches, I think you don't have a legal leg to stand on."

The sheriff proceeded with the arrest, and Anne wound her way through the bystanders toward Ben, who stepped out into the rising wind and met her in the middle of the road. Rain fell in large, warm drops, and the wind whisked Anne's hat away, tumbling end over end down the street. He pulled her into his arms and held her close against him.

"How did you know what was happening?" he asked against her hair.

"Bernadette Sisk warned me. I wasn't leaving you to face this alone, Ben." There were tears in her voice. Another strike of lightning lit up the sky, and Ben caught her hand in his and tugged her next to him as they hurried back inside the shop. He pushed the door shut, and they stood in the lamplight, their breath coming fast.

"Anne—" He swallowed hard.

Anne moved toward the worktable and picked up his piece of carving. She froze.

"I was just carving something—" he began.

"It's me."

"It is you." He smiled weakly. "I am glad you can recognize it."

"It's…beautiful." She shook her head slowly.

"You're beautiful, Anne." Didn't she know it? "I know that when I asked you to marry me, I said I wanted something more practical. I know I asked that you'd prioritize my daughter, and that we'd build a life together. But…"

Her gaze flickered toward him uncertainly.

"But I love you. I do. I love you, Anne, and I don't want merely some practical arrangement for my daughter's benefit. I want your heart too. I want—" He swallowed. "I hope you might love me in return."

Anne looked up at him, her eyes filled with tears. "You do?"

"I don't know how to win my wife's heart, but I am going to try. If you will let me. Just know that is my intent."

Anne brushed a stray tendril of hair out of her face. "I love you too, Ben. I realized something while I rode through a gathering storm to find the sheriff. My home is with you and Molly now. If we have to leave, we leave together. I will do my best, and may God grow my abilities. I am your wife, Ben."

His wife. His own precious, beautiful wife. There was no sweeter word.

"For better or for worse," he breathed, looking down at her in wonder.

"For as long as we both shall live."

He lowered his lips to hers and pulled her close into his arms. He wanted to surround her, protect her, provide for her, and make her the happiest woman on this green earth. He felt richer than any mogul in New York City with Anne's love.

"Let's go get Molly," he whispered. "And then... I think Molly will do just fine on her own in her room. Anne, will you sleep next to me tonight?"

Color touched her cheeks. "Yes, Ben."

This was marriage, and he'd never felt so grateful in his entire life.

The next morning, Anne, Ben, and Molly sat around the breakfast table, with cream of wheat in ceramic bowls, doused in fresh milk. Anne's heart was filled to the brim, and Molly looked between her father and Anne with a curious expression on her face. She seemed to sense that something had changed, although she didn't know what.

"Let us pray," Ben said, and they all bowed their heads. "For this food, we are thankful. For my wife and my daughter—Lord, You have truly blessed me. Hold us together always."

"Amen," Anne murmured, and she lifted her eyes to meet her husband's loving gaze.

There was a knock at the front door, and Ben pushed back his chair to see who was there. Anne went to fetch the sugar bowl, and as Ben opened the door, she looked out to see who might be on their step this early in the morning.

A portly, older man came inside. He had a big white mustache and a suit that was buttoned right up. He doffed his hat, and his gaze moved over the shop slowly. A customer? But then Molly pushed past Anne and dashed toward him.

"Grandpapa!" she shouted.

The old man bent down and gave Molly a hug, tears shining in his eyes. There was some commotion, and introductions were made. Ike Rumsfeld kissed Anne's fingers gallantly.

"Did you get my gift, madam?" Ike asked.

"Gift?" she murmured.

"There—" He pointed at the crate. "I sent it weeks ago, as a way to mend fences. Ben, I was wrong. I pushed you away, and I realized what an old fool I was. I wanted Molly to have that tea set—now, while she can grow up with it. Then it can go to her home when she marries. It belongs with Eliza's daughter, not me."

"It was incredibly thoughtful of you, sir," Ben said. "I read about the robbery."

"Ah, yes." Ike shook his head. "It made me realize that the most important things in life aren't carted off and sold by a thief. I got your telegram saying you were about to get married, and at first I admit I had to sort through my own anger. But it turns out, Ben, that I was just very, very sad about the loss of my daughter. So I got on the next train to come out to tell you in person that I am putting you in my will. For Eliza's sake."

Ben's gaze whipped over to Anne.

"Sir, that isn't necessary—" Ben began.

"For Eliza's sake," Ike repeated firmly, and then he smiled kindly at Anne. "And for Anne's, don't you think?"

Anne didn't know what to say. They would be provided for, that much was clear. And so would Molly. But uncertainty wormed up inside of her. It didn't change the fact that Anne would never be a shining society wife.

"Sir, we will be making our home here in Last Chance," Ben said. "I promised my wife, and I intend to keep my word."

Ike looked at Anne thoughtfully then nodded. "I understand. But perhaps you'll come to New York at Christmas and let an old man see his granddaughter. Perhaps Anne would enjoy shopping on Ladies' Mile. My treat, of course." Ike turned toward her with a sad smile. "I hope you will say yes."

"To a visit?" Anne smiled. "Yes, of course. And sir? I would like to say that I truly am sorry for your loss."

Ike put a warm hand on her shoulder. "You are a treasure, Mrs. Huntington."

"She is," Ben agreed.

The family visited together that day, and when the men settled by the woodstove with mugs of strong coffee next to them, there was another knock on the door. It was Elizabeth Bertrand.

Anne knew her husband had to tell Miss Bertrand that he'd not be able to complete the commission. She watched in sympathy as he explained the situation.

"Oh, never mind the cherry wood. The old oak tree in the grave-yard was hit by lightning last night," Elizabeth said. "I asked the reverend if we could have the wood for the pulpit. It seems appropri-ate, and the reverend agrees with me. That tree can continue to be a part of our dear church. But I am not a carpenter, and I don't know what will work and what won't. So I am asking you."

"Yes, that is an ideal solution," Ben said, and he looked at Anne in awe. "God certainly provides, doesn't He?"

Ike pushed himself to his feet and came over to where Miss Bertrand stood. He gave a little old-fashioned bow.

"Benjamin, perhaps you would introduce me to this lovely crea-ture," he said.

Elizabeth blinked at him.

"Elizabeth Bertrand, this is my father-in-law, Ike Rumsfeld," Ben said.

"Charmed." Ike took Elizabeth's fingers and kissed them. "Please, come sit with me. I feel like we will have much in common."

Perhaps there was another romance starting here tonight, Anne thought with a rueful smile. The Lord worked in mysterious ways!

The town of Last Chance had begun with the same sort of pro-vision. It started with a graveyard, then grew into a town, and a church was built for the faithful. Then the oak tree was struck by lightning, and a pulpit would be lovingly carved and placed at the front of the church.

Last Chance had started with a graveyard, and Anne's marriage had started with a practical agreement. But even the humblest of beginnings could flourish when placed fully in God's capa-ble hands.

LEGACY OF LOVE

by

SANDRA ORCHARD

The strongest oak of the forest is not the one that is protected from the storm and hidden from the sun. It's the one that stands in the open where it is compelled to struggle for its existence against the winds and rains and the scorching sun.

—Napoleon Hill

CHAPTER ONE

Last Chance, Iowa

Present Day

Reining in her borrowed horse, Rachel Jones basked in the serenity of Stephens State Forest. Last night's rain intensified the contrast between tree bark, emerging leaves, and the colorful May wildflowers carpeting the forest floor. The air's rain-cleansed scent with a hint of pine reminded her of childhood hikes with her dad in these very woods. A pang of sadness piggybacked the memory, but she pushed it away, not willing to let her mom's thoughtlessness steal her joy. Not today.

Curtis Shoemaker, their handsome guide, drew up alongside Rachel, and the appreciation in his deep blue eyes as he surveyed the landscape reassured her that her new colleague was a kindred spirit. "Welcome to your new home."

Home. Excitement swelled Rachel's chest. With 15,500 acres split among seven separate locations, Stephens was the largest state forest in Iowa and had been her number one pick to launch her career after completing her Forestry Master's last month. She didn't officially start work for another week, but she'd jumped at the opportunity to participate in this guided weekend equestrian camping trip. She couldn't have hoped for a better employee orientation to the Lucas County branch of the state forest.

"This is where we'll make camp," Curtis announced to the small group, consisting of, besides her, a half-dozen employees of a small start-up company on what their supervisor billed as a team-building adventure.

After Rachel set up her tent, she found Curtis trying to coax damp wood into flame. His sandy-blond hair, damp from perspiration after wearing a riding helmet all day, hung in curls that skimmed the edge of his collar. He'd shed the plaid fleece he'd been wearing, unveiling a slender build beneath his T-shirt. She shifted her attention back to the paper he was adding to the firepit as fast as the flames devoured it. "I hope we're not depending on that fire to cook tonight's meal."

"Not a fan of raw hot dogs?"

"That would be a no."

His chuckle rescued her. "Don't worry. I packed two camp stoves. The group takes care of their own meals. And I'll cook ours. Hot dogs aren't even on the menu."

"No?" She injected a curious lilt to her voice. "Are you a gourmet cook as well as an expert horseman and forester?"

"Ha. Hardly. But we are having my world-famous chili con carne."

"Ooh." She drew the word out enthusiastically by adding a couple of extra syllables. "I'm intrigued." He'd stopped the group every mile or so to ask the riders, especially the novices, how they were doing and to share interesting factoids about the forest and the forestry's mission. But until now, he'd scarcely addressed her, although his gaze often seemed to stray her way. "And how'd this *world* renown come about?" she teased, hoping to establish a comfortable camaraderie. "Didn't you say you've worked *here* every summer since you were sixteen and full-time since college?"

Mimicking her playful attitude, he tapped his index finger to the side of his nose like a TV detective. "Exchange students from around the world come here, not to mention visitors."

"And they've all sampled this famous chili of yours, have they?"

Curtis shrugged. "Not all of them. But those who have said it was the best they'd ever tasted."

"Well, I can't wait to try it then."

Blushing, Curtis ducked his head and returned his focus to the soggy kindling. She'd noticed his shy reactions when a couple of women from the team-building group expressed interest in more than information about the forest's flora and fauna. Considering the women were pushing forty, Rachel had assumed Curtis felt intimidated by their attention. But *she* was hardly intimidating, was she? Maybe she hadn't shrugged off her bristly mood over her mom's bombshell as effectively as she'd hoped. She shoved aside the thought, determined not to let the loss ruin her weekend.

Rachel frowned at the smoldering fire. "Maybe we could phone the office and ask them to send out someone on a four-wheeler with dry wood?"

"I already made the request this morning. But someone has to come from Red Haw State Park, and no one's gotten here yet."

"Forgotten, maybe?"

"Maybe, but probably just busy with visitors, since this is the first really nice weekend we've had this spring."

By the time Rachel finished exploring the immediate vicinity on foot and gave her horse a rubdown and a special treat, Curtis had a fire burning and a delicious smelling pot of chili simmering on the camp stove. The rest of the group kept to themselves, laughing and eating and basically ignoring her and Curtis.

"Hungry?" he asked.

"Starving."

He chuckled in that low rumbly way she'd decided she quite liked then ladled a generous helping onto a tin plate for her.

After thanking him, she took a moment to bow her head and silently thank the Lord for the food, the exquisite weekend, and the wonderful job she'd soon start. When she looked up, she was surprised, and oddly encouraged, to see Curtis's head bowed. Was her new colleague a fellow believer? She bit her lip, hesitant to ask, not wanting to put him on the spot if he was merely being respectful.

He scarcely said more than half a dozen words through supper.

"This chili is delicious," she praised when she couldn't stand the silence any longer.

He beamed. "The secret is in the sweet chili sauce I use as a base. My gran cans it from scratch."

"Ah, so this is really your gran's world-famous chili recipe."

The instant their gazes touched, crimson, brighter than the scarlet paintbrush blooms, crept into his cheeks. "You got me."

Rachel smiled warmly, hoping to allay his seeming embarrassment at her teasing. "You're fortunate to have such a special legacy. I never knew my grandmother, and my mom isn't much of a cook. So, sadly, we don't have a single family-favorite recipe."

"I'm sure Gran would be happy to share hers." His voice cracked. "If you'd like it, that is." He surged to his feet and relieved her of her plate.

"I would. Thank you." Before she could add anything more, he busied himself cleaning the dishes. "Here, let me take care of those. You cooked. You shouldn't have to clean up as well."

He looked as if he wanted to argue, but a gangly male staff member chose that moment to zip in on a four-wheeler laden with dry firewood, and he brought their exchange to an abrupt end.

Curtis expelled a relieved sigh at the sight of his friend Ian and quickly excused himself to Rachel. He'd felt tongue-tied from the moment he met her and couldn't for the life of him stop the infernal way his cheeks heated every time she talked to him. Her shoulder-length, strawberry blond hair framed her face in a mass of curls that would be the envy of his sisters. And she was so nice. Not like girls at college who'd made it their mission to make him feel like an idiot and then tease him over the way he blushed.

"Oh wow," Ian said as he helped Curtis unload the firewood. "You sure landed a plum assignment this weekend—a camp full of pretty women."

Curtis snorted and motioned to the group of women still eating. "They're all at least a decade older than us."

Ian jutted his chin toward Rachel. "Our new forester's not. I heard she's only twenty-four. Please tell me you're at least talking to her."

"Of course I'm talking to her." Curtis focused on the wood he was stacking, hoping Ian wouldn't ask for details. Ian was a good friend. A fellow geek. Or rather a reformed geek who was doing his best to help Curtis overcome his debilitating shyness around women.

"Because you've got to remember that you're a great guy. But if you don't talk to the woman, you're never going to give her the chance to find that out for herself."

Curtis could feel his ears heating at his friend's pep talk.

Ian shook his head then good-naturedly slugged Curtis's shoulder. "I'm serious. Just pretend she's one of the guys."

Curtis rolled his eyes. The woman's petite athletic build, not to mention those expressive green eyes and heart-stopping dimples, ensured she could *not* be mistaken for one of the guys.

"Okay, okay," Ian said. "That's probably not the best suggestion. Did you know that until 1870 all trees were felled with axes?"

"What's that got to do with anything? And I think you're wrong about the date. There were crosscut saws around before then."

"You're right. But they were useless because they were always jamming in the wood."

"Is there a point to this history lesson?"

"Yeah, remember when loggers changed to using saws?"

"When they came up with a better design."

"Exactly. They discovered that if they changed the depth of every other tooth, they would clear the sawdust that jammed the saw."

Curtis narrowed his eyes at his friend, clueless to the point he was trying to make.

"Don't you get it? That minor adjustment revolutionized the industry."

"Okay." Curtis wondered if his friend had been out in the sun too long.

"One minor adjustment," Ian enunciated slowly. "That's all you need to make. You don't talk to women, because you're afraid they'll reject you. And some will. But it's not the end of the world. You need to push past your fear and be yourself. Just like you pushed past your fear to rescue that kid who fell through the ice last winter."

"His life was on the line."

Ian shrugged. "Maybe your life *is* on the line…your future happiness at least."

Curtis rolled his eyes and shook his head over his friend's melodrama.

Ian headed off, and dusk soon pushed into the forest despite the longer days.

The group of women monopolized the fire, so Curtis lit a lantern and, after retrieving his carving knife and a piece of maple from his saddlebag, sat apart from the group to quietly whittle. Sensing someone watching him, he glanced up, and his gaze tangled with Rachel's. Her sweet smile set his pulse rioting, and the next thing he knew he'd sliced his thumb. "Ouch." He pressed the cut to his lips.

Rachel sprang to his side and offered him a tissue. "I'm so sorry I distracted you."

"It's not your fault I'm clumsy," he muttered, making a point of avoiding looking into her lovely face.

"Hardly," she scoffed. Picking up the wood he'd dropped, she admired it from every angle. "Your carving is exquisite." She blinked repeatedly as if fighting tears.

Her unsettling reaction must have shaken his tongue loose, because he found himself chattering on in a desperate effort to keep her from crying when he had no idea why she would. More likely, the smoke had gotten into her eyes. "I started out carving toy animals and dinosaurs in my spare time for my young nephews," he rambled. "Soon visitors took notice, and a few commissioned special pieces as souvenirs of their visit. Eventually, I accumulated enough unique pieces that a local curio shop in Last Chance invited me to sell them there on consignment."

"That's fantastic!" The enthusiasm in Rachel's voice sounded genuine, not like the feigned compliments of the college girls who'd relished their hazing assignment to humiliate him all those years ago. But almost reflexively, his guard shot up again anyway.

Rachel stroked the hair of the miniature doll he'd been carving, and a silent tear rolled down her cheek.

His heart thumped.

Swiping at her damp cheek with the back of her hand, she said, "My great-great-grandfather carved dolls like this."

Unnerved by the wobble in her voice, Curtis blathered, "My sister's expecting her first daughter, so I figured it was time I tried my hand at a doll."

Rachel set the doll back on the table. "Will you make her a dollhouse too? And furniture?" She clasped her hands and dropped them into her lap, as if attempting to restrain herself from picking up the doll once more.

The curious response made his mind whir with questions, and it took him a moment to realize he hadn't answered hers. "I haven't thought that far ahead. But maybe. My sisters always loved playing with their dollhouse when they were little."

"Me too. Well, minus an actual dollhouse. Although I did build a pretty cool makeshift one from cardboard boxes one year. My dad told me his great-grandfather built an elaborate dollhouse full of carved miniatures for his daughter, my great-grandmother."

"Your dad didn't inherit an interest in carving?"

Rachel chuckled. "No. But my great-grandmother's collection was handed down to the daughters of each generation."

"Since none would've been passed on to your dad, does that mean you missed out?"

"Actually, he persuaded a childless aunt to pass her share of carved miniatures on to me." Rachel's gaze drifted to the treetops. "My dad died a year later, when I was ten."

"I'm sorry," Curtis whispered.

But Rachel continued as if she hadn't heard. "Somehow playing with those dolls always made me feel as if my dad was right there with me." She sighed. "But when I got home from school a couple of weeks ago, I discovered my mom had given them to a thrift shop. And of course, they'd already been sold."

"That's rough."

Rachel ducked her head. "I'm sorry. I promised myself I wasn't going to stew on the loss anymore. But my dad used to bring me camping here, and I guess being back has roused a lot of memories, and then seeing your carvings..."

"I'll put them away." He set his knife into its case.

"Oh no. Don't stop on my account. I'd love to watch how you make them. I'm not usually so emotional. Honest." She scraped at the tabletop with her thumbnail. "I just can't believe my mom didn't have a clue how important the miniatures were to me."

"Maybe I could help you track them down. The owner of the curio shop that sells my carvings has a lot of connections. If you give me descriptions of your miniatures, or better yet, have pictures, I could pass those along to him so he can ask his contacts to keep an eye out for them." Curtis wasn't sure what had compelled him to make the offer, but the way Rachel's hope-filled gaze clung to him made him feel ten feet tall.

"Would you?"

"I'd be happy to try," he said. He prayed he wasn't building her hopes for a devastating crash.

⁓ Chapter Two ⁓

The next Friday, Rachel parked outside her new home and unloaded her suitcases.

Due to budget constraints, on-site staff housing at Iowa State Parks and Forests was no longer an option. But thankfully, Curtis had told her about an opening at this house in Chariton, shared by several twentysomething staff members, himself included.

Curtis pulled into the driveway behind her in a black pickup. "Hey, you made it." He rushed over and relieved her of a couple of suitcases. "Did you get my message that I might already have a lead on your miniatures?"

Her heart leaped. "So soon? That's fantastic."

"Yeah, I sent the pictures you messaged me to the curio shop, and it turns out someone recently emailed them about a dollhouse and miniatures they want to sell."

"But I—"

Curtis cut her off with a raised hand. "I know you didn't have a dollhouse, but Gary, the shop owner, said some of the miniatures look identical to ones in your picture."

"Seriously?" Rachel pressed her hand to her chest, almost afraid to believe finding them could be this easy.

Curtis set down the suitcases and opened the photo app on his phone. "These are the pics the seller sent the shop." He thrust his phone into her hands.

She swiped through the first four or five pictures and then gasped. "That's my doll!"

"It sure looks like it, doesn't it? I'm thinking the collector must've picked up your pieces at the thrift shop to add to a collection they already had and now they want to sell them. Who knows, maybe it's a long-lost relative who got some of the other figures your great-great-grandfather carved."

"Wouldn't that be amazing?" Rachel scrolled through the rest of the pictures, hope swelling in her heart. "Dad was an only child, and I never really knew any of his aunts and uncles or cousins."

"Well"—Curtis returned the phone to his pocket and lifted the suitcases once more—"my friend emailed the collector about you, so we might soon get the chance to meet them."

Rachel frowned. "I wonder why this person wouldn't want to keep the set. If it's a descendant of my great-great-grandfather, I mean."

"Their loss is your gain." Curtis disappeared inside with her suitcases, and she hurried behind him with an armload of boxes.

When she'd come by to tour the place on Monday, she'd been shown her room and told the guys weren't permitted upstairs, where the women's bedrooms were. She supposed carrying luggage and furniture up for them qualified as an exception. The guys' rooms were downstairs and similarly off-limits to the girls. The main floor rooms—kitchen, dining room, living room, rec room, and sunroom—were all common areas.

Ten minutes later, Rachel and Curtis carried the last of her belongings to her room and Curtis left with a promise to let her know as soon as he heard back from the curio shop owner.

"Wow," exclaimed Lara, a coworker who had the room next to Rachel's, "you brought a lot of stuff."

"Everything I own. My mom's remarrying and selling our house, so it was either bring it here or pay for storage."

Lara laughed. "My mom threatens to move to try to get me to go through my junk."

"Be happy she doesn't dejunk it herself," Rachel groused, immediately embarrassed by the bitterness that crept into her tone at the thought of her mom's cleaning spree. It was hard enough saying goodbye to her childhood home without returning from school to find every last remnant of her dad's life—his favorite books, his favorite painting, his favorite CDs—already stripped from the walls and shelves.

"My mom wouldn't dare," Lara said in a tone that promised dire consequences if she did. "The last time she made that mistake, I was six. She gave away my Tickle Me Elmo, and I cried for weeks. After that, she promised to never give away any of my stuff without asking again."

Rachel offered a polite smile and turned her attention to unpacking. In fairness to her mother, she had asked. But the question about sorting through Rachel's old things had been so general, she'd never imagined Mom would lump the carved miniatures into that category.

She'd avoided her mom since discovering the loss, and for the last week had packed her belongings while Mom was at work. She spent her evenings on her laptop scouring the internet for doll collector sites in the hope that whoever purchased her miniatures from the thrift store might brag about the find to fellow collectors.

She knew she needed to forgive her mom for giving them away, but the hurt was still too raw and her mother's apology too…insincere. Well, insincere probably wasn't the right word. More like exasperated that Rachel expected her to know how important the miniatures were to her. But she should have known. A mother should know.

Then again, these days Mom acted more like a lovesick teenager than a mother. Not that Rachel begrudged her the second chance at love if that's what she wanted. She'd been alone a long time. But given the crater-sized hole Dad left in their lives when he died, Rachel couldn't fathom wanting to risk her heart like that again.

Lara opened a box of Rachel's books. "Would you like me to put these on the bookshelf for you?"

"You don't have to do that. I'm sure there are lots more exciting things you'd rather be doing after working all day." Rachel's phone pinged an alert for one of the social media doll collector groups she'd posted to asking for help.

Lara sashayed over to Rachel and peered over her shoulder. "You're into doll collecting?"

"Not exactly. My mom inadvertently gave away my special carved miniatures, and I'm trying to get them back."

"Ah, the dejunking spree?"

"Yeah." Rachel smiled at a heart-hugging emoji Curtis had added to her post. During their camping trip, she'd learned that Curtis didn't do much on social media. She didn't either. But he'd suggested that joining online groups might be a good way to find her miniatures. She hadn't realized he'd planned to do his own online sleuthing by joining a few too.

"You got a hit?" Lara asked.

Rachel tossed the phone back into her purse. "No, just someone showing they care."

Curtis watched the dining room doorway as he filled his glass with soda. Most nights everyone fended for themselves for meals. But two nights a week, everyone in the house shared a meal, and tonight was one of those nights. The guys barbecued ribs—a favorite among the group. "Do you think I should've messaged Rachel to tell her it's dinnertime?" he asked Ian.

"Looks like she got the message anyway." Ian jutted his chin toward the door, and Curtis caught a glimpse of strawberry blond hair a second before soda overflowed his cup and drenched his hand.

"Oh great." He grabbed extra napkins and cleaned up the mess then followed Ian to the dining table.

"Don't worry. I don't think she noticed," Ian whispered as they sat down.

"What does it matter?"

"Yeah, right. You're telling me you're not interested in her?"

"I'm saying she wouldn't be interested in me."

"How many times do I have to tell you? Not all women are—"

"I know what you're going to say," Curtis interjected. "Save your breath."

"Is this seat taken?"

Curtis startled at Rachel's voice and knocked his soda glass. "Ah!" He grabbed the toppling glass with one hand and a napkin with the other.

"The chair on my side is dry," Ian volunteered.

Sopping up the spill, Curtis kicked his friend's shin.

Rachel thanked Ian sweetly then dragged the dry chair to Curtis's side of the table.

Curtis grinned. Oh yes, he liked this woman. "Are you all settled into your room?"

"Well enough. Have you heard anything more from the curio shop?"

"Not yet. Sorry."

"Hey, isn't that shop open late on Friday nights?" Ian chimed in. "You should take her. Introduce her to Last Chance, Iowa—the place people are dying to get into." Ian chuckled at his lame joke.

"That's a great idea," Rachel exclaimed. "Do you mind? I mean, I could go on my own if you have other plans tonight."

Ian snorted.

Curtis gave his ever-so-helpful friend another swift kick, eliciting a satisfying "oomph." "No, I'm not busy. I'd be happy to take you."

An hour later, Curtis gave Rachel a brief history of Lucas County as they drove through the rolling countryside, past fields green with hay or newly plowed. "The curio shop is up ahead, just past Last Chance cemetery."

"Oh." Rachel chortled. "So that's what Ian meant by people are dying to come here."

"His jokes can be in bad taste sometimes," Curtis said softly, thankful she didn't seem as disturbed by the quip as she might have been if her father's death were more recent.

The clapboard exterior of the curio shop appeared as old as most of the eclectic selection of goods they sold. Nestled between an equally dilapidated pottery shop and a tack shop, the trio of buildings represented the entirety of Last Chance's business district. Curtis guided Rachel inside as the old-fashioned bell above the door announced their arrival. Not that it helped the elderly shop owner much. Between his penchant for whistling and tendency to let his hearing aid batteries go dead, Gary rarely heard the bell.

Not spotting him about, Curtis called his name.

Gary bustled out of the backroom. "Curtis, good to see you. I was going to call you tonight."

"You've heard from the dollhouse seller?"

"No. That's what I needed to tell you." Gary caught sight of Rachel, and his expression brightened. "Is this your girl?"

Curtis's face flamed. "This is Rachel. The woman I told you about."

"Yes, yes." Gary beamed at her. "Pleased to meet you, my dear."

"The pleasure is all mine," Rachel responded. "I can't tell you how grateful I am for any help you can give me in tracking down my miniatures."

Gary frowned. "Ah. About that."

Not liking the hesitancy in Gary's voice, Curtis tensed.

"I'm afraid I can't reach the person who I think has them," Gary continued. "My emails are bouncing."

The light in Rachel's eyes snuffed out. Her shoulders sagged, and her smile drooped.

"What do you mean they're bouncing?" Curtis pressed, sorry he'd mentioned the lead to Rachel before securing contact information.

"The first email I sent, telling the collector I found an interested buyer, seemed to go through okay. But when I didn't hear back after a day and a half, I sent a second. That one and all the others I've attempted to send since have returned as 'no such mail recipient.'" He emphasized the last part with air quotes.

Curtis shook his head. "That makes no sense."

"The person must have deleted their email address," Rachel said, sounding defeated before they'd even started.

"But why?"

"I suppose they didn't want to be found." Gary fiddled with his hearing aid. "I mentioned in my first email that the buyer might be a distant relative. If I had a suspicious mind, I'd wonder if that spooked them."

Visibly shaken by the notion, Rachel braced a hand on a nearby table. "I don't understand. Why would it?"

"It might if they didn't come by the collection honestly."

Rachel drew in a sharp breath.

"Didn't you tell them that Rachel's pieces were donated to a thrift store by mistake?" Curtis asked, struggling to keep his frustration from coloring his voice.

"No, I didn't see the point."

"What's the email address?" Curtis asked. "Is there any clue in that?"

Gary shrugged. "Only if the initials E.L. mean something to you. It's 'EL0211.' A Gmail address." He looked at Curtis. "But you can track the original email's IP address and find them that way, right?"

Curtis snorted. "Maybe if I were a hacker instead of a forester." He turned to Rachel. "How about you? Any hacking skills?"

"Only with an axe, I'm afraid."

He chuckled, heartened that she could still manage to joke despite how disappointed she must be.

Gary scratched his beard. "I suppose it's possible Fletcher got to them."

"Fletcher? Who's Fletcher?" Curtis fisted his hands. He wasn't a violent man. But seeing Rachel's disappointment was enough to compel him to want to confront this Fletcher person, if not duke it out with him.

"He's an avid collector. Some would say fanatical."

"And you told *him* about your emailer?"

Gary winced. "Sort of. I ran into him at an auction last night, and I might've mentioned that I had a lead on some Huntington pieces he'd want to see, if they didn't turn out to be what you were looking for."

"Might've mentioned?" Curtis failed to keep his exasperation out of his voice. Gary was a good guy. But… "What were you thinking?"

The man groaned. "I wasn't. Sorry. Fletcher revels in getting my goat. I wanted to turn the tables on him for once."

"Can you give us his contact information, so we can talk to him?" Rachel's soft voice quelled their rising tension.

Gary shook his head. "I can't. He's a mysterious sort. Shows up at auctions from time to time. But no one seems to know where he lives or has ever heard of him reselling or trading anything he's bought."

Rachel frowned.

"To be honest, I wouldn't be surprised if Fletcher wasn't even his real name. There's an old Chevy Chase movie called *Fletch*. And this guy looks a lot like the beach bum Chase pretends to be in the movie."

"Oh yeah, I know the one you mean," Curtis said. "Chase's character is an undercover reporter with the last name Fletcher, but he takes on other identities to get his story."

"That's right."

Rachel sank into a chair. "So we're searching for a collector who might have the initials E.L. and is looking to turn a profit, or an elusive eccentric collector, and neither of them wants to be found."

"I'm afraid so." Gary drew a folder from beneath the counter. "But I did do some research you might find interesting. The miniatures EL sent me a picture of were carved in the early 1900s by Benjamin Huntington."

"I've heard of him," Curtis said. "He settled right here in Last Chance after his father disinherited him from the family railway business in New York City. He's well known among carving enthusiasts for a nativity scene he carved for a local church back then."

"That's right. He lived here with his wife Anne York Huntington and his daughter from his first marriage, Molly."

Rachel surged to her feet. "My great-grandmother's name was Molly."

"That would make Benjamin Huntington your great-great-grandfather."

"I didn't know his name," Rachel said. "And I certainly didn't know he was a famous carver."

Gary pulled a copy of a newspaper clipping from his folder and slid it across the counter. "This is a picture of the nativity Curtis mentioned."

Rachel gasped. "Mary's face looks just like *my* doll's." She skimmed the article. "I don't recognize the surname, Huntington, but I guess that makes sense, since our line comes from his daughter and her married name would've been different."

"If you wander around the cemetery, you might find their grave markers and some for their descendants. The Lucas County Historical Society might also be able to help you trace your family tree."

"That's a great idea." Curtis typed the names listed in the article into his phone. "A little more digging could score us the names of relatives still in the area who might know about the miniatures. Are you game to tour the cemetery and see what we can learn?"

Rachel tugged her lower lip between her teeth, her gaze wary.

"After that, we can check obituaries."

She inhaled deeply. "I guess it's our best chance at this point."

Fifteen minutes later, Curtis found Benjamin Huntington's headstone, and from there, markers for two sons and another daughter, besides Molly. Apparently after the newspaper article about the nativity was written, he'd had three more children. Curtis continued searching for Molly's gravesite and found it in the next row. "Rachel, over here." He pointed to a headstone that confirmed Rachel's hopes.

Rachel stared at the name, clearly straining to hold her tears. "Molly Huntington Jones, beloved daughter, wife, and mother."

Curtis gently touched the small of Rachel's back. "You okay?"

She swiped at her eyes. "I'm sorry. You must think I'm silly. It's not like I knew any of these people."

"You're remembering your father."

She nodded. "And I think I recognize this name." She led Curtis to the headstone she'd been reading when he called her to Molly's. "Naomi Jones Billings. I think she was my dad's aunt."

"The aunt who gave him your miniatures?"

"I'm not sure." Rachel pulled out her phone. "I'll call my mom and see if she recognizes the name or can remember dad's cousins' names." She held up a finger as her mother picked up. "Hey, Mom. Do you remember Dad's aunt's name?"

Her mother's response brought a smile to Rachel's face.

"And what about his cousins' names?" She turned the phone to speaker so Curtis could listen in.

"Oh, honey, I can't remember those."

"Did Dad have a family tree written out anywhere?"

"Not that I ever saw. Funny you should ask though, because last week I got one of those scam emails, claiming your father was the cousin of a recently deceased somebody Michaels who died intestate."

"Seriously?" Excitement flashed in Rachel's eyes. "Maybe it wasn't a scam. Can you forward it to me?"

"Oh, honey, I deleted it."

"No! Wait, we can recover it from the computer's trash bin."

"I'm afraid I emptied that too." At Rachel's groan, her mother rushed on. "I'm sure the sender was someone who gleaned enough private information from the internet to make us think the email was legitimate. You hear about people falling for that all the time and giving away information that allows the scammer to steal their banking information."

Rachel's shoulders fell. "Did the email ask for that kind of information?"

"No, it just asked for your email address because they were trying to contact descendants about the estate."

"Mom." Irritation threaded Rachel's voice, and she shot Curtis an apologetic glance. "You should've forwarded the email to me to decide how to respond."

"I'm sorry, but I was sure it was a scam. Who ever heard of inheriting from cousins, let alone cousins once removed?"

"Okay, Mom. I need to go. I'll talk to you later." Rachel ended the call and fisted the phone in her hand, looking as if she wanted to hurl it. "I can't believe she deleted the email."

"Hey, it's still a great lead," Curtis reassured her. "We can check recent obituaries for anyone with the last name Michaels. They always list next of kin."

"Yes!" Rachel squealed, then she immediately sobered. "Only, if this supposed cousin of my dad's died intestate, any other relatives who stand to inherit part of the estate might not be thrilled about my showing up on the radar."

Curtis grimaced. "Yeah, that might explain why our would-be seller disappeared so abruptly."

CHAPTER THREE

As Curtis drove, Rachel silently prayed someone at Happy Haven Retirement Home would be able to help them. They'd spent most of Saturday morning and a good part of the afternoon combing through obituaries and historical records at the library. From the moment Rachel shared her devastation over losing her beloved miniatures, he'd helped her launch a full-scale search. In fact, if not for his contact with the curio shop, she might never have learned about the recent demise of a long-lost relative—Vivien Michaels.

Granted, the email Mom deleted might still have been a phishing scheme. But Rachel didn't care about claiming an inheritance, only about getting back her miniatures.

Unfortunately, the obituary didn't name the estate's lawyer. Not that they would have been able to reach him or her over the weekend. And the funeral home was too preoccupied with a funeral in progress and afternoon visitations to tell them anything more than Vivien had resided at Happy Haven.

The instant Curtis parked outside the home, Rachel jumped from his pickup. But as she stared at the elderly residents wandering in and out of the front doors, her feet glued themselves to the ground. "Do you think they'll tell us anything?"

"You never know until we try." Curtis came around the truck and stood beside her. He must have sensed her fear that this would be another dead end, because he slipped his hand in hers and squeezed. "Ready?"

The rasp of his calluses against her skin matched his husky tone, and both were oddly comforting. She and Curtis had known each other only a few days, but in that time, they'd become fast friends—something she rarely experienced. Well, *never* experienced. Not since meeting her BFF the first day of kindergarten. The same friend who'd moved away the summer Dad died.

Rachel inhaled deeply. She'd been plagued by random morbid thoughts ever since Mom began stripping the house of mementos— things that reminded her of Dad and her cut-short childhood. "I suppose the worst they can do is kick us out."

Curtis's throaty chuckle chased away the chill that had shivered through her at the prospect. "If they do, then we befriend all the kind-looking residents strolling the grounds on this beautiful after-noon until we find one who knew Vivien Michaels."

Vivien Michaels. The obituary said she'd died two and a half weeks ago, leaving behind no husband or children, only a stepdaughter and step-granddaughter. But under Iowa state law "steps" had no stake in the estate—a factoid Curtis's research had uncovered. Everything they had dug up matched the scenario painted by Mom's email. But was that because Vivien was Dad's cousin? Or, as Mom presumed, because some-one tried to use a real death to swindle unwitting supposed relatives?

"I appreciate you coming with me," Rachel told Curtis.

"I'm as eager as you are to solve this mystery." His wink boosted her spirits.

Researching together was fun—an adventure. Would he still want to hang out with her if they recovered the miniatures today? She wasn't good at dating. Her last roommate said she had a bad habit of cutting bait at the slightest hint things were getting serious. She shook her head. Since when did she entertain the prospect of dating anyone? Curtis was a friend helping her out. That was all. It couldn't be more. They were colleagues. And it would be way too awkward working together if they tried dating and wound up having a nasty breakup.

Curtis nudged her arm. "We going in?"

"Yes."

Once inside, Curtis took the lead. "My friend here is a relative of Vivien Michaels," he said to a young man mopping the hallway. "We understand Mrs. Michaels is a resident who recently died."

The young man chuckled. "Oh, we all knew Vivien."

"Friendly, was she?" Rachel asked, taking her cue from Curtis's suggestion they befriend other residents. Befriending staff might garner even more information.

"Oh yeah. She—"

"Finch, back to work," a balding man in a dark suit scolded. "Sorry, ma'am." The man stroked his neatly trimmed beard. "Sean is a personable sort, but he makes a habit of chatting more than he mops. The residents love him, of course, but they'd soon tire of dirty floors if we didn't keep after him." He reached for the office door. "May I help you with something?"

"No, that's all right. I think the receptionist will be able to help us."

"Okay. Good day then," he said, and disappeared into the office.

Rachel led Curtis to the receptionist's desk and inquired about Vivien.

"I'm afraid Vivien's room has already been cleared out." The receptionist tapped more keys on her computer keyboard and studied the screen. "Her stepdaughter, Maribel, was the only next of kin in our records, and it says here she left instructions to have everything donated to the local thrift store."

"We've been trying to connect with Maribel," Curtis said. "Do you have a phone number or mailing address you could give us? Now that everyone is on cell phones, it's so hard to update our contact information."

The woman squared her jaw and studied first Curtis then Rachel. "I'm afraid I'm not allowed to give out that kind of information."

"Of course, we understand," Rachel assured her. She pulled a Stephens Forest business card from her purse and jotted her name and phone number on the back then handed it to the woman. "But could you contact her on our behalf and ask her if she'd be so kind as to get in touch?"

The receptionist rubbed the business card between her fingers and glanced over her shoulder at the door labeled ADMINISTRATOR that the man in the dark suit had disappeared through. Finally, with a heavy sigh, she said, "Yes, I suppose I can do that."

Rachel thanked her and turned to leave.

Curtis snagged her arm and pointed to a collage of photos on a bulletin board in the hallway. "Look at this." He tapped on a photo of a smiling white-haired woman posing beside a handcrafted dollhouse filled with carved miniatures.

Rachel gasped. "Is that Vivien?"

A portly gentleman pushing his walker past them glanced up at the question. "Yup, that was our Vivien. My great-grandchildren are going to miss skipping down to her room to play with her miniature dolls. She loved to see the children playing with them."

A lump lodged in Rachel's throat, threatening to cut off her airway. She swallowed hard. "Do you, uh"—she cleared her throat—"do you know what became of the dollhouse?"

Sean Finch stopped mopping, looking as if he might answer the question for them, but resumed mopping when the man shook his head.

"Vivien's stepdaughter took it, I imagine," the man said. "Although Maribel's daughter is already a teenager, past the age of playing with dolls. It's a shame Vivien didn't leave the dollhouse here in the common room. Maybe more of our grandchildren and great-grandchildren would be eager to visit longer."

"Come along, Mr. Wilson." A health-care aide hurried the talkative gentleman away. "It's time for your medication."

Rachel clapped her hands together, scarcely containing an exuberant *whoop*. "Did you hear that?" She returned to the receptionist's desk. "Excuse me, again. Just one more question. Which thrift store were Vivien's belongings taken to?"

"There's only one in town. Odds and Ends on East Street."

Rachel turned to Curtis. "You thinking what I'm thinking?" Without waiting for a response, she dragged him outside then squealed, "This is it!" She made a show of crossing her fingers. "Now we just need to hope no one has bought the dollhouse yet."

Curtis opened his mouth to respond then clamped it shut. The dollhouse could still be there. He doubted it. But it could be. If she stopped long enough to think about it, she'd realize that it was likely picked up by the person who contacted the curio shop. He hoped he was wrong for her sake.

"What's the matter?" she asked.

He winced, annoyed that she'd sensed his mood so easily. "I don't want you to be disappointed." He glanced over his shoulder at the nursing home and caught sight of someone watching them through one of the windows. He squinted for a clearer look, but the curtain slipped back into place, shielding whoever had been there.

Rachel squeezed his arm. "You're a good friend."

The warmth of her hand, of her voice, did funny things to his heart, and it took a moment for his feet to get the message it was time to move.

He escorted her back to his truck and, a few minutes later, they found the Odds and Ends shop around the corner from the nursing home. Curtis snagged a parking spot in front. The shop consisted of one large room with aisle after aisle of clothes racks. Around the perimeter, shelves filled with everything from shoes to board games covered the walls. Several customers browsed through the clothes, but cashiers were free, so Curtis headed to the closest one, while Rachel scoped the store's perimeter.

"I don't see the dollhouse," she said when she returned, her tone subdued.

Curtis asked the manager if she recalled a dollhouse donation coming in from Happy Haven and if by chance a regular customer bought it.

"You're the second couple to ask after that dollhouse," the manager said. "It must've been something special."

"So, it was here?" Rachel exclaimed.

"No. I would have snatched it up myself if it had been. I've been looking for a dollhouse for my granddaughters for months."

"Did you get the names of the other couple?" Curtis asked.

She shook her head. "They were in their late teens. I've never seen them in here before. But they were adamant the dollhouse had to be here. The fellow got angry when I insisted it wasn't. Kind of scary angry."

At Rachel's shudder, Curtis edged closer, hoping his presence would ease her concerns. According to the obituary, Vivien Michaels didn't have any immediate blood relatives, which could mean Rachel had as much right to the family's legacy as any other distant relative, no matter how much they ranted. And knowing how much the miniatures meant to her, even if the ones given to her by her father weren't among them, he'd do whatever he could to help her find them and stake her claim. "Could you describe the couple?"

The manager shrugged. "At my age, teenagers all look the same. The fellow had some kind of tattoo on his arm."

They thanked the manager for the information then headed outside. "Well, the description doesn't fit the Fletcher guy Gary was worried about. Any idea who else might be hunting for the dollhouse?" Curtis asked.

"Not a clue. And considering everyone and their grandmother seems to be getting tattoos these days, the manager's description of the guy doesn't help us."

"No, but remember what the resident said about Vivien letting visiting children play with the dollhouse? I'm thinking one of them, a little older now, might've recognized its value and asked what became of it after she died."

"And was told the same as us."

"Exactly."

Rachel frowned. "Only…somewhere between Happy Haven and the thrift store, someone else got their hands on it."

"Someone who must have overheard the stepdaughter's instructions to the retirement home, regarding Vivien's belongings."

"Or a resident, visitor, or staff member who observed her room being cleared."

Curtis nodded. "Or that. Either way, it seems we have a mystery to solve."

The sun glinted in Rachel's hair as she tipped her head back and smiled up at him. "*We?* You still want to help me keep looking?"

"Absolutely. We can't quit now." Curtis tore his gaze from her sweet smile and yanked open the passenger door for her.

She gasped. "You've been robbed!"

CHAPTER FOUR

Rachel pulled out her phone. "I'll call the police."

Curtis clapped his hand over her phone. "Don't bother. I didn't have anything worth stealing."

The warmth of his fingers and certainty in his tone stilled the tremors that had overtaken her at the sight of his glove box contents strewn over the passenger seat.

He leaned inside his truck and riffled through the items. "My ownership and insurance cards are still here, and my maps. I can't think of anything that's missing." He shoved the things back into the glove box. "It was probably a kid looking for easy change. I rarely bother locking my truck."

"This is exactly why I lock mine." That and she'd seen too many movies where bad guys hid in the back of a woman's car, waiting for a chance to pounce. She glanced behind the seat before settling into it, just to be safe.

Curtis started the truck and looked at the dashboard clock. "It's not too late. Do you want to give the retirement home another shot? We could talk to more residents this time or the housekeeping staff who cleared Vivien's room."

"If you don't mind. Then I'll treat you to pizza afterward."

"You don't have to do that."

"It's the least I can do to thank you for all your help." She silenced any further protest with a mock stern look that earned her a hands-in-the-air surrender. "Keep your hands on the steering wheel!"

"Okay, okay, bossy."

She chuckled, thankful his earlier shyness that had caused him to blush every time they spoke had blossomed into an easy camaraderie. By the time they reached the retirement home for the second time, the clouds had blotted out the sun. "Looks like the drop in temperature has driven the residents inside."

"They likely went in for dinner."

"Oh, I never thought of that. Now might not be the best time to go back in."

Curtis shrugged. "We could grab a pizza first or eat at the local diner."

"Let's go to the diner."

Fifteen minutes later they were settled in a corner booth in a fifties-style diner, waiting on two orders of the day's special. They surfed the internet on their phones, researching Iowa estate law.

"According to this article," Rachel said, then read from her phone, "'an estate can avoid probate altogether if there are no valuable assets, such as real estate, jewelry, artwork, etc. and if bank accounts are jointly held.' That could be Vivien's situation."

"Although if the email your mom received was legit, then someone must've applied to administer her will."

"Hoping to win entitlement to her assets, you mean?"

"Yeah. And the most logical person to do that would be her stepdaughter."

"Who we haven't managed to locate." Rachel set down her phone and sighed. "Unless we hack into the retirement home's computer for her phone number or that receptionist actually gives her my message and she responds, we're still at square one."

"You have to watch the newspapers," the server interjected, setting their plates of meat loaf on the table. "Sorry, I couldn't help overhearing. But you always see lawyers' notices about estates in the newspapers, right?"

"That's true," Curtis said. "And we should check the newspaper's archives too."

"Need anything else?" the server asked.

Curtis turned a high-wattage smile up at her that hit Rachel with a ping of what almost felt like jealousy. "You wouldn't happen to know a woman by the name of Vivien Michaels or her stepdaughter Maribel?"

The young woman thought for a moment. "Sorry, doesn't ring any bells, but I don't usually learn customers' names, only faces."

"No worries. It was a long shot. Thanks."

Rachel gaped at him as the server walked away. "For someone your friend Ian claims to be so shy, you're a whole lot braver about talking to strangers than I am."

The rosy color she'd grown so used to seeing in his cheeks returned. He shrugged. "When I need information, I guess I don't feel so intimidated."

His response begged the question—did he find *her* intimidating? She squirmed, not sure she wanted to know the answer.

"What's wrong?"

"Wrong? Oh." She grappled for a thread of their earlier conversation. "I guess I feel weird presenting myself to some lawyer as if

I'm after Vivien's estate. No matter what the law says, I think the estate should go to her stepdaughter, or whoever was actually a part of her life, rather than some stranger."

"You can tell the lawyer that you're only interested in keeping the dollhouse in the family."

"Except from everything we've read, the dollhouse likely isn't considered valuable enough to go through probate. The receptionist at the retirement home clearly believed it was sent to the thrift store without question."

"Or maybe the reason it didn't make it there is because Vivien's stepdaughter already took it home."

"And if she wants it, she should have it." Rachel bowed her head to give silent thanks for the meal. To her surprise, Curtis prayed aloud, not only thanking God for the food, but asking for guidance in finding Rachel's family miniatures. "Thank you," she whispered when he was done. They'd never talked about faith, and she was touched he'd pray for her that way.

He slid his hand across the table and gave hers a quick squeeze. "I can see how important this is to you." He picked up his fork and sampled the meal before adding, "And if Vivien's stepdaughter is the one who emailed Gary's curio shop looking to sell the dollhouse, she doesn't value it like you do. Does she?"

Rachel shrugged.

"I understand your hesitancy to agree. I've had friends with stepparents who meant as much to them as their own mother or father and who would likely treasure a token of their adopted family heritage. But clearly Maribel only wants to make money off the dollhouse."

Rachel pushed her food around on her plate with her fork. "I see what you mean…*if* she's the one who emailed the curio shop. Her initials don't match the emailer's signature, remember."

"Unless EL isn't initials. El could be her nickname, short for Maribel."

"Hey, yeah, that makes sense. Only, if she is our emailer, then she's unlikely to get in touch with me, even if the receptionist passes along my message."

"There are other ways of finding people. With how popular Vivien's dollhouse must've been with children, a lot of visitors and residents would likely have also met Vivien's stepdaughter and might be able to tell us where Maribel works or lives, which could very well be local. After all, seniors who don't retire to a sunny state tend to choose retirement homes near their children."

"Or in the communities where they lived all their lives, no matter where their loved ones live."

"Are you determined to be pessimistic about this?"

Rachel chuckled at his teasing. "I'm sorry. It just seems so hopeless. And I feel guilty about monopolizing all your free time on rabbit trails."

"I work in the woods. Following trails is one of my specialties," Curtis quipped, surprised by how easy he found talking to Rachel. If only he could control his infernal blushing. What must she think of that? She sure wouldn't think it was manly.

"Speaking of trails, we need to address the erosion issues on some of the equestrian trails or a horse is going to take a tumble." Her eyes twinkled at the clever topic switch.

Oh boy. Horses wouldn't be the only thing tumbling if she kept looking at him like that. His heart might be next. He dropped his gaze to his plate and cleared his throat. "I, uh, noticed a few riders have already blazed their own trails to get around the worst areas."

"And I'm concerned they'll only create a bigger mess."

"We can post signs saying the trails are closed for regeneration."

"But before we do, we need to scout out and clear appropriate reroutes to thwart our would-be trailblazers."

Curtis nodded. "I'd planned to do invasive insect checks Monday, but that can wait a few days if you want my help scouting options."

"I'd appreciate it. A few areas could be remedied with basic shoring up, but you'll have a better idea how long that will take the students to complete."

"Yup, I spent many summers on that detail."

By the time they'd settled on a plan of action for Monday's workday, they'd both finished their meals and were ready to revisit the retirement home. Curtis attempted to pay for the meal, despite Rachel saying it was her treat, but she must have anticipated the maneuver, because she paid for it at the counter on her way to the restroom.

"Next time," he insisted as he opened his truck's passenger door for Rachel, "dinner is on me."

Her eye-twinkling grin sent his heart into somersaults.

A few minutes later, as they strode into Happy Haven, they ran into the same chatty caretaker heading out that they'd met on their earlier visit. "Back so soon?" he asked.

"Yes, we hoped someone might be able to tell us where we could find Vivien's stepdaughter, Maribel. You wouldn't happen to know where she lives or works, would you?"

Sean glanced toward the office, which was now dark. "I don't. I'm sorry. But you know, even if I did, I could get in trouble for sharing private information about a resident. Any of the staff would."

"Except Maribel isn't a resident. And neither is her stepmother anymore."

Sean smirked. "True. Why do you need to find her anyway?"

"We're interested in learning more about Vivien's dollhouse. We believe the miniatures in it were carved by my friend's great-great-grandfather."

"Wow, that's cool." The guy smiled at Rachel.

Rachel tugged her bottom lip between her teeth, looking suddenly self-conscious.

"I tell you what." Sean shoved his car keys back into his pocket and motioned toward the common room, where a TV blared and several residents sat watching the news. "I'll introduce you to Hazel Crumb. She spent a lot of time with Viv. If anyone knows how to find her daughter, she would."

"Thanks." Curtis turned to allow Rachel to precede him. "We appreciate it."

A floral, fruity scent enveloped Hazel, reminding Curtis of his gran. And the deep smile lines bracketing her lips and eyes put him immediately at ease.

After Sean introduced them and explained their interest in the dollhouse and finding Vivien's stepdaughter, Hazel warmly clasped Rachel's hands. "Vivien would have loved to have met you, my dear. She was so proud of her great-grandfather's work and never tired of sharing his story."

Rachel blinked rapidly, her eyes gleaming with moisture. "I would've loved to have met her. Sadly, I didn't know of her relation to my late father until yesterday."

"That's the way these days. Families don't seem to have big reunions like they used to when I was a child. Many of them are too scattered across the country, I suppose."

"My dad was an only child, so I never knew any aunts and uncles or cousins on his side. I'm told Vivien was his cousin, but if I ever met her, I don't recall. My dad died when I was ten."

Hazel squeezed Rachel's hand. "Oh, you poor dear." She turned her attention to Curtis. "And is this your beau?"

His face heated. *Just a friend* was on the tip of his tongue, but he couldn't bring himself to say it. Maybe because deep inside, being *just* a friend didn't seem like enough. So instead, he extended his hand. "Pleased to meet you, ma'am."

"Oh my, call me Hazel." She returned his handshake, her warm grip firm. "Now, sit down here, and I'll tell you everything I know about Vivien and Maribel and Vivien's lovely granddaughter, Lita. Lita would be in to visit her gran far more often than her mother. The last few months, she brought a boy with her, Evan something or other. She fancied herself in love with him, I suppose. But to be honest, he made me nervous with all those tattoos." She glanced at Sean Finch. "No offense."

Sean, who presumedly also sported a tattoo, grinned. "None taken, Hazel. I'll leave y'all to get acquainted. I need to get home."

"Thanks for your help," Rachel called after him.

"Such an affable lad," Hazel commented. "Now, where was I?"

"Lita's boyfriend, Evan," Curtis prodded, wondering if the two could be the curio shop's mysterious emailer. EL could stand for Evan and Lita.

"Oh yes. We've had a few things go missing around here the past few months. Pilfering mostly, but the night Vivien had her heart attack, a resident's antique ruby ring was stolen right off her finger as she slept. At first, the staff tried to suggest it fell off somewhere or fell in the sink when she washed, since she'd lost a lot of weight lately, but they never managed to find it. Sean, bless his heart, even took apart her sink's plumbing to check the P trap." Hazel shook her head. "The pilfering stopped after that night."

"Which is the last night Lita and her boyfriend would've visited the home?" Curtis mused.

"Exactly."

Curtis exchanged a glance with Rachel. Chances were good if they found Lita, they'd find Vivien's dollhouse…providing they got to her before she sold it.

They spent another half hour speaking with Hazel, and although she couldn't offer an address, she did remember that Maribel was a hairdresser who worked in Chariton.

As Curtis and Rachel walked out to his truck, he said, "I'm thinking Lita and Evan are the ones who emailed Gary about selling the dollhouse. Remember it was signed EL? Could be their initials. Lara went to Chariton High. We could ask her if she still has any contact with some of her teachers. A teacher might be able to give us an in to finding Lita."

"But if they sent Gary the email that would mean they already have the house."

"Yeah. Lita probably scooped it from her grandmother's room before the rest of Vivien's belongings were packed up." Curtis held the passenger door open for Rachel.

"But after hearing Hazel's description of them, I was thinking Lita and Evan are the couple who visited the thrift shop *looking* for the dollhouse." Rachel climbed into the truck then shot him a frown. "Except if that's the case, Maribel, Lita's mother, can't be our EL either, because Lita would've known if her mother brought the dollhouse home, don't you think?"

"Well, I don't see why she'd have kept it a secret from her daughter." Curtis closed Rachel's door and quickly rounded the truck to climb in himself. "Your theory does make more sense though. Maribel told the home to ship Vivien's belongings to the thrift store, like the receptionist said. When Lita found out, maybe she was upset because she wanted it or because her boyfriend said they could flip it for a quick buck."

"So they went to the thrift store to get it back. Only it wasn't there."

Sighing, Curtis jabbed his keys into the ignition. Suddenly, their supposed leads didn't feel as promising as he'd thought. "Where to next?"

Rachel already had her phone out and was tapping the screen. "According to this, there are six beauty salons in Chariton." She glanced at the time. "But it's too late to hit any of them now. I can phone them after they open tomorrow and ask if Maribel works at any of them."

"Tomorrow's Sunday."

"Oh, right." Rachel squinted at her phone screen. "Three of them will be open. I can try those at least. If I find her, would you want to come with me to talk to her?"

"Absolutely. But I can't tomorrow. My brothers and sisters and I made plans to attend our parents' church then Dad's barbecue to celebrate Mother's Day."

"That's tomorrow?" She turned a little green, and he was pretty sure it didn't have anything to do with the reflection of her cell phone screen on her face.

"You forgot?" He chuckled. "That makes me feel a little better. My sisters always get on to me and my brothers for forgetting special dates. At least you still have time to plan something. She lives close enough for you to drive there for the day tomorrow, right?"

Rachel's gaze remained fixed on her phone's now blank screen, her thumb swiping a frenetic rhythm across the corner. "I think she might've made other plans."

"I'm sorry," he said softly. He had assumed she and her mother would be close, having lost her dad at such a young age.

"It's my own fault. We haven't been on the best of terms since I got back from school and found out she'd given away my minia-tures, not to mention disposed of every other reminder of Dad, thanks to her whirlwind effort to get the house ready to be sold."

Curtis nodded. Having three sisters, he'd learned that saying as little as possible and letting them talk out their problems was usually the safest way to avoid becoming the surrogate target of their angst for daring to presume he could fix what was wrong. And on especially good days, they figured out how to fix their problems themselves and gave him the credit for helping them arrive at their own conclusions. He hoped Rachel was as adept at problem-solving.

Rachel searched his face and must have seen something in his expression that encouraged her to continue. "She asked me as I packed my car to start the new job if I'd come back to town for church Sunday. But I didn't know it was Mother's Day." If she had, would she have responded differently? Deep down she'd known her mom was really asking *Will I see you?* Rachel just hadn't realized the significance of the day. "I told her I planned to look for a church closer to my new place."

"You could surprise her."

Rachel shrugged.

Curtis opened his mouth to urge her to reconcile with her mom but stayed the impulse. He didn't know Rachel well enough to offer unsolicited advice, no matter how much he itched to. And he had a sinking feeling how he responded could be a major test of their fledgling friendship.

CHAPTER FIVE

Mother's Day dawned as gloomy as Rachel felt. She'd tossed and turned the entire night, reflecting on Curtis's advice. She'd always longed to have a big brother to turn to with her problems. Only, the way her heart fluttered when Curtis looked at her wasn't exactly a sisterly reaction.

She'd been embarrassed to admit to him that she hadn't felt all that magnanimous toward her mother lately. But Curtis seemed to understand. Not that being upset over the loss of her miniatures excused her behavior. Mom deserved better. Rachel yanked her brush through her hair, but it proved as difficult to untangle as her emotions. Knowing how ungenerous and unforgiving she'd been acting didn't make trying to reconcile any easier.

She showered and dressed and then, resisting the coward's way out, grabbed a quick breakfast and drove the forty-five minutes to her home church. Arriving with five minutes to spare, she sat in their usual pew halfway up the aisle. But Mom never showed.

"You're here!" A friend of Mom's bustled her young grandchild into the pew and sat beside Rachel. "Your mom didn't think you were coming, so she and Jerry went to see his mom in Sioux City."

Rachel admitted she forgot what day it was when her mom asked if she'd be back.

Mom's friend patted Rachel's hand. "She'll be sad she missed you."

Thankfully, the worship team's invitation to join them in the opening hymn spared Rachel from having to respond. But she should have known the pastor's sermon would be related to mothers, given the occasion. It made her feel even guiltier about the cold shoulder she'd given her mom lately. Rachel closed her eyes and silently prayed for help to truly forgive her mom. In particular, the "keeping no record of wrongs" part the apostle Paul exhorted. Because as hard as Rachel tried, she couldn't seem to let it go.

Not feeling up to chatting with folks after the service, Rachel slipped out during the closing hymn and drove to the house. She'd leave Mom a nice note and maybe look around to see if there was anything she still wanted to bring with her to Chariton. Or better yet, weed the flower beds as a little Mother's Day gift.

Reaching the house, Rachel stomped on her brakes.

An open house sign sat on the front lawn, and cars lined the street. A tangle of emotions she couldn't define clogged her throat. Who held an open house on Mother's Day?

An unfamiliar car, presumably the Realtor's, sat in the driveway, and Rachel couldn't bear to walk into her own home like a stranger. She drove on and parked at the playground down the street and then tried calling her mom.

Mom's voice mail picked up.

"Hey, Mom. I hoped to find you at church today and treat you to lunch for Mother's Day. I'm sorry I missed you and"—she cleared her throat—"um, for how I've treated you lately. I hope you're having a good day." Rachel bit her lip. "I do love you. I hope you know that even when I get mad."

The voice mail app beeped and disconnected the call. Rachel stuffed her phone back in her pocket and set off again. She drove with no destination in mind. Eventually, she ended up in Last Chance, but the lone trio of shops was as dead as the occupants of the cemetery. She parked there and wandered among the headstones. Finding her great-great-grandfather's grave once more, she remembered her intention to phone all the Chariton beauty salons to try to locate Maribel. Rachel sat on a nearby bench and tried the first number on her list.

The call lasted long enough to confirm no Maribel worked there, and then Rachel's phone battery died. "Figures!" She stuffed her phone into her pocket and headed back to her car. Reluctant to return to the staff house just yet, she found a food truck in the vicinity of Stephens Forest and grabbed some lunch. Then she traded her sandals for the hiking boots she kept in her trunk and spent the rest of the day exploring trails.

Monday morning, Rachel awoke to the aroma of brewing coffee and frying bacon. Outside, the sun peeked over the horizon. She quickly dressed for a long day of horseback riding to map and mark trails and then found Curtis in the kitchen packing lunches, snacks, and water to bring along while Lara made breakfast for everyone.

Curtis closed the flap on one of the backpacks and passed it to Rachel. "I figured with all the miles we want to cover, we should pack enough to keep us going for a good ten hours. And I asked Wellmount Stables to trailer a pair of horses to the parking lot for us by seven thirty."

"Perfect. Thanks."

They shared a hearty bacon and eggs, toast, and fruit breakfast with the rest of the staff then headed to the Whitebreast Unit of Stephens Forest in Curtis's pickup. "Did you see your mom yesterday?"

"No." Rachel's hand strayed to her phone stuffed in her pocket. She'd grabbed it off the charger at the last minute and noticed the missed call alert, but she wanted to wait until she was alone before listening to Mom's voice mail. "I tried," she admitted softly. "But she'd already made other plans." Rachel injected a cheery note into her voice. "How was your day?" She'd resisted the impulse to ask him earlier, precisely because she hadn't wanted to reciprocate.

"Awesome." His gaze sliced to the rearview mirror then, sounding oddly distracted, he added, "One of my sisters organized a badminton tournament after lunch. And Mom—" Curtis jerked the wheel to the right and turned onto a side street.

Rachel grabbed her armrest as the truck's momentum threatened to propel her across the seat. "This isn't the right road, is it?"

"No." He drove another few hundred yards, watching the mirror more than the road.

"What's going on?"

"Hang on."

Rachel braced herself as he swerved into a farm lane.

He waited for a car to pass then reversed out of the lane and headed back toward the road they'd turned off of a moment earlier.

He glanced once more in the rearview mirror and, for the first time, she noticed his white-knuckled grip on the steering wheel. She twisted in her seat to try to spot what had him so agitated. "Curtis? What's going on?"

"I think someone was following us."

"What? Why?" She bobbed her head left then right, but couldn't see any vehicle, let alone a suspicious one.

"I don't know. Saturday night I noticed a dark sedan behind us the entire drive home from Happy Haven. But I didn't think much of it until the same kind of car pulled onto the road behind us when we left the house this morning." Curtis glanced at the rearview mirror then made a left back onto their original route.

"There's no one behind us now," Rachel said. "Maybe it was a fluke."

Curtis's shoulders relaxed. "Yeah."

"Because why would anyone want to follow us? You don't have a crazed stalker ex I should know about, do you?"

"Ha. No. You?"

Rachel shook her head emphatically. "I never date a guy long enough to get attached."

Curtis glanced across the seat. "I'd be more concerned about a guy you turned down from the get-go."

Rachel laughed. "You're kidding, right? I'm hardly the kind of woman a guy would obsess over." Then, remembering Curtis's emptied glove box, she frowned. Could she have attracted the attention of an obsessive personality? Someone who'd seen her with Curtis?

"You thought of someone?" Curtis asked.

She shrugged off the ridiculous notion someone would obsess over her. "No." She couldn't remember the last time a guy had so much as attempted to make a pass at her...if she didn't count the silliness of Curtis's buddy, Ian.

Curtis turned into the parking area for the trailhead where they planned to start. But after climbing out, rather than heading over to the stable hand already waiting for them with their horses, he strode the ten yards back to the entrance and scanned the road, clearly still concerned. "I don't see anybody." He rejoined her with a self-deprecating chuckle. "To be honest, my first thought was it's someone who doesn't want us finding Vivien's dollhouse."

"Seriously?"

He shrugged. "I probably watch too many suspense movies."

Rachel chuckled. "Well, I'm happy to know you've got my back." She pulled their packs from the truck. "Although, out here, hopefully the only predators we need to worry about are coyotes."

They saddled their horses and, after arranging a time for the stable hand to return, they set out. The Whitebreast Unit boasted more than thirty miles of equestrian trails. And thankfully, during the first three hours of riding them, they encountered nothing more threatening than a chattering squirrel. "I'm ready to take a coffee break," Rachel announced. "How about you?"

Curtis pulled out his cell phone. "Sure. There's decent cell reception here, so we could get a start on calling those beauty salons to locate Maribel." Curtis dismounted and pulled a thermos from his pack.

"My thoughts exactly." Rachel swung her leg off her mount, and Curtis handed her a steaming cup of coffee.

"They do say great minds think alike," he quipped with a wink that warmed her faster than any cup of coffee.

Oh man. She needed to get a grip. She focused on her phone and copied half the list of beauty salons into a text to Curtis. "I'll call the first shops on my list, and you can try the ones I've just texted."

With a nod, he pulled out his phone then wandered to a fallen log and took a seat.

She chose a sunny stump several yards away so she could privately listen to her mom's voice mail first.

Honey, thank you so much for your call. Knowing you tried to see me means the world to me. I'm so sad I wasn't there. I know I hurt you, and more than anything I wish I could turn back the clock and undo my mistake. I hope we can get together soon. I love you with all my heart.

Rachel gulped down the emotion welling in her throat. She'd been so bent on reclaiming the only tangible connection she'd still had to her dad that she'd taken her mom for granted. Sabotaged the relationship she had with her here and now. Hadn't Dad's sudden death taught her anything?

Curtis waved his hand at Rachel then gave her an exuberant thumbs-up.

Rachel hurried over to him.

He recited his phone number then disconnected. "Maribel starts work at one, and her boss promised to have her call me as soon as she comes in."

"Awesome!" Rachel swigged the last of her coffee. "Then we'd better get back to work."

At twelve forty-five, Curtis suggested they break for lunch. They found a fallen log to sit on in a clearing and ate in silence while they waited for Maribel's call.

When one o'clock came and went, Rachel motioned to his phone. "Did you check that you have cell phone reception here?"

Curtis glanced at the screen. "Four out of five bars and still well charged. Maybe Maribel didn't arrive early enough to call before her first client appointment."

Rachel hoped that was all it was. By one fifteen she'd finished eating. "We'd better get back to work. We can't sit here all day waiting."

"Better yet, I'll phone the salon again." Curtis tapped redial and turned on the phone's speaker. When an employee picked up with a cheery *How may I help you,* Curtis asked to speak to Maribel.

A moment later, Maribel came on the line, and Curtis explained why they were calling.

"I'm so sorry. My daughter was never into dolls, and it never occurred to me to hang on to the dollhouse in case someone else in Vivien's family would want it."

"So, you're saying you *don't* have it?" Curtis clarified.

Maribel expelled a loud sigh. "I don't. No. I told the home to donate everything. I never even realized Vivien might have living relatives until I applied to administer her estate and they said they'd have to search for blood relatives first."

"That's understandable. But about the dollhouse. Happy Haven told us your instructions. But when we visited the thrift store where they said the stuff was sent, the manager there said no dollhouse came in."

"That's strange. Maybe one of the home's staff members asked to keep it. I could call and ask if you like."

"We'd appreciate that." Curtis gave her his phone number.

"I'll text you once I hear anything, okay?"

"That'll be perfect."

Rachel listened carefully to the exchange to try and gauge how honest Maribel sounded. "I believe her. Do you?" she said the moment Curtis disconnected.

Curtis shook his head, half shrugging. "She *could* be buying herself time to stash the dollhouse someplace we won't find it, but I think she's telling the truth. In fact, now that I think about it, I'm wondering if the administrator might be the one who scooped the dollhouse."

"Really?" Rachel frowned, but then remembered something. "The receptionist did give his office door a nervous glance when we asked about Vivien."

"And he looks like a well-groomed version of Gary's description of the elusive collector. Fletcher."

"I didn't catch the administrator's name."

"Neither did I, but Gary seemed to think Fletcher was an alias anyway. And if that guy mussed his hair, instead of slicking it smooth with styling gel, I could see the resemblance to the beach bum in the *Fletch* movie."

Excitement bubbled up in Rachel, as pure and promising as the natural spring they'd come across on that morning's ride. "Wow, solving this mystery is turning out to be pretty easy after all."

"Don't count your lumber before the logs are milled," Curtis cautioned in a forester's twist on the old adage. "At this point, Maribel's only speculating that a staff member asked for it. And if it was Fletcher, or whatever his real name is, he might've given his staff a gag order."

"Who's being the pessimist now?" Rachel teased.

Four hours later, as they pulled into the driveway back at the house, Curtis grinned at the text that came in. "Good news. A health-care provider at the home took Vivien's dollhouse for her granddaughter. Maribel has forwarded me a phone number and address." He grimaced. "Oh, wait. This might not be good."

"What?"

"Her name is Evelyn Lupin—initials E.L. She could be Gary's would-be seller."

"You think she lied about wanting to give the dollhouse to her granddaughter?" Rachel fidgeted with her seat belt buckle. "Because if she gave it to a little girl already, there's no way I could ask for it back. But if she lied, and just took it to sell it…"

"I think we should clean up and have a quick bite to eat then drive straight to her house."

"You don't want to call first to make sure she's home?"

"No, because if she is our EL, I'm more concerned she'll hide the dollhouse if we tell her we're coming."

"Ooh. Has anyone ever told you you have a devious mind?" The admiration in Rachel's voice assured him that in this case, she thought that was a good thing.

"It's not so different from catching unwanted pests. To catch them, you've got to think like them. And trust me, since taking on this job, I've had lots of practice dealing with pests of every description." He winked.

Rachel's giggle, accompanied by the grin she flashed him before dashing inside, kicked his confidence up a notch.

Ian, who'd apparently been eavesdropping as he washed his car, swaggered over to Curtis the instant the screen door slapped shut behind Rachel. "Look at *you*, hanging with the new girl."

"I'm helping her."

"Uh, huh." Ian elbowed Curtis and then feigned the accent of a kung fu master. "You have chosen wisely, Grasshopper. Perhaps it is time the student becomes the teacher."

Curtis flicked the brim of his friend's ball cap. "Just following your advice and being myself." He strode inside before Ian could grill him on the nature of his relationship with Rachel. At this point, the last thing he wanted to do was analyze it.

An hour later, they turned onto Evelyn's street to find a police car in her driveway.

"Please tell me that's not the woman's house," Rachel pleaded.

Curtis double-checked the house number against the address in the text he'd received. "I'm afraid so. Maybe selling ill-gotten dollhouses isn't her only racket."

Curtis parked across the street from the house so they could decide how to proceed.

"Do you think we should knock while the police are still there?" Rachel asked.

"It might be safer."

Rachel looked taken aback by his blunt remark. "You think she could get violent over our asking about the dollhouse?" Disbelief colored her tone. "It's not as if I'm asking her to just hand over a priceless heirloom. I'm willing to pay a reasonable price for it."

"Yeah, but she might not be a reasonable person." Curtis scrutinized the home's windows for some indication of what was transpiring inside.

The front door opened, and a female police officer stepped out, spoke to a woman standing in the doorway, and then left in the cruiser.

"C'mon, let's go now." Curtis hurried Rachel across the street and up the driveway. At their knocking, the front room's curtain shifted, but no one came to the door. Curtis rang the doorbell. Again. And again.

A minute later a burly guy emerged from the house next door and crossed the lawn, his hands fisted, his expression snarly. "Ship off. The last thing she needs is a pair of salespeople trying to hoodwink her into buying something she doesn't need."

"We're not salespeople," Rachel protested. "I need to speak to Evelyn about the dollhouse she brought home from the retirement home after its owner died. My great-great-grandfather made it, and I want to keep it in the family. I'm even willing to pay her so she can buy her granddaughter a different house."

The man's gruff exterior softened. "Just a second." He took out his cell phone and tapped the screen. A moment later, a phone rang inside the house. "Hey, it's Jack. The folks at your door are here about a dollhouse." He frowned at Evelyn's response then said, "The woman sounds real cut up about losing it. Maybe you could at least—"

The front door opened, and a red-eyed woman appeared in the doorway. She nodded to her neighbor. "Thanks, Jack. I can take it from here."

He pocketed his phone. "Do you want me to stick around for a bit?"

"No, that's okay."

Curtis shook the man's hand. "Thanks for your help."

"No problem. Hope you find what you're looking for."

Rachel's attention was already on Evelyn. "I'm so sorry. We've clearly caught you at a bad time."

The woman still wore her work uniform and had obviously been crying. Curtis gulped, suddenly feeling like a bully for laying on the woman's doorbell, when for all he knew she'd just received news from that police officer that a loved one had died or something.

Evelyn stepped back to allow them inside then motioned them toward the front room. It had been completely tossed. "I came home to find I've been robbed."

CHAPTER SIX

Curtis stared at the contents of drawers and shelves strewn about the woman's living room. The fact that the woman who'd taken the dollhouse would be burgled soon after Maribel called Happy Haven about it was too big a coincidence to ignore, especially given the black sedan following them this morning. What if chasing after this dollhouse endangered Rachel?

"This is awful," Rachel commiserated with the woman. "Why would a thief make such a mess of the place? You think he'd just want to get in, grab the valuables, and get out."

"Could've been looking for something, maybe," Curtis said.

Evelyn sighed. "That's what the officer said. Or maybe they got angry when they discovered I had nothing worth stealing."

Curtis fit a sofa cushion back in place. "I'm surprised they didn't take the game console."

Evelyn shoved aside the contents of an overturned drawer with her foot and invited them to take a seat. "They took what little cash I had in the place, but nothing else that I can see. It makes no sense. What could anyone want from me?"

Rachel perched on the edge of her seat. "We're here because I'm hoping you still have Vivien's dollhouse." Rachel explained about her father's gift. "Maribel said you wanted it for your granddaughter, and if you've already given it to her, I wouldn't think of asking for it back.

But if I could buy even just one of the dolls and a couple of the other miniatures to have as keepsakes, it would mean so much to me."

The woman crumpled. "I'm sorry. I wish I had it to give to you. But my germophobic daughter vetoed accepting the century-old *relic*, as she called it." Evelyn sniffed and sank deeper into her chair. "I suppose you're the interested buyer the curio shop in Last Chance found."

Rachel sat a little straighter. "That's right."

Evelyn shook her head and repeated her apology. "When the shop owner emailed me to say he'd found a relative interested in the dollhouse, I panicked."

"What did you do with it?"

At the urgency in Rachel's voice, Curtis's heart squeezed. She'd pinned so much hope on recovering her miniatures, as if somehow that might be a salve for her grieving heart. Having both his parents and grandparents still, he couldn't begin to understand what the loss of a parent felt like, especially at the young age Rachel lost her dad. But how raw it still seemed after more than a decade surprised him a little. Was it the upheaval of saying goodbye to her family home, or starting a new chapter in her life after graduate school, or maybe seeing her mom ready to move on and remarry that had churned up unresolved grief?

Not that he knew much about grief, besides the horrible sadness of losing his beloved dog at fifteen. Then again, that was twelve years ago, and the memory of how deeply the loss cut still kept him from wanting another dog.

"Please understand. I thought I'd be in trouble for taking the dollhouse under false pretenses," Evelyn continued. "Which I didn't. I honestly wanted to give the dollhouse to my granddaughter."

"I believe you," Rachel soothed, although she leaned toward Evelyn as if it took all her self-control to endure the woman's lengthy explanation without repeating her question.

Evelyn emitted a mewling sound and, shaking her head, dabbed at her eyes. "If only I'd known you'd be so understanding…"

"We know you deleted your email address, presumably so we wouldn't be able to track you down," Curtis prodded, unable to endure the belabored torment she was putting Rachel through.

Evelyn blinked and stiffened her spine. "Yes. And then I gave the dollhouse to a thrift store."

"Which one?" Rachel's voice lifted an octave.

"I don't know the shop's name. I didn't want to leave the dollhouse at a place where people might know me, so I took it to a small one near Last Chance. The sign said the money went to missions. I hoped that if you went to the Last Chance Curio Shop looking for the dollhouse, you might visit the thrift shop too."

Doubting there'd been any such altruistic motive in her choice, Curtis pulled out his smartphone and searched for thrift stores near Last Chance. The closest listed were all right there in Chariton. He pulled up a map of the vicinity of Last Chance then turned the screen toward Evelyn. "Whereabouts on the map?"

She cocked her head and reoriented her body, as if mentally driving the route. Finally, she pointed to a spot on Mormon Trail east of Last Chance, in the middle of nowhere.

Rachel thanked her and rushed him outside. "I know by now the place will be closed, but do you mind if we drive there and at least learn its name? That way I could leave a phone message or maybe a note under the door, asking them to hold the dollhouse for me if they still have it."

"Of course, we can go now. But you do realize Evelyn's explanation kiboshes our theory that your miniatures might've been added to the dollhouse collection she tried to sell to Gary."

"Yes, but they are part of my family's legacy. I'm sure of it. And if I can't have the exact ones my dad gave me, at least I'll have keepsakes very much like them. Keepsakes I can pass down to my own children one day."

Curtis pictured an adorable pair of towheaded children with Rachel's curls and his blue eyes. His hands went slick on the steering wheel. That kind of thinking would only lead to a whole lot of disappointment.

When he reached Mormon Trail, he turned east away from Last Chance, since he'd never noticed any other shops between the intersection and the curio shop, besides the ones on either side of it. At Highway 69, he pulled to the side of the road. "We must have missed it."

"You don't think she sent us on a wild-goose chase, do you?" The anguish in Rachel's voice tore at his confidence.

"Maybe she mixed up her directions and the shop is the opposite way. I'll turn around." This time he slowed to a virtual standstill at every farmhouse and peered down the driveways.

"Evelyn could've lied about not having the dollhouse."

Curtis shook his head. "I can't see it. If she was after money, she would've taken you up on your offer to pay her. She seemed genuinely remorseful to me."

"Yes, to me too."

Last Chance.

As Curtis passed the town sign, Rachel twisted her hands in her lap. "The town's name feels a little too prophetic for comfort. If we find this shop and another doting grandmother or pigtailed little girl has beaten us to the dollhouse, the chances of ever owning it are slim to none."

"I'm sorry. If I hadn't told Gary *why* you were looking for the miniatures, he wouldn't have mentioned the familial relation in his email to Evelyn and spooked her."

"You couldn't have known. And I certainly don't blame you."

He appreciated her saying so, but it did little to assuage his regret.

"You jumped right into helping, which is more than I can say for my mother, who gave them away in the first place." Rachel winced. "Sorry, that sounded harsh. I've honestly forgiven her." Her gaze dropped to her tangled fingers. "I came to the realization yesterday that my time with Mom this side of heaven is too precious to waste nursing a grudge. But clearly, I still have to work on letting go of the resentment."

"We're all works in progress."

Rachel's nod gave him the courage to go on.

"And sometimes, we just can't see the forest for the trees."

Rachel chuckled. "You do like your forest metaphors."

"Yeah, that one's not exactly original. But my point is that unlike us, God sees the big picture. And for myself, I've found that if I let Him steer, instead of continuously wrestling back control, He works things out for our good, like the Bible says."

"I hope so."

So did he. He'd known her scarcely more than a week, yet everything in him wished he could take her hurt away.

Four miles west of Last Chance, they still hadn't spotted the shop. Curtis pulled another U-turn. "Let's stop by Gary's. If this thrift store exists, he'll know where it is."

"Won't his shop be closed by now?"

"Yes, but Gary lives above it."

Curtis parked behind Gary's car in the driveway, and a moment later the outside light came on. By the time they reached the side door, Gary had pushed it open. "Curtis, what brings you out tonight? Do you have more carvings for me?" Gary's gaze lit on Rachel, and his voice rose excitedly. "Or did you locate the dollhouse?"

"We have a lead on where it might be. We found the woman who emailed you." Curtis relayed Evelyn's explanation for why she severed contact. "She claims she donated the dollhouse to a thrift store outside of town on Mormon Trail, but we couldn't find it."

"Ha, no you wouldn't. Not unless you drove past on a Saturday or Wednesday. Come in. Come in."

"So the shop does exist?" Rachel clarified as they climbed the stairs to the second-story apartment.

"Sure does." Gary put on coffee then showed them to his cozy living room and explained. "A retired couple runs the thrift store out of their barn, and the proceeds go to supporting a youth drop-in center in Lucas."

Rachel shook her head. "How do they expect to draw in customers without a sign? We drove four miles in each direction, actively looking for it, and didn't see it."

"They set a sandwich-board sign on the road when they're open. They have a bay door around the side of the barn where locals know they can drop off donations during the week. I suspect the couple opted not to put out a permanent sign to keep anyone passing by from dumping who-knows-what any time of the day or night."

"I've heard that can be a problem for secondhand shops," Curtis acknowledged.

Gary disappeared into his kitchen and returned a moment later with a tray of steaming mugs and a plate of cookies. "I'd be happy to visit them tomorrow and ask about the dollhouse. If they'll sell it to me on the spot, I'll bring it back here for you. Otherwise, I'll ask them to hold it for you until they're open."

Rachel clapped her hands together and pressed them to her chest. "That would be wonderful! Thank you." She shot Curtis a giddy grin.

He handed her a mug of coffee then sipped his with mixed emotions. Once they recovered the dollhouse, would Rachel want to spend time with him outside of their work? Although he had several years' seniority with the DNR, she had far more qualifications. Would she want to go out with someone who was beneath her in that sense? If they didn't work at the same place, maybe the disparity wouldn't be an issue. But if they became romantically involved, the work relationship might be awkward.

He shook his head. The notion she'd even be interested in dating him was a pipe dream anyway. Ian's crosscut saw lesson flitted through Curtis's thoughts. He gritted his teeth. If pushing past his fear that she could never see him as more than a friend ruined their friendship, then it wasn't worth it.

Rachel muffled a yawn. "I hate to cut our visit short, but I'm beat."

"We can get going." Curtis carried the tray of empty coffee mugs back to the kitchen and thanked his friend for all his help. "I'll carve a couple more miniatures for you by next week."

Gary's gaze strayed to Rachel, then he winked at Curtis. "No hurry. You've had more important things on your mind."

Curtis's face heated at Gary's teasing tone. Winning Rachel's favor hadn't been his motive for helping her. He led the way down the back steps, grateful for the growing darkness, then opened the passenger door for Rachel.

The appreciative smile she flashed him as she climbed in let loose a bevy of butterflies that had no business being out after dark, let alone fluttering around inside his stomach. He hurried around the vehicle and focused on driving. He couldn't deny that the more time he spent with Rachel, the more he liked her and, maybe, secretly wished there could be more to the partnership than solving a mystery.

"Is something wrong?"

"What?" he squawked, startled out of his ruminating. "Why would you think that?" He glanced at her and wished he hadn't, because the concern in her gaze left him tongue-tied.

"You've been so quiet since we left your friend's."

Realizing he'd driven more than halfway home without saying a word, Curtis fixed his attention on the road and tightened his grip on the steering wheel. "I was thinking I'm going to miss our mystery-solving adventures now that we've located the dollhouse."

"Should we moonlight as freelance detectives? We could try to solve the retirement home's jewelry heist Hazel mentioned."

His grip relaxed at her whimsical tone. "There's an idea. We can print business cards that say no mystery is too small."

Rachel nodded, clearly enjoying the playful plotting. "I can see it now. We'll become famous for tracking down stray cats."

"And cat burglars," Curtis added with feigned seriousness. "Don't forget about Evelyn's burglary." He parked the car in front of the staff house.

"Of course. How could I forget that?" Laughing, she reached across the seat and clasped his arm.

He stilled, even as her touch sent his pulse galloping. The air between them seemed to become charged. He searched her gaze, wondering if she sensed it too.

A bang on the driver's-side window made them both jump and broke the moment.

"You two going to sit there all night?" one of the summer staff members bellowed as he and another fellow headed inside, laughing.

Rachel pulled back her hand and ducked her head. "I guess we should go in. I have another early day tomorrow."

"Yeah. I'll let you know when I hear from Gary."

"Thanks, Curtis. For everything." And with that, Rachel hurried into the house without so much as a backward glance.

He'd embarrassed her. Being caught by the others sitting in the car, looking like they might be…what? About to kiss. He snorted and rolled his eyes. Kiss, right. In his dreams.

He pushed open his truck door and trudged toward the house. For a few moments, while bantering with Rachel, he'd felt light enough to soar, but as he climbed the porch steps, he felt as if he slogged through marshland. And the cricket serenade sounded more like snickers.

CHAPTER SEVEN

Rachel hummed as she entered the kitchen the next morning.

"Sounds like someone had a fun evening," Lara singsonged. "How many nights in a row have you been out with Curtis?"

"It's not like that," Rachel protested, even as she recalled the way he looked at her in the car last night when she touched his arm. She'd hoped he might kiss her.

"Earth to Rachel." Lara's teasing voice jerked Rachel from her thoughts.

"Sorry, what was that?"

Lara laughed. "Yup, you keep telling yourself it's not like that."

"We're just friends." A friend who had her thinking about one day having children, when she'd never so much as contemplated having a serious relationship, let alone getting married and having kids. Rachel withdrew a couple of bread slices from the bread box and tipped them into the toaster slots. "He's been helping me locate some family heirlooms. That's all." She closed the bread box with an emphatic slap and then, turning toward the fridge for jam, caught a flash of green disappear from the doorway.

"Oops," Lara said. "Something tells me that's not what Curtis hoped to hear."

"Curtis heard that?" Rachel's heart dipped at Lara's nod. She hurried after him to…to…what? Tell him she just said that to get

Lara off her back? Somehow, she doubted that would make him feel any better.

She slowed her steps. Did he think there was something more than friendship developing between them? Did he want there to be? Did she?

Stopping abruptly, she gripped the back of a living room armchair. In school, she'd had the excuse of prioritizing her studies to avoid romantic entanglements. But that wasn't the only reason she did. She remembered all too well listening to her mom cry herself to sleep after Dad died. And then seeing her college roommate spiral out of control and lose a year of studies after being dumped by the supposed love of her life.

It wouldn't be fair to let Curtis think there might be more between them. Not when her modus operandi was to cut out before a relationship got serious, especially given they'd still have to work together. No, it was better this way.

Their extracurricular activities would die a natural death once they recovered the dollhouse and miniatures.

"You okay?" Lara whispered from behind her.

"What?" Rachel spun around. "Oh yes. Just remembered something I need to do."

"Don't forget your toast. It's getting cold." Lara's gaze strayed to the front window at the sound of Curtis's truck starting. "Aren't you working with Curtis again today, rerouting trails?"

"No. I have planning committee meetings." A text alert spared Rachel from facing any more probing questions. The sight of her mom's name tugged at her conscience. With everything that happened yesterday, she'd forgotten to call Mom back. When she was in school they used to talk for a few minutes every night, often longer. That was, until Mom started dating again. Then the calls grew more infrequent.

And after Rachel's third worried call to assure herself Mom was okay, only to learn she'd been out on a date, again, Rachel had stopped calling if she didn't hear from her. Then, when she had come home between graduate school and the new job and the whole miniatures-giveaway fiasco erupted, resuming their old heart-to-heart talks had seemed too difficult.

Rachel's stomach clenched as she skimmed her mother's text.

"Bad news?" Lara prodded.

Rachel glanced up, having forgotten all about Lara. "Huh?"

"The text. You look like you just found out your dog died or something."

"Oh. No." Rachel tucked her phone into her pocket to respond later. "It's my mom. She wants to come for a visit."

"And you don't want her to?"

"It's complicated."

"When some of the guys' mothers come by, they bring care packages. Things like cakes and cookies. It's great."

Rachel chuckled, recalling Mom's care package delivery treks to college and grad school during exam week every year. "Yeah, that sounds like my mom too." She pulled out her phone and texted back. It'd be great to see you. We're ordering Chinese for supper. You're more than welcome! Could you be here by 6?

A thumbs-up emoji blipped on Rachel's screen almost instantly, followed by Can't wait to see you!

A fat tear plopped onto her phone screen, and Rachel swiped at her eyes. She'd been too hard on her mom after learning she'd given away the miniatures. It had to have been hard for her going through a lifetime of memories alone. How many crying jags had Mom endured while deciding what she could bear parting with? Maybe she'd hoped to spare Rachel the emotional roller coaster. Maybe. That was the way the mom she'd always known would have thought. But lately…she'd been different.

Curtis spent the morning gathering data in Stephens Forest on insect infestations of the newest invasive species. He found several trees with the heartwood already turned to dust, not unlike how his own heart felt after overhearing Rachel's declaration this morning. He extracted a sample and added it to the day's collection. He didn't even know why he let what she'd said get under his skin like an ash borer digging under the tree bark. If asked, he too would have said that he and Rachel were just friends. He wouldn't have dared presume there was more between them. But something about her tone had reminded him of the freshman girls commissioned to humiliate him and his buddies during Frosh Week.

His phone's ring mercifully yanked Curtis from his brooding. He glanced at the caller ID then picked up. "Gary, do you have good news for us?"

"Not yet. The farmhand taking care of the Bakers' animals said they won't be back until the weekend. And he's not sure if they arranged for someone else to open the shop tomorrow. Unfortunately, he doesn't have a key himself, so we couldn't check for the dollhouse."

"Did he have a phone number for the Bakers?"

"He did, but was reluctant to share it, which I understood. He texted my question to them for me, though, along with my phone number, and we taped a note on the door in case someone else comes in to run the shop in the meantime."

"That's great. We really appreciate your help."

"Rachel seems like a special girl." His tone intimated he was fishing for information.

"Yes, she is. The forest service is lucky to have her."

Gary burst into laughter. "You do know she likes you? I'd dare say at least as much as you like her."

Curtis winced that his interest was that transparent. Wait a minute. Did Gary say…? "You think she *likes me* likes me?" Curtis cringed at how much like a pubescent boy that sounded.

"She'd be a fool not to. You're a great guy. You just need to get out of your own way."

Okay, that didn't sound as hopeful as he'd supposed.

"Oh, sorry. Gotta go. I have a customer. I'll call when I have more news."

"Appreciate it." Reveling in having an excuse to chat with Rachel, Curtis opened his contacts to find her number. But then his thoughts strayed to the conversation he'd overheard between her and Lara, dampening his enthusiasm, and he opted to send a quick text instead.

Her terse "thanks for letting me know" response didn't come through until an hour later, confirming he'd made the right decision. Only the confirmation didn't improve his mood any.

He continued collecting samples and happened upon an ideal hunk of maple for carving. He studied the wood and pictured a squirrel holding a nut. Maybe he could carve it for Rachel, as a keepsake—a reminder of their time together hunting down her miniatures. The concept for the squirrel expanded and grew as he finished his job for the day. By the time he'd delivered the samples he'd collected, he couldn't wait to get started on the new piece. He parked at one of his favorite scenic spots, where he could enjoy the sights and sounds of nature while he whittled.

The piece soon emerged from the wood as he stripped away the unnecessary layers. Too bad figuring out Rachel's true nature, and feelings toward him, wasn't as easy. Curtis flicked his carving knife against the wood with a snort. What made him think she had feelings for him? *Flick.* Or thought about him when he wasn't around? *Flick.* Gary's supposed observations? *Flick.* Gary was an old romantic. More so now that his wife was away visiting her ailing sister. *Flick.* "Ow!"

Curtis jerked his sliced thumb to his mouth to staunch the blood. This was what entertaining thoughts about a woman did to him. When would he learn? His cell phone rang. And his traitorous heart leaped...until he glanced at the screen. He tapped the screen. "Hey, Ian. What's up?"

"Where are you? You were supposed to pick up the Chinese food tonight, remember?"

Curtis looked at his watch. "Sorry, I lost track of time. Can you phone in the order, and I'll head over now?"

"Sure thing."

Turning onto their street twenty minutes later, he spotted a familiar-looking woman emerge from a car parked on the street in front of the house next door. She retrieved a clear plastic bin from the trunk. But as Curtis passed her and pulled into the driveway, he couldn't figure out why she looked familiar. Must just have one of those faces. He grabbed the bags of food.

Rachel stepped out of the house smiling his way, and his spirits lifted.

Then loud voices rose from the street.

"What are you doing?" a woman demanded. "You can't—Help! Stop, thief!"

Rachel blanched. "Mom?" She catapulted off the porch.

Curtis dropped the food bags back into his truck and raced after her.

The woman he'd seen as he drove in—Rachel's mom?—was chasing a guy in a dark hoodie down the street. "Stop!" she screamed again.

Curtis sprinted past Rachel and her mom and raced after the guy.

Half a block later, the guy cut across the street and ducked through a row of hedges. But the plastic bin he'd snatched snagged in the bushes.

Curtis caught hold of one end of it and tugged. The lid popped off, revealing a collection of carved wooden miniatures. Rachel's miniatures?

The startled instant was all the time the guy needed to rip the container from Curtis's grip.

Curtis plowed through the hedge after him. The guy hoofed it around the corner of a house. Curtis chased after him. But by the time he reached the corner, the guy was unlocking the door of a dark sedan. He lunged into the car and sped off before Curtis could reach the curb.

Curtis squinted at the plate but caught sight of only an *S* and a *K* before the car disappeared around the corner.

Curtis trudged back to where Rachel and her mother waited expectantly. Did Rachel know what was in the stolen bin? Curtis slowed, the magnitude of his failure weighing each step. He couldn't bear to meet Rachel's gaze, so he focused on her mother instead. "Sorry, he got away."

CHAPTER EIGHT

The anguish in Mom's wail wrenched Rachel's heart. "What is it? What was in the bin?"

Mom's eyes filled with tears. "Your miniatures. I found your miniatures."

"My miniatures?" Rachel froze. "I don't understand. You found them? Where? How?"

"Let's talk inside." Curtis prodded them toward the house. "I got a partial license plate on the thief and the make of his car. We can call the police."

Mom shook her head. "The police will hardly be willing to launch a manhunt over a stolen bin of children's toys."

Rachel's heart twisted. *Mom found my miniatures. Brought them to me. And now they're gone. Again.*

"Maybe not," Curtis acknowledged. "But we need to report the situation." He withdrew his phone and punched in 911. "This isn't the first time I've noticed a dark sedan lurking around the neighborhood. I don't know if this was the same guy. Or why he'd snatch a bin of toys. But the police will want to know what's going on. Maybe you're not the first person he's confronted."

Mom nodded, but her sagging shoulders said she didn't hold out much hope.

While Curtis relayed a description of the thief and his car to police, Rachel retrieved the bags of food from his truck and carried them inside to their waiting housemates, who were apparently oblivious to what had just unfolded on the street. Maybe Curtis was right. Maybe this wasn't the first time something like this had happened in the neighborhood. She hadn't met any of the neighbors yet, let alone chatted about the goings-on. Mom hung back, probably not eager to meet Rachel's housemates for the first time with red-rimmed eyes.

Rachel handed Lara the takeout bags. "Start without us. We'll fill our plates in a bit." She led her mom to the relatively private sunroom at the back of the house and then enveloped her in her arms. "It's so good to see you. I'm sorry for the way I've been acting lately."

"No, I'm sorry. I should've realized how much the miniatures your dad gave you meant to you."

Rachel guided her mom to a chair and sat kitty-corner to her, their knees almost touching. "How did you find them? I went to the shop and tried posting on social media. Did everything I could think of."

Mom's eyes teared up once more. "I asked the thrift store manager if I could post signs at each cash register and on the bulletin board, asking whoever purchased them to contact me. I found a picture of you playing with them as a child and included how very important they were to you and that they'd been donated by mistake."

Rachel sniffed. "You did that for me?"

"Of course. I hated the rift my thoughtlessness caused." Her mother reached across the space between them and swept Rachel's hair from her face. The back of her fingers tenderly stroked Rachel's cheek before she dropped her hand to her lap once more. "A local reporter noticed my posters and ran an article about my quest to find the miniatures."

Rachel swallowed a sob. "That's so cool."

"And it worked. The same day the article was published the person who bought the miniatures called me. Fortunately, he hadn't yet given them to his niece as he'd planned. He wouldn't even let me buy them back from him. Said he was just glad he could restore them to you."

"Amazing," Curtis interjected, stepping into the room with a tray of Chinese takeout cartons and a pair of plates. He set it on a side table. "The others said you hadn't eaten yet."

Rachel smiled at him through a sheen of tears. "Mom, this is Curtis. He's the guy I mentioned who's been helping me try to find the miniatures. And we think we have a lead on others carved by Dad's great-granddad, along with a dollhouse."

"Really?" Mom's face brightened for the first time since she'd arrived. "That's marvelous." Then she frowned. "What did the police say about the prospects of finding our thief?"

"They're coming by to take your statement—a description of the guy if you can supply one. Unfortunately, I only saw him from behind, and with the hoodie on, I didn't even see his hair color."

"I'm afraid I scarcely glimpsed his face," Mom said. "Once I realized his intention, I focused on hanging on to the bin." She shook her head. "I don't know what came over me. If it had been anything else, I would've let the creep take off with it rather than risk escalating the situation. But I couldn't let the miniatures go.

Not"—she shot Rachel a sorrowful glance—"not after everything I've put you through."

"Oh, Mom. I'd rather have you unharmed." Rachel pulled her into another hug. And that truth seeped through her entire being.

By the time their hug ended, Curtis had slipped from the room.

Half an hour later, after they'd picked at cold Chinese food, Curtis came back into the room. Rachel knew he had heard enough to know her mom was frustrated with her inability to offer a useful description of the thief to the officer.

"You said you were focused on the bin," he said to her. "Did you notice his hands? Maybe a ring he wore?"

Mom had been studying her own hands, but at this last question, her attention snapped to the officer. "He had a tattoo on his arm!"

"Can you describe it?"

Mom frowned. "I only glimpsed part of it when his sleeve slid up as he grabbed the bin. It was drawn in black ink and looked like a snake tail, or… No, a dinosaur tail. It had triangle armor spikes."

Curtis who'd remained standing by the door, met Rachel's gaze. "Lita's boyfriend?"

"Who's Lita?" Mom asked.

Curtis explained about their search for the miniatures and their suspicion that the young couple might have tried to reclaim the dollhouse that Lita's mom instructed the retirement home to donate to the thrift store. "One of the residents mentioned the boyfriend had a tattoo. We never met them, so I have no idea what kind of tattoo it is." He met Rachel's gaze again. "But I think it's high time we found out."

After Rachel's mom left, Curtis found Rachel brooding in the backyard, shoulders hunched, her arms wrapped protectively around her middle. If he'd held on to the bin a little tighter, run after the thief a little faster, this night could have turned out so much different. He longed to draw Rachel into his arms and drive away her heartache. But he'd lost his best chance at being her hero. He ventured to the edge of the patio, not sure she'd even want to talk to him. "You okay?"

She spun around, and the torment in her gaze lashed a gaping hole through his chest. "I feel terrible that my mom could've been hurt tonight because of my obsession with"—her voice broke—"finding my miniatures."

He rushed to her and rubbed his palms up and down her arms to still her trembling. "None of this is your fault."

When her gaze lifted to his, his world tilted at the mixture of emotions in their watery depths. "Thank you for all you've done for me." Her gaze dropped to the vicinity of his chest.

After all he'd done? He let the thief get away, and she thanked him! He loved this woman.

He gulped at the wayward thought. *Loved?* The word was as foreign to him as happening upon a bandicoot in Stephens Forest. Yet, the notion burrowed deep into his chest and refused to give ground. Who was he kidding? He'd lost his heart to her the moment she'd taken an interest in his carvings during the camping trip.

He might have lost his bearings for a little while after over-hearing what she said to Lara. But he knew she wasn't like those college girls. She'd never led him on. She'd never laugh at him. His fingers curled around the squirrel he'd carved this afternoon. His heart pounded as he withdrew it from his pocket. "I carved this for you."

"For me?"

"It's no substitute for what you've lost, but…"

She reached for it, the graze of her fingers against his palm caus-ing his heart to skip a beat. "It's beautiful."

"I was thinking that when squirrels root around for the nuts they've buried, it must be like a treasure hunt for them, so I thought this squirrel admiring his acorn might be a fun memento of our hunt for your miniatures."

"Thank you. I'll treasure it always." A fat tear dripped down her cheek.

"Hey there." Tamping his inhibitions, he hooked his fingers under her chin and lifted it until their gazes tangled once more. "We're not done yet. Don't give up hope."

A feeble smile trembled to her lips. "No. Having my miniatures back isn't worth anyone getting hurt over."

"I've been thinking about that since Officer Scott left." Needing to put a little more space between them so he could think clearly, Curtis took a step back. "Don't you think it's strange that our thief was so obsessed with hanging on to the bin?"

"What do you mean?"

"To anyone but you or a collector, they're only toys." Curtis paced, his theory forming more clearly in his mind. "So why would he hang on to the bin so doggedly, at the risk of getting caught, even after the lid popped and he could see they were just toys?"

Rachel's head tilted. "What are you suggesting?"

"Remember the black sedan I spotted following us yesterday morning?"

"Yes."

"I think the driver is our thief. He must've overheard us asking about the dollhouse, either at the retirement home or the thrift shop, and has been keeping an eye on us ever since, hoping we'd lead him to it. When he spotted your mom carrying a bin labeled dollhouse miniatures, he must've assumed they were from Vivien's dollhouse."

Rachel sank into a lawn chair. "You still think Lita's boyfriend is the thief?"

Curtis hunkered down next to Rachel's chair. "After I gave him the slip yesterday morning, he would've realized we were onto him and maybe resorted to parking on the next street to spy on our comings and goings."

"How would he have known where we live? You think he followed us home from Happy Haven after our visit?"

"Maybe. Or he's the one who emptied my glove box outside the thrift store. He could've gotten my address from the car ownership or insurance paperwork I keep in there."

Rachel nodded. "It does all seem too coincidental to not be connected. But that's a lot of trouble to go through to recover toys that have scarcely more than sentimental value. Sure, the miniatures are hand carved and antique, but how much could he hope to get by hawking them?"

"Maybe he's not interested in the miniatures so much as what's inside one of them?"

Rachel's brow furrowed. "Huh?"

"Think about it." Unable to resist any longer, Curtis reached for Rachel's hand. Her fingers were cool but warmed quickly once he folded them in his. "Lita and her boyfriend visited Vivien the same night the ruby ring was stolen." He stroked Rachel's bare ring finger with his thumb. "And if the alarm went up before Lita was ready to leave her grandmother, he'd want a place to stash the ring in case staff started searching people—a place no one would think to look."

Rachel's eyes widened with understanding, and she squeezed Curtis's hand. "Inside one of Vivien's miniatures!"

His heart almost burst at her exuberant touch, giving wings to his theory. "I'm thinking that since Lita didn't ask her mom to save her gran's dollhouse for her, she must not have known what her boyfriend did. He likely figured they'd visit again in the next day or so and he could slip it into his pocket with no one the wiser."

"Only Vivien died, so they had no excuse to return!"

"Bingo."

"Do you think we should tell Detective Scott our suspicions?"

Curtis hesitated. "At this point it's only speculation that we're looking at one and the same thief. Not enough for him to secure a warrant to search the kid's house or car."

"He could at least confirm whether or not Evan drives a black Corolla with an *S* and a *K* on the plate."

Curtis pushed to his feet and, still holding her hand, drew Rachel to hers. "I was thinking that maybe we could talk to Lita instead." At Rachel's abrupt inhalation, Curtis skimmed his thumb across her wrist. "Hear me out. If we can convince Lita that we're only interested in recovering your miniatures, perhaps she'll tell us where Evan dumped them. I suspect he'll have chucked them as soon as he discovered the ring wasn't among them, since the miniatures your mom had were not the same ones that went with Vivien's dollhouse."

"And if she doesn't know anything about what he's been up to?" Rachel pulled free of his hold, and the cool air that swooped between them sent a chill through his chest.

"We'll worry about crossing that bridge if we come to it."

Chapter Nine

At Curtis's suggestion, Rachel used her phone to call Maribel, since his number might be recognized. Rachel's insides swirled as the number rang.

"Hello?" came a younger voice than Maribel's.

"I'm sorry, I must have the wrong number," Rachel blurted.

"Are you looking for Maribel? This is her daughter, Lita."

Rachel glanced at Curtis. She was supposed to ask Maribel for Lita, to learn if she was home without alerting her, or her boyfriend, to their interest. They hadn't expected Lita to answer her mother's phone.

Say yes, Curtis mouthed.

"Yes, is she home?" Rachel threw in the last part to confirm they weren't out somewhere else together.

"Yup. Hang on a second."

"Wait! I, uh, I was just checking so I could pop around to, um, give her something." Not entirely a lie. They had information to give her if Curtis's theory panned out. "But I forgot your address."

Lita rattled it off without a second's hesitation.

Rachel's heart pounded at the subterfuge. "Thanks. I'll see you soon." She disconnected before the girl could ask who she was then beamed at Curtis. "I got their address!"

Curtis palmed his keys. "Great. Let's go."

Rachel dashed upstairs to put Curtis's gift into her room for safe-keeping. Like the sun breaking through the clouds on a gloomy day, the tenderness in Curtis's voice, in his touch, had lifted her spirits.

"I was thinking," Rachel said as Curtis drove them to Maribel's, "if my mom hadn't given away my miniatures, we might never have become such good friends."

Curtis grinned across the seat at her. "Maybe our friendship is one of the ways God is working things together for good." He blushed. "I didn't mean to imply—"

She smiled. "That's okay. I know what you meant. I'd had the same thought." Their friendship was quickly becoming as precious to her as the miniatures for which they searched.

Ten minutes later, dark purple-gray clouds gathered on the horizon in the descending dusk as they rang Maribel's doorbell.

Maribel opened the door with a wide smile that immediately faltered. "Uh, hi. May I help you?"

Taking the lead, Curtis introduced himself as the person she'd spoken with the day before. "We hoped to talk to you and your daughter about Vivien's dollhouse."

Confusion flitted across Maribel's face. "My daughter? Like I told you on the phone, she was never into dolls. She was fine with me donating it."

"Actually..." A teen girl's voice sounded from deeper in the house. "I've kind of changed my mind about that, Mom."

"Really?" Looking flabbergasted, Maribel motioned Curtis and Rachel inside. "You'd better come in."

Lita, dressed in black from head to toe with the only splash of color a streak of dark purple in her black hair, didn't strike Rachel as the kind of girl who'd be sentimental about a dollhouse. The impression solidified Rachel's suspicion that Lita and her boyfriend's search for the dollhouse was for nefarious reasons.

After they'd taken seats in the living room, Rachel casually asked Lita, "You're not seeing your boyfriend tonight?"

"He had to work."

"Where does he work?" Curtis asked.

"I think he said he was chicken catching tonight for some farmer his friend knows." Lita spoke without pretense, and Rachel wondered if Lita was oblivious to what her boyfriend had really been up to this evening…if their theory about him was right.

If he'd kept her in the dark, then coming here might not only *not* bring them any closer to recovering the miniatures, but Lita might inadvertently, or deliberately, tip off her boyfriend that they were onto him. Which meant they could be in real danger.

Lita straightened in her seat. "Did you bring Gran's dollhouse with you?"

"No, we haven't located it yet," Curtis said, which was the truth. They knew where it *might* be but couldn't confirm it until the proprietors returned from their trip.

"Oh." The girl sagged.

"Why the sudden change of heart over the dollhouse?" her mother asked, echoing the question racing around Rachel's mind.

Lita pushed to her feet. "Evan convinced me."

Oh, I bet he did. Rachel surreptitiously stole a glance at Curtis.

"Evan said his sisters were always super into dolls. And he thought that one day"—Lita edged toward the doorway, her voice fading—"if I have girls, I might be sorry I didn't save the dollhouse for them."

"I see." Maribel's clipped tone betrayed her discomfort with the possibility, although Rachel suspected her displeasure had more to do with learning her teenage daughter was already contemplating her future family with her boyfriend. Maribel directed her attention to Rachel. "No matter how Lita feels, we understand that, as a blood relative, keeping the dollhouse is your prerogative, and we certainly wouldn't begrudge you that." She snagged her daughter's gaze. "Would we?"

Lita shrugged in typical noncommittal teenage fashion.

"We wouldn't," Maribel repeated firmly.

"The thing is"—Curtis projected his voice toward Lita, who now hovered in the doorway, looking ready to bolt—"giving Lita the dollhouse might be an option Rachel would consider if…"

Rachel's heart quickened, wondering what on earth Curtis was thinking, because although she might not have known of the dollhouse's existence a week ago, reclaiming her great-great-grandfather's entire collection to hand down to future generations had become as important to her as regaining the connection they represented to her father.

"If what?" Lita asked.

"Well, if her own missing miniatures were restored to her, the situation would be different. You see, her mom was able to get them back. But when she brought them to the house to give to Rachel this evening, a guy in a hoodie snatched the entire bin from her and ran."

"Seriously?" Lita turned from the doorway, sounding genuinely indignant.

Rachel nodded. "I was devastated all over again."

"That's horrible," Maribel said, "but I don't understand why that would bring you here."

"Because we think Lita can help us recover Rachel's miniatures."

"Me? How am I supposed to do that?" Lita sounded confused, and Rachel didn't think she was faking.

"Rachel's mother said the thief had a dinosaur tattoo on his arm," Curtis explained. "Or maybe it was a dragon?"

Lita stiffened. "And you think it was Evan?"

It was Curtis's turn to sport the noncommittal shrug. "A Happy Haven's resident mentioned he has a tattoo."

"A wyvern. Not a dragon."

"Wyvern is just another name for dragon, honey," Maribel reasoned.

"But he can't be in two places at once. And he's working tonight."

"Catching chickens," Curtis said, deadpan.

"Yes."

"Is that a job he does frequently?"

"No, I think this is the first time."

"Is the tattoo the only reason you think Evan is your thief?" Maribel asked, her manner much less hospitable than it had been when they first arrived. "Because not everyone with tattoos is a hoodlum, you know. Once you get past his somewhat intimidating exterior, Evan is a kind, honest young man."

"It's not the only reason, no." Curtis regained control of the conversation with the acumen of a seasoned detective, and Rachel silently thanked the Lord for bringing him into her life. "We also suspect he mistook the miniatures for Vivien's."

Lita slouched back into a chair. "And you think Evan would steal them so he can give them to me? That's just stupid."

"Actually, we believe he was after something hidden in one of Vivien's miniatures."

"I'm not aware of anything my stepmother kept hidden in any of her miniatures," Maribel said, "so, I doubt Evan would be."

"You don't understand," Rachel chimed in. "A ring was stolen at Happy Haven the same evening Lita and Evan last visited Vivien. And we believe the jewel thief hid the stolen ring in one of your stepmother's miniatures."

"So you think Lita and Evan saw what he did?"

Rachel exchanged a glance with Curtis. That possibility hadn't occurred to her, but whether Evan stole the ring in the first place or not didn't make him any less culpable for snatching the bin of miniatures away from her mom.

"And you think that's the real reason they want the dollhouse?" Maribel continued. She turned to her daughter. "Did you see anyone near your gran's dollhouse?"

"No. We were the only ones who visited her room that night."

"Did either of you leave the room at any time?" Curtis asked.

"Sure. To use the restroom. We both did at different times."

Curtis nodded. "Were you both still in your gran's room when the alarm went up about the theft?"

"Yeah, they went into lockdown. Closed everyone's room door and asked that no one leave."

"Did Evan step out of the room at any point before that?"

Lita's eyes narrowed, and she surged to her feet, hands fisted at her hips. "Now you're calling Evan a jewel thief? Evan is a good guy. He wouldn't do anything like that."

Curtis patted the air and urged her to sit back down. "So you didn't see him fiddle with any of your gran's miniatures while you were there?"

Lita flinched, and her mom must have noticed too, because she reached for her daughter's hand. "Did you?" Maribel asked gently.

"Sure, but he's done that lots of times when we visit. He thought the house was cool. That's why he couldn't understand why I told you I wasn't interested in keeping it."

Maribel's gaze shifted to Rachel, and she could read the doubt in the woman's eyes.

Doubts must have begun to niggle at Lita too, because she teared up. "After we learned the dollhouse was donated to the thrift store, he took me to go buy it back. I thought he was showing me how much he cares about me. That he's thinking about a future with me." She sniffed.

Rachel didn't see any reason to tell her that the dollhouse never made it to that particular thrift store.

Maribel wrapped Lita in her arms. "Oh, honey. We don't know anything for sure."

Lita sat back and, balling her hands, scrubbed the moisture from her eyes. "Have you told the police your suspicions?"

"We haven't. We want to give you both a chance to do the right thing. To return the miniatures to Rachel. And if the dollhouse is found, return the ring to its rightful owner."

"Okay," Lita agreed. "I'll talk to Evan."

When she made no move to do so, Rachel prodded, "Could you phone him now?"

"He won't be able to answer if he's in the middle of chicken catching," she pointed out.

"*If* he is," Curtis said softly.

With a huff, Lita tapped her phone's screen. A few seconds later, she said, "Hey, Evan. Call me when you get a chance. Thanks."

Drawing her bottom lip between her teeth, Rachel slanted a silent *what now?* in Curtis's direction.

"You don't happen to have those apps on your phones that allow you to see where each other are, do you?" Curtis asked Lita.

"No. We trust each other." She turned her phone over and over in her hand and slanted a scowl at her mom. Rachel could only surmise her mom had wanted to track her daughter in a similar fashion.

Curtis squared his jaw, clearly not ready to call it a night without some sort of confirmation they were on the right track. "Then do you know his license plate number?"

"His motorcycle plate, you mean?"

"No. His car plate," Rachel corrected.

"He doesn't have a car," Maribel said.

Rachel's heart kicked into a frenzy. If Evan didn't drive a car, he wasn't their guy.

"Does he have access to a black sedan?" Curtis studied Lita intently. "Maybe his parents' car."

"No. They drive a minivan."

"What about a friend's car?" Curtis pushed.

Rachel mentally shook her head. If Evan wanted to follow them without being noticed, wouldn't a motorcycle have been a smarter choice? Why switch vehicles with a friend? Unless he realized he wouldn't have room to carry the dollhouse on his bike. Then again, he wouldn't bother, would he? Not if all he was after was the miniature holding the ring.

Lita squirmed, presumedly recognizing the implication if she answered *yes.* "Not any friend I know."

"Okay." Curtis pushed to his feet and extended his hand to draw Rachel up. "We apologize for interrupting your evening, and if we've jumped to the wrong conclusion. But please know that what matters most to Rachel is recovering the beloved miniatures her father gave her before he died. So, if you can make that happen, we won't ask questions. Fair enough?" He squeezed Rachel's hand as if seeking confirmation, and she nodded her agreement.

Lita crossed her arms over her abdomen and seemed to shrink into herself. "All right. But I'm sure you're wrong about Evan."

As much as Rachel wanted to say "I hope so" for Lita's sake, she merely nodded again, because if they *were* wrong, she held out little hope of ever finding her miniatures again.

Chapter Ten

Rachel tossed her rubber boots into her trunk and slammed the lid. Skipping work wasn't an option, even if she'd rather race to Last Chance to see if there was a signboard on the road for the elusive thrift shop. Or surveil Lita to see if she'd lead her to Evan and the black sedan getaway car.

"Hey," Curtis called, hurrying out of the house, "I have to go to the Unionville unit today too to assess insect infestations. You mind carpooling?"

"Not at all. Be glad for the company." The Unionville unit of Stephens Forest consisted of eleven distinct parcels of land, none of which she'd ever visited. "My map app says the drive is almost an hour. I planned to hit the parcel that spans Appanoose and Davis County off 440th Street today."

"Works for me." Curtis slid into the passenger seat as she climbed behind the wheel. "You'll want to park at the 440th Street entrance. The other entrance is on a dirt road that's not regularly maintained, and with all the rain we've had, it could be dicey."

Before today, Rachel had never noticed that Curtis wore cologne. But she really liked the sandalwood scent that teased her senses as he turned to fasten his seat belt.

He tilted his head. "You forget something?"

She cleared her throat. "Uh, no. Just thinking." She reversed out of the driveway and headed east. "I'd hoped to hike in from one entrance before lunch and the other entrance after lunch." The Unionville unit had no recreational facilities, but it was popular with wildlife watchers, hunters, and backcountry hikers. "I've been asked to update the forest management plan for the entire unit. But before I can strategize a vision for the future, I need to assess the forest's current state."

"Of course."

"The Asteria Boulevard entrance is the only access point to the DNR service lane, which will be the fastest route for me to gather a comprehensive view of the area. But I do have all-wheel drive, so getting to it shouldn't be a problem."

"Great. We can always hike the half mile in from the main road if need be." Curtis shifted his seat back to accommodate his long legs. "I guess you haven't heard from Lita?"

"No." Rachel frowned. "I'm afraid even if Evan is our thief, he'll deny it. Because if he loves Lita, he won't want her to know he's a thief."

Curtis snorted. "Yeah, a smart guy knows no woman wants to be hooked up with a thief."

Rachel felt Curtis's gaze on her and glanced his way. The empathy in his eyes squeezed her heart.

"I'm sorry. Maybe we should've taken our suspicions directly to the police."

"I haven't given up hope," she said firmly, as much to convince herself as him. "Besides, like you said, the police need hard evidence to get a search warrant. I just have a bad feeling that if our theory about Evan's motive for snatching my miniatures is true, he likely dumped them as soon as he discovered his mistake."

"Me too." Curtis grimaced. "And if he was worried we'd hop into a car and chase him, he likely drove a long ways before stopping to check."

Struck by an idea, Rachel sat straighter. "If we find out where he lives, we could map his most likely route from our house to his."

"Great idea." Curtis shifted to face her, the excitement in his voice matching hers. "We can check out any secluded areas along the route where he might've stopped to search his stash."

"My thoughts exactly."

The drive passed quickly in Curtis's company, and they soon reached the forest parcel she needed to assess. She drove past the entrance, opting instead to first see if the dirt road would be navigable. Reaching Asteria Boulevard, she peered up the rutted road marked by the odd muddy puddle. "My car should be able to handle this." A minute later, she turned into the parking area and glanced at her watch. "How about we meet back here at eleven?" Since Curtis would be regularly stopping to collect samples, she anticipated covering a lot more ground than he would. "Then we can drive to the other section after lunch."

"Sounds good." Curtis pulled out his cell phone. "The cell signal is decent. So if you change your mind on the time, give me a call."

"Will do." Deciding she wouldn't need her rubber boots, she shrugged into her backpack and checked her pocket to confirm she had her map and compass. The GPS on her phone was great, but she'd learned from experience that she couldn't always count on getting a signal. "My plan is to survey the forest east of the road first. Then I'll head back here to the service lane. That way it'll be easier to gauge my time."

As she crossed the road, she noticed they had company. Only the driver had pulled off the road halfway to the entrance. "You okay?" she called out.

He waved and climbed back into his vehicle. Probably decided not to risk taking his low-lying car through the water-filled ruts. She paused to see if he'd turn around, but he didn't start his car. Checking his map, maybe?

She continued into the woods. Since the spring turkey-hunting season ended yesterday, and no self-respecting poacher would drive anything less macho than a pickup truck, she doubted the driver was anyone to worry about. He'd likely ventured out to watch the wildlife, maybe take some photos. The hazy sunshine was perfect lighting for picture-taking today.

Rachel slogged through the forest, picking up the occasional trail forged by animals and/or people, and was pleasantly surprised to find a wider variety of trees than she'd expected. She was so absorbed in her work that when a call came in from a number not in her contacts, she almost dismissed it. Then, at the last second, thinking it could be Lita, she swiped the screen to answer it.

"Rachel? This is Lita."

Rachel's spirits soared. "I'm so glad you called."

"I don't have the news you were hoping for, I'm afraid." The girl's voice wobbled.

Rachel sank onto a fallen log. "Oh?"

"Evan swears he didn't steal anything, and I believe him. He even showed me a scratch he got on his arm from chicken catching last night."

"Okay." Rachel fought to keep her voice even, to accept what the girl said at face value, even though her first thought was he likely got the scratch from cutting through the hedgerow. "I appreciate your asking him. And I'm sorry for..." She swallowed hard.

"That's okay. I get it. I've got to get to class. I figured you'd want to know."

"Yes."

Lita disconnected before Rachel could repeat her thanks, which was just as well, because she didn't feel all that grateful. Her dad would have reminded her that when God closes a door, He opens a window. But what if Evan lied to Lita? The reality was they still didn't know for sure one way or the other if he was their thief.

Rachel forced her attention back to the task at hand. She noted areas where the forest would benefit from managed harvesting to give saplings room to grow and to strengthen the health of the trees overall. An hour and a half later, she returned to the parking area.

Curtis was nowhere in sight.

With more than an hour before their agreed upon meeting time, she only stopped long enough to grab another water bottle from her car. *That's strange.* She was sure she'd locked the car. She glanced around, but nothing appeared out of place. Remembering Curtis's riffled glove box, she popped hers open. Everything seemed in order.

Straightening, she muttered, "Mom's run-in last night has me paranoid." Then she reminded herself that Evan should be in school right now. As if to convince herself she had nothing to fear, she purposely left the car unlocked this time. After all, if Curtis returned before she did, he'd appreciate being able to get in.

She jogged the length of the service lane for a quick overview of the area then trekked back slower, pausing frequently to take notes. The wind whistled eerily through the trees. Suddenly, the snap of a twig made her jump. "Curtis, is that you?"

Silence. Even the birds stopped tweeting. The eeriness of it hit her like a mass of creepy-crawlies skittering over her skin.

She squinted through the trees and listened. She saw nothing unusual. Heard nothing unusual. Then, just as abruptly, the squirrels resumed their chattering and the birds their chirping. Telling herself it was nothing, she finished jotting the note she'd been making. But her shaky script betrayed how unconvinced she was. She took out her phone and tapped Curtis's name in her contacts.

"What's up?"

"I'm heading back now on the service lane. I left the car unlocked so you can get in if you get there before me."

"Is something wrong?"

Her grip on the phone tightened. "Why would you ask that?"

"You sound…I don't know, uneasy, maybe."

Were her emotions that transparent? "Everything's fine. Honestly. I think I'm just still keyed up from last night."

"I've finished here, so I'll meet you on the service lane."

"You don't need to do that."

"I want to," he said, and the tenderness in his voice soothed her trembling.

Curtis sprinted to the parking lot to drop his samples at the car and, to his relief, found the lot otherwise empty. Of course, someone could have hiked in from the other parking lot or up Asteria. He locked the car then jogged up the service lane to meet Rachel.

Because Rachel hadn't sounded fine.

Five minutes later, she came into view and greeted him with a "Hey" that sounded more relaxed.

He found himself hoping he had something to do with the change. "Hey, yourself. Get everything you want?"

She'd attempted to tame her strawberry blond curls into a high ponytail, but a wispy, errant ringlet had broken loose and brushed her cheek. Suddenly, his fingers itched to do the same.

Rachel patted her notepad against her leg. "Yeah, I—" Her cell phone rang, and she signaled him that she'd just be a second then dug the phone from her pocket. "It's Lara." She tapped the speaker button on her screen. "Hi, Lara, what's up? Curtis is with me, and you're on speaker."

"We've been burgled," their housemate blurted, sounding breathless and shaky. "I came home to pick up a sweater and found the back door forced open. He went through all our rooms. Kicked open the doors that were locked. It's—it's a mess."

Rachel's face went ashen.

Curtis squeezed her hand. "Have you called the police? Is someone with you now?"

"They're on their way, and so is Ian. The intruder busted Ian's moose bank that had the money he was saving up for his vacation. They must've only been interested in cash and jewelry, because none of our laptops or other electronics seem to be missing."

"That's good at least. Let the police know we can tell them what, if anything, we're missing when we get home after work. Okay?"

"Yeah, but Curtis"—Lara hesitated, and he braced himself for worse news—"do you think this is connected to the guy who stole the stuff from Rachel's mom?"

The pained noise that escaped Rachel's lips turned him inside out.

"Maybe. Mention it to the officer who takes your statement. Two incidents in two days might inspire them to look a little harder for this guy."

Rachel hit disconnect and held his gaze. "I hate to sound like a broken record. But this is too much of a coincidence for the thefts to not be connected, don't you think? It sounds like the same MO as Evelyn's burglary. I think this guy is looking for the dollhouse."

"This guy? You don't think it's Evan?"

"He'd be in school right now."

"Kids skip classes."

She squirmed. "Yeah, I guess. The thing is—Lita called earlier. Evan claims he's not our thief. I'm just not sure if we can trust that he's telling the truth."

"C'mon. The sooner we have our lunch and get what we need from the other section, the sooner we can get home and figure out if there's a connection between all these thefts."

Back at the car, Rachel grabbed a sandwich from her pack and, after taking a bite, set it on the console next to her seat to start the car. But when she turned the key, the engine cranked without starting. She tried again. Same thing.

"Stop and pop the hood," Curtis instructed. "At this rate, you'll drain your battery before it starts."

"What do you think the problem is?"

"Could be a clogged fuel filter or bad spark plugs." Curtis lifted the hood and sucked in a breath.

"That bad?" Rachel asked.

Curtis grimaced. "No, it's just that we don't have the tools to check any of those things on your engine. I'm not even sure where they are." He pulled out his phone and googled *my Subaru Forester cranks but won't start.* Besides the possibilities that had immediately come to mind, they listed a blown fuel pump fuse. Next, he googled where to find fuses in a Subaru Forester. He quickly found a short and simple video. "Thank you, Lord, for YouTube video nuts." He popped the fuse box cover on the dash. "Now, according to the fuse list in this video, number eleven controls the ignition system." He compared Rachel's array of fuses to the diagram and, thankfully, it was identical. Curtis jerked back. "That can't be right." He reached across the seat and pulled the owner's manual from the glove box, which, in retrospect, he should have done in the first place. "It is right. But then that means—"

"What?" Rachel blurted, holding the driver's side door open for him.

"The good news is your fuse isn't blown."

"Okay," she responded. "The bad news?"

"Someone's pulled it."

"Pulled it? What do you mean, pulled it? You mean someone's been in my car? I knew it. I was sure I'd locked it before I headed out. I tried to convince myself I was just being paranoid. That's why I left the car unlocked after that."

Curtis caught her arms. "Breathe."

She locked gazes with him as if clinging to a lifeline and sucked in a deep breath.

"Now let it out slowly."

She did as he instructed, closing her eyes as her breath hissed from her lungs. Then suddenly her eyes snapped open. "What if pulling the fuse isn't all he's done?"

CHAPTER ELEVEN

While they waited for AAA, Rachel shimmied under her car and traced the brake lines and gas line with the flashlight on her phone to assure herself they weren't tampered with as well. At the same time, Curtis scrutinized the engine. Nothing else appeared amiss. By the time AAA arrived and got her car running again, Rachel was ready to call it a day and, thankfully, Curtis agreed.

But staring at her bedroom's splintered doorjamb, she regretted being in such a hurry.

Drawing in a fortifying breath, she pushed open the door. Her knees faltered, and she gripped the edge of the bureau to steady herself. The mattress was overturned, the drawers dumped, the pockets of her clothes turned out, every book was pulled from the shelf, and the contents of her jewelry box were scattered over her desktop.

She scanned the items. A small gold cross, a silver locket, several gold chains of varying lengths and thicknesses, and a myriad of costume jewelry. Nothing seemed to be missing. Just like at Evelyn Lupin's burglary.

Because nothing here would have fetched enough to bother trying to fence? Or because the thief had only been after the missing ring?

But he had taken Ian's money. A glass container stuffed with coins and bills was apparently too tempting for any thief to resist, even one with a shopping list. Rachel fingered her gold cross—a gift from her mom on her thirteenth birthday. "Why, Lord?"

The Bible verse *where your treasure is, there your heart will be also* whispered through her mind. She'd never thought of herself as the type obsessed with accumulating treasure on earth. She wasn't into clothes and shoes and jewelry like many of her college cohorts. She kind of prided herself on living simply. Yet her obsession with the miniatures had caused nothing but trouble.

Spying the carving Curtis gave her peeking out from under a book, she rescued it and tweaked its chubby cheeks. Okay, not *nothing* but trouble. Her newfound friendship with Curtis was a gift. And treasure hunting with him was fun if she ignored the burglaries and her car's missing fuse.

But if she was honest with herself, in her hurt and anger over Mom disposing of the miniatures, she had lost sight of her truest treasure—her relationship with Jesus. *Help me keep my priorities straight, Lord. To care more about the things that matter most to You—people…loving them, treating them right, forgiving their wrongs.*

"Knock, knock."

Rachel glanced toward the open door. "Mom!" She sprang into her mother's arms. She was long past the stage of asking her mommy to kiss her boo-boo better, and she'd stopped believing in platitudes that claimed everything would be okay the day her father died. But Mom's arms enfolding her was sweet comfort. "What are you doing here?"

"I tried calling to see how you were after last night's excitement."

Was that only twenty-four hours ago?

"And when I couldn't reach you, I called Curtis. He told me what happened."

Mom had Curtis's phone number?

Mom squeezed her tighter then stepped back. "Now enough of this touchy-feely stuff," she teased, mimicking a phrase Dad used to say when his girls got too emotional. "Let's get this room tidied."

With a fresh burst of energy, Rachel gathered her books while her mother returned clothes to their hangers.

"After your dad died, our counselor cautioned that people who've been hurt tend to latch on to control as a coping mechanism for their fear of a future they're no longer willing to trust to God."

Rachel stiffened, wondering where her mom was going with this. Her room had just been broken into, and her car sabotaged. Surely Mom didn't think now was the time to give her a lecture on trusting God. Had she forgotten that Rachel never found their counseling sessions all that helpful?

"Maybe that's why when things like this happen"—Mom motioned to the chaos in the room—"it takes every ounce of self-control not to be a helicopter parent."

Rachel giggled. Her mom had never seemed like an overprotective parent.

"But I thank God you weren't alone in those woods today. And that you don't live alone."

"Yeah, me too." Rachel watched her mom fold clothes. And maybe for the first time *really* saw her. All this time Rachel struggled to understand why Mom would want to risk losing another husband when Dad's passing had left such a giant hole in their hearts. But that wasn't what she was doing at all. She was refusing to let fear rule her life.

Rachel had to admit she did remember the counselor's lecture about how her quest for a semblance of control could become like an idol that usurped God's rightful place in her heart. At ten, she hadn't had a clue what the woman was talking about, except that the image of a carved wooden idol had stuck in her mind. And the carved wooden miniatures she'd spent the past few weeks trying to track down were too freakily similar a parallel to ignore.

Rachel stifled a shudder. "I'm sorry, Mom."

"For what, sweetheart?"

"For not being more supportive of your relationship with Jerry."

"Oh, honey. I understand how hard it is for you to see me with someone else. And to sell our family home."

"Yes, but I was just thinking about me, about how your relationship with Jerry affected me. I never considered how lonely you must've felt rattling around in that house full of memories while I was away at school for months on end."

Hugging a stack of folded shirts to her bosom, Mom beamed at Rachel. "I'm so proud of you."

Rachel cocked her head, confused about what her mom was referring to but certain it meant she forgave her.

Chuckling, Mom stuffed the folded shirts into a drawer. "One day, you'll have a child of your own and understand a mother's pride."

A child of her own? She'd always told Mom she didn't plan to marry. At Mom's wink, Rachel blushed. Had Mom guessed her fondness for Curtis?

Who was she kidding? She'd gone way past fondness.

Mom moved on to straightening the bedcovers. "I suppose the police weren't any more optimistic about finding today's burglar than they were yesterday's thief?"

"No. We reported the sabotage on my car too. But they didn't send out an officer, just noted the incident in the burglary report."

"I saw the fingerprint dust around the broken door downstairs. I'm kind of impressed they've put as much effort into this as they have," Mom admitted. "Especially since nothing of significance was stolen and no one was hurt."

Curtis appeared in the doorway. "Our theory this is all connected to Happy Haven's ring theft helps, I think. Excuse my interruption. I thought you'd like to know that we ordered in pizza for supper and it just arrived."

"Well, I should go," Mom said.

"You're welcome to join us for supper."

Mom gave Rachel another hug. "I won't, thanks. I only wanted to make sure you were okay."

"I am. And don't worry"—she picked up her ball cap and fitted it back on the stuffed bear sitting on her bed—"I'm hanging up my detective's hat. I don't plan on giving bad guys any more reasons to bother us."

Curtis hated that Rachel blamed herself for the burglaries, but let her declaration go by without comment. The next couple of days, he tamped down his impulse to urge her to not give up the hunt, and instead, surreptitiously kept his eyes peeled for trouble. When on Friday there'd still been no update from the police, Curtis took a circuitous route home from work to scope out the high school parking lot for a black Corolla, then Maribel's place, and finally Happy

Haven. But he didn't spot a single car like the one their thief drove. He even scanned the ditches for Rachel's bin of miniatures, but the byways were remarkably litter-free.

Friday evening, he and Ian challenged Rachel and Lara to a game of badminton, pleased she was at least still happy to spend time with him. After the girls slaughtered them amidst much laughter, Curtis drew Rachel aside and drummed up the courage to broach the subject of Vivien's dollhouse. "Tomorrow is Saturday. And I'd like to take you to Last Chance to see if the thrift store is open."

Rachel hesitated.

"I haven't seen anyone suspicious hanging around since the burglary. I think he's realized we don't know where the dollhouse is any more than he does."

"But we do," she whispered.

"*Maybe* we do. We don't know if it's already been sold."

"It is too good an opportunity to pass up, isn't it?"

"I think so. I'd hate to have done all this research into finding it only to let it slip through your fingers now. And I don't see how our driving there to check out the store could possibly put anyone else in danger."

Rachel grinned. "You had me at tomorrow is Saturday."

The next morning, Curtis's chest felt ready to burst as he waited for Rachel to join him in his truck. He struggled to wipe the grin from his face, since as far as she was concerned, they were driving to the thrift store on the off chance somebody would open the shop even though the proprietors were out of town. But Gary had called him at dawn to say he had the dollhouse waiting for Rachel at his shop.

She jogged out of the house, apologizing for taking so long. "I'll kick myself ten ways to Georgia if I find out we missed reclaiming the dollhouse because I made us late."

Curtis laughed at the image conjured by her quirky remark. "I'm sure you have nothing to worry about." He averted his attention to the road, not nearly as confident he could keep his excitement from her.

She gnawed on her bottom lip and wrung her hands.

"Don't be nervous."

She sat on her hands, her cheeks flaming crimson. "I can't help it. For the last two days I've been telling myself it doesn't matter if we find them. They're just *things* after all."

"As a carver myself, I'd like to think they're a little more than that. I'm sure your great-great-grandfather carved them with love for his daughter and perhaps even the wistful hope that they would continue to bring joy to the generations that followed. Like my grandmother's recipes do in our family."

"Yes. They're part of my family's legacy. And with the miniatures from my dad in some ditch or dumpster, this could be my last chance to secure a piece of that legacy."

"From an aptly named town too." Curtis winked.

"Let's hope so."

At the trepidation rattling her voice, he realized he couldn't make her wait any longer to hear the good news. "Gary called."

"About the dollhouse?" The scarcely banked hope in her voice drew a grin to Curtis's face. Her eyes brightened and, sitting straighter, she twisted in her seat to face him.

"Yes." Curtis hadn't thought his smile could get any bigger, but the joy in Rachel's eyes did crazy, wonderful things to him. "The thrift store owner got his farmhand's text and instructed a volunteer who helps in the shop to deliver the dollhouse to Gary's place. The owner knew the dollhouse, because when it came in, he was so impressed with the craftmanship, he set it aside, planning to sell it at auction."

"But he's giving it to us instead? Just like that?"

"Yup. No charge."

Squeezing his arm, she squealed, "I can't believe this! I'll definitely make a huge donation to the charity their shop supports. Pull over."

"Pardon me?"

"You need to pull over." She pointed to an area ahead. "There."

He did as she requested and shifted his truck into park.

She immediately jumped out of the passenger side and turned back to look at him. "Aren't you coming?"

Watching her in bewilderment, he unlatched his seat belt and slid across the bench seat and out her door.

The moment his feet hit the ground, she launched herself into his arms. "Thank you!"

Laughing at her exuberance, he spun her around as they hugged.

"What were you thinking, telling me while you were driving?" she needled. "You had to know such fantastic news calls for a celebratory hug."

He ended their spin. "Yeah, I'm an idiot."

The instant her feet touched the ground, her face tipped upward and the light in her green-brown eyes drew him like a moth to a flame. He dipped his head and inhaled, savoring the fragrance of her wild curls before pressing his lips to hers. Her posture softened against his, and his eyes slipped closed. Never in a million years would he have imagined them sharing their first kiss at the side of the road, but the moment was perfect. His fingers tangled in her hair as he drew her closer, not wanting the moment to end.

A car passed and tooted its horn encouragingly.

Her lips smiled against his, and he reluctantly ended the kiss but continued to hold her close. Her eyes were a forest he could get lost in for hours. A tiny sigh escaped her lips, and he wondered what she was thinking. But he didn't have the courage to ask.

She didn't shy away from his perusal, giving him hope that she didn't regret their impulsiveness. Because his only regret would be if she didn't want it to happen again. Somewhere in the middle of that kiss, he'd surrendered his heart to her, and he didn't think he could bear to go back.

Her lips twitched with some unspoken thought, and his heart stuttered. "Uh, I guess we better get going. Gary will be wondering what happened to us." At her nod, he opened the passenger door and gave her a hand stepping up into the truck.

The moment he turned the key in the ignition, something unloosed Rachel's tongue. "I can never thank you enough. Without your help I never would've so much as dreamed of seeing my great-great-grandfather's dollhouse. A detective I'm not," she jabbered on, scarcely taking a breath. "When I moved out of my place at grad school, I couldn't even tell you what used to be in the jar that'd started growing something in the back of my fridge."

He laughed, adoring her nervous, nonsensical rambling. Funny how the more nervous she sounded the more confident he grew.

CHAPTER TWELVE

Rachel's legs wobbled as she and Curtis stepped into Gary's office at the back of the curio shop. "I'm actually shaking," she admitted.

Curtis laced his fingers through hers and squeezed her hand. "I've got you."

His gaze wandered over her face, and her thoughts flew to their kiss. She pressed a hand to her chest, still feeling sparks dancing about like fireflies on a clear June night.

"Huh-hum." Gary pretended to cough into his fisted hand, and when he had their attention, motioned to the dollhouse with an arm-twirling flourish.

Rachel gasped at the sight. The house was two stories painted a lovely blue, with white porch columns in front. Inside there were eight rooms, all decorated in ornate Victorian style from tiny crystal chandeliers to carved wooden furniture, mirrors, lamps, and even a fireplace.

Curtis studied the minute mantel clock. "The detail he includes in even the tiniest pieces is incredible."

With trembling fingers, Rachel reached for one of the dolls, the male one. She traced the facial features with her fingertip, and her heart pinched. "He looks a little like my dad. I remember his dimpled chin."

Curtis examined the furniture. "Your great-great-grandfather was incredibly talented. The drawers in these tiny bureaus even open." Curtis pried one open with the tip of his fingernail.

Rachel gasped. "And they'd be a perfect-sized place to hide a ring." She reached for the second bureau. "This drawer's stuck."

Curtis fished a penknife from his pocket. "Try using this."

Rachel handed him the bureau instead. "You do it."

A moment later, Curtis withdrew a stunning ruby ring in a delicate, antique gold setting.

Gary whistled. "That's got to be worth a pretty penny. If that ruby is real, we're talking five figures."

"Our theory was right," Rachel exclaimed. "That must be the stolen ring."

"We'd better call the police and let them know. They might want to try to get fingerprints off this." Curtis frowned. "I guess I shouldn't have touched it with my bare hands."

"Uh." Gary sheepishly repositioned a carved chair. "I'm afraid I washed everything when I set it up."

"I'm sure the ring's owner will simply be happy for its safe return," Rachel soothed.

"And who knows?" Curtis added. "Maybe if we return the ring without implicating anyone, Evan and Lita will return the favor."

Rachel shivered, not wanting to get her hopes up. This many days later, she feared her bin of miniatures had already found its way to the landfill.

Curtis called Detective Scott's direct line, but he was out on another call, so Curtis told the receptionist he'd call back later. "What do you think about returning the ring to its rightful owner ourselves?"

"That's a great idea. Knowing how stressed I've felt waiting on news about the dollhouse, I'd hate to make her wait until the police get around to returning her ring."

With the dollhouse carefully wrapped and stowed in the back seat of his truck cab, Curtis drove Rachel to Happy Haven. As crazy as it seemed, the moment he held the ruby ring in his fingers, he wished it'd been his to offer to Rachel. What would she have thought if he'd heeded the impulse to drop to one knee and offer her his heart?

He mentally rolled his eyes and shook his head. Yeah, that would have freaked her out. Probably sent her running for the hills. They'd known each other less than a month after all. Only... The kiss they'd shared when she made him stop the car had felt like maybe she felt the same way about him as he did about her.

His heart pummeling his ribs, Curtis parked in the visitor parking at Happy Haven Retirement Home but made no move to climb out of the car. "I'm going to miss not having an excuse to spend so much time with you," he admitted softly.

"Do we need an excuse?" Her head tilted, and the smile that lit her eyes made his heart soar higher than the treetops. "I like spending time with you."

"You do?"

She squirmed. "Only, I'm afraid I've never been good at relationships, um, romantic ones I mean."

"I haven't had much practice myself."

Her cheeks grew rosy. "Until I lost the miniatures, I hadn't realized how much my dad's death still impacted me. But getting to know you and, I guess, finally seeing my mom through adult eyes, has helped me realize that I've been stuck in the past because I was afraid. Afraid of losing someone I love again." She reached for his hand. "I don't want to live in fear anymore."

Awed by her candor, he drew her hand to his lips and brushed a soft kiss across her knuckles. "From the first day we met, you've given me the courage to overcome my fears too. For me it's been fear of rejection."

Humiliation, really, but he'd prefer she remain blissfully unaware of just how undatable most women had found him in college.

"Rejection? You?" She scoffed. "I find that hard to believe. You're a great guy. A girl would have to be crazy not to want to go out with you."

Grinning, he pressed another kiss to her hand. "And you are great for a man's ego."

They agreed to continue the conversation later and headed into Happy Haven. The moment the home's administrator learned of the reason for their visit, he escorted them himself to Mrs. Ruby Bowen's room. He knocked on the woman's door, but there was no response.

"Wait here," he said. "I'll find out if anyone knows where she is."

A large picture window overlooking the grounds behind the building drew them down the hall. Passing a resident's open door, Curtis glimpsed the maintenance guy on a ladder, changing a light bulb in the ceiling fixture. Curtis tapped on the doorframe. "Hey, you'll never guess—"

At the sight of the dragon tattoo on Sean's arm, Curtis bit back his news about finding the stolen ring. Could Sean be the thief?

He'd seemed like such an affable guy.

Sean fitted the light fixture cover into place then climbed down the ladder and tugged his sleeves back to his wrists. "What were you saying?"

"Nothing. Sorry, I thought you were someone else."

"You know more than one maintenance guy who works here?" Sean cocked his head, narrowing an eye and widening the other in an expression he might have meant to be teasing.

But Curtis couldn't help stiffening in response. He looked at Rachel, but she was examining a poster on the wall. "Ha, no, I suppose not."

Sean folded his ladder. "What brings you two back here? Ever find that dollhouse?"

"Uh." Curtis mentally debated how to respond. Telling him yes might spur Sean to target them again, but would telling him they were here to return the ring put its owner in danger? Curtis's gaze dropped to Sean's toolbox, and he wondered if he'd find a pilfered something or another in it even now.

Curtis shook his head. Lita's boyfriend was the thief. Wasn't he?

"Here's Mrs. Bowen." The administrator strode toward them pushing a stately looking woman in a wheelchair. Her hair was perfectly coiffed, her makeup tasteful, if not a tad too heavy on the face powder, and her posture ramrod straight. To Mrs. Bowen, the administrator said, "This is the young couple who found your ring."

Something clattered in the room behind them, and Sean muttered an apology as he gathered his tools.

"Shall we sit by the window, and you can tell Mrs. Bowen your story," the administrator suggested, ignoring Sean.

The window afforded a view of gently rolling hills dotted with flowering crab apple trees of every color.

"The grounds are gorgeous," Rachel said.

The administrator beamed. "We're proud of them."

From the corner of his eye, Curtis caught sight of Sean leaving the room he'd been in and letting himself into one across the hall. If he had a master key to every room, surely they would have taken steps to rule him out as the thief from the first report of pilfering. Unless the pilferer and the jewel thief weren't the same person. Curtis let that possibility roll around in his brain a moment.

"Right, Curtis?"

Hearing Rachel say his name, Curtis shook the thoughts from his mind. "Sorry, what?"

"I was telling Mrs. Bowen what an adventure we've had hunting down the dollhouse."

"Oh yes." Curtis offered Mrs. Bowen a warm smile and noticed that while he'd been spinning yarns in his mind, Rachel had already returned the ring. Mrs. Bowen slipped it onto her pinky, not bothering to attempt to slide it over the gnarled joint of her ring finger. "Searching for the dollhouse was a true treasure hunt, complete with pirates trying to foil our success," he added with a wink.

"Pirates?" Mrs. Bowen's eyes sparkled with keen interest. "How interesting. *Treasure Island* was my favorite book as a child. Who were these pirates?"

"We aren't sure," Rachel admitted. "Someone who wanted to get their hands on the dollhouse and who knew we were looking for it."

"The lengths they were willing to go to recover it," Curtis continued, "were what raised our suspicions that they weren't after the dollhouse so much as something they'd hidden inside."

Mrs. Bowen clasped her hands with a loud clap. "My ring."

"Yes. Hazel told us it went missing the night before Vivien died. And we theorized that her death and the resulting dispersal of her belongings made it difficult for the thief to return to her room to recover his hidden booty before it was gone."

"How exciting!" Mrs. Bowen exclaimed.

The administrator, who'd taken a seat beside Mrs. Bowen's wheelchair, leaned forward. "What did they do that made you suspicious?"

By the time Curtis finished telling their story, Mrs. Bowen had paled considerably. "That's terrible. I'm so sorry recovering my ring caused you so much trouble."

Rachel covered the woman's hand with her own. "Please don't feel bad. Finding the dollhouse was very important to me because my great-great-grandfather crafted it. Finding your ring inside was just a happy coincidence."

"My one regret," Curtis interjected, "is that we didn't manage to recover Rachel's miniatures. They were a gift from her father, who died when she was ten, and very special to her."

A tear slipped down Mrs. Bowen's crinkled cheek, leaving a trail through her face powder. She reached her other hand across her lap and covered Rachel's hand, now nestled between her own. "Losing one's father is so hard. Vivien once told me that her dollhouse reminded her that Jesus has gone on ahead to prepare a home for us in the next life. And if her great-grandfather had put such love and care into fashioning every element of a child's toy house, she could scarcely imagine how wonderful the home that awaits us in heaven will be."

"I never thought of it that way," Rachel said.

The administrator cleared his throat, clearly discomfited by the display of emotion. "Well, I should get back to my office." He shook Curtis's hand, then Rachel's. "Thank you again for all your help."

"Our pleasure," they said as one voice.

Mrs. Bowen caught Rachel's hand. "Sit awhile longer. Please."

Rachel settled into a seat beside Mrs. Bowen, and Curtis pulled up a second chair.

Mrs. Bowen smiled down at her ring. "This was my mother's ring. My father gave it to me after she died." Mrs. Bowen's gaze sought Rachel's. "That's why I know how important recovering those miniatures must be to you."

Rachel nodded, her eyes filling with tears.

Mrs. Bowen pressed her fist to her chest. "But you'll always have him in your heart. And that's where it counts. You'll see his smile in your children's smile and hear his laughter in their laughter."

Rachel visibly gulped, and when her gaze strayed to Curtis's, his world tilted on its axis.

CHAPTER THIRTEEN

"Shall we head home?" Rachel said to Curtis after they'd left Mrs. Bowen.

"There's one more thing I'd like to check first."

"What's that?"

"I can't shrug off the feeling that Sean has something to do with the thefts."

Rachel stopped and gaped. "But he's the one who introduced us to Hazel so we could learn more about the dollhouse."

"And knowing we were looking for it, could've followed us. Then when Maribel called here asking about the dollhouse, he could've overheard someone say Evelyn took it home."

"So he burgled her house," Rachel whispered.

"Could be. I'm curious what he drives."

"How do you propose we figure that out without waiting until quitting time?"

"No problem. I overheard Sean tell a nurse he'd be done at noon today."

Rachel glanced at her watch. "Then we need to get out to the parking lot, or we might miss him."

"The trouble is there are two. One in front and one in back. I suspect the employees park in the rear because that's likely where they clock in, but the other day when we were here, Sean left out the front."

Rachel caught up to a kitchen staff member pushing a food cart. "Excuse me. Could you direct me to the staff locker rooms?"

The young woman motioned toward the elevator. "Go to the ground level and turn left."

"And do staff park in the back lot?"

"Most do, I think."

Rachel thanked her for the information, and Curtis tapped the elevator call button. "We should split up. How about you check the front lot and I'll check the back?" He handed her his truck keys. "If you don't see a black Corolla with *S* and *K* in the license plate, get my truck and meet me around back."

"Will do." Rachel dashed out the front door and scanned the parking lot. Spotting four black sedans scattered throughout the lot, she sprinted from one to the next. One had *S* and *K* on the plate, but it wasn't a Corolla. The sole Corolla had a NANAROCKS vanity plate. Rachel texted Curtis: No LUCK. DRIVING AROUND.

Curtis shrank behind the stairwell on ground level and texted Rachel. THE CAR'S HERE! CALL OFFICER SCOTT.

At Rachel's thumbs-up emoji, Curtis checked the time. Eight minutes before noon. Curtis couldn't be 100 percent sure the black Corolla he'd spotted near the back door was Sean's. Not until he clocked out. But Sean fit the description of their thief. And if there was the remotest chance he still had Rachel's miniatures in his car, Curtis wanted it searched before Sean left the premises.

Curtis gritted his teeth. Should he have waited outside to confront Sean? Ensured the black Corolla belonged to him first? His gut told him Sean had been up to something in the residents' rooms earlier. Up to more than changing light bulbs. He'd been nervous.

Then again, maybe seeing them with Mrs. Bowen and the administrator had been enough to trigger his nerves. Would he be brazen enough to steal again after the police had launched an investigation?

Whistling alerted Curtis to someone's approach. Peeking around the corner, he spotted Sean carrying a ladder and toolbox into the storage room opposite the men's locker room.

Soundlessly, Curtis snuck to the door and peered around it.

The dimly lit room was small, no bigger than eight-by-ten, lined with shelves overflowing with everything from light bulbs to plumbing supplies. Sean hunched over his toolbox, his back to the door. The next instant, he straightened and stuffed something into his front pants pocket then snapped the lid shut.

Before Curtis could formulate a plan, Sean turned toward the door. He jolted at the sight of Curtis but covered his surprise with a smooth, "Was there something you needed?" Sean pulled his cell phone from his pocket and glanced at it. "My shift ends in a few minutes, so if you have a repair request, I'll have to leave it for my boss."

"Is that your toolbox or Happy Haven's?" Curtis asked.

"Excuse me?"

As Curtis had hoped, the question threw him. "The toolbox. Does it belong to you?"

"No. The home supplies all our tools." Sean moved toward the door, clearly not interested in chatting, and expecting Curtis to step out of his way.

Curtis held his ground. "Aren't you curious why I ask?"

"Look, I'm expected somewhere and don't have time for twenty questions." Sean motioned to the doorway Curtis blocked. "Now, do you mind?"

Curtis braced his hands on the doorframe. He'd probably already tipped Sean off that they were on to his thieving. If he let him out of his sight before the police arrived, Sean would dump whatever he'd slipped into his pocket before he could be caught with it.

Advancing shoulder first, Sean shot him an amused look then suddenly slapped off the lights and catapulted a bony elbow straight into Curtis's gut.

Curtis staggered back. "Stop!" He gulped air. Sean had already disappeared from the hall. Curtis dashed after him. "The police are on their way."

Sean hit the exit door's crash bar at a run.

Curtis raced after him.

Sean blipped his key fob, and the black Corolla's door lock clicked open.

Curtis lunged for him but only managed to snag the tail of his jacket.

Sean shed the jacket and dove into the driver's seat, almost slamming the door on Curtis's fingers when he tried to grab it.

Curtis slapped the window. "Why run?" he yelled. "They know where you live. Running only makes it worse."

The car's engine roared to life, and Sean threw the car into reverse.

Curtis leaped back before the side mirror clipped him.

But before Sean was halfway out, Rachel sped down the hill into the lot and careened to a stop behind Sean's car, blocking his escape.

"Out of my way," Sean yelled and laid on his horn, but he didn't try to ram the truck. With a row of cars in front of him and a car on either side, Sean was boxed in.

The sound of his horn drew curious staff and residents from the building. Then the wail of an approaching police siren added to the excitement. Officer Scott whipped his car around to face Curtis's truck, flanked by a police cruiser.

Sean must have concluded he was beat, because he turned off his car's engine.

Rachel jumped from the truck, and Curtis scooped her into an exuberant hug. "Way to block him in! That was smart thinking."

She grinned. "What can I say? I'm not just a pretty face."

Still holding her around the waist with one arm, he reached up and cupped her cheek with his other hand. "But such a pretty face."

She blushed at the compliment—a response that looked so much better on her than it had ever felt on him. "I'm glad you picked up on Sean's caginess. I never would've guessed it was him. He seemed so nice."

"He hasn't admitted to anything yet. But the way he ran sure makes him look guilty."

"Officer Preston will take your statements." Officer Scott motioned to the police cruiser. "And we'll take it from here."

"Could you search his trunk before we go? See if he still has Rachel's miniatures," Curtis asked.

"Unless he grants us permission, we'll have to wait on a search warrant."

"Seriously?" Rachel blurted. "He tried to flee. He's obviously hiding something."

"Trust me. Suspects concoct a slew of excuses for running. Some are even believable. But don't worry. We'll ask him about the miniatures. And we'll let you know if we locate them."

Rachel nodded, although her expression said she wasn't happy.

CHAPTER FOURTEEN

After they'd given the officer their statements, Rachel handed Curtis his truck keys.

"Home?"

"I think we should pay Lita a visit. We owe her and Evan an apology."

Curtis winced. "Yeah, I guess we do." His gaze strayed to Sean now sitting in the rear of the police cruiser. "Despite our mistakes, we make an impressive crime-fighting team. Mrs. Bowen has her ring back. The real bad guy is in custody. And we've recovered at least part of your family's legacy."

Rachel offered a tremulous smile. Realizing they were guilty of making horrible false allegations against Evan dulled her elation over the dollhouse's recovery.

Curtis gave her hand a squeeze before starting his truck and carefully navigating his way between police vehicles. "You know... almost every crime show I've watched depicts cops interrogating at least one wrong guy as if he's guilty."

Rachel sighed, appreciating his effort to lighten her mood. But their accusations weren't the only thing weighing on her mind. Evan and Lita wanted the dollhouse. And maybe Lita deserved it more than Rachel. Even if she wasn't the legal heir. She'd been close to Vivien. Rachel hadn't known her at all.

Then again, Lita hadn't wanted the house when her mother first asked her. Would she give it the care it deserved and pass it on to her children's children one day?

Rachel's chest tightened. Hadn't she been as thoughtless toward the specialness of the miniatures her dad had given her? If she'd truly valued them as a legacy to be preserved for the next generation, her mother would never have considered giving them away.

Rachel winced at the reminder they were still missing. Relinquishing the dollhouse to Lita would be so much easier if she at least had the precious carvings her father had given her.

"They'll forgive us," Curtis said encouragingly. "You can't beat yourself up over this. They understand how important the miniatures are to you. Our promise not to turn them in for taking the ring if they simply returned them proved that."

"I hope so."

When Curtis and Rachel arrived at Lita's home, a motorcycle sat in the driveway. Curtis parked behind it. "Looks as if they're both here."

"Hmm."

Lita burst out the front door and barreled toward them. "You've got some nerve coming back here. I told you Evan didn't do it. And you made me think the worst about him."

"You heard?" Curtis asked.

"My friend works at Happy Haven. She called and said they arrested some maintenance guy."

"Yes." Rachel stepped closer and lifted her chin to force herself to meet Lita's hard gaze. "And we came to apologize for our horrible accusations."

Evan joined Lita on the walkway in time to hear the apology. He curved his arm around her waist. "I'm used to everyone assuming the worse about me. When I got angry about it, my mom said it's my own fault and that if I don't want people to be so quick to judge, I should change my look."

Rachel ducked her head, knowing she'd been equally quick to judge, since his tattoo was so similar to the thief's.

"But like I told Lita. This is who I am. I like my hair long and wearing black and riding a motorcycle and my tattoos. If people can't see past them to the nice guy I am, that's their problem, not mine."

Rachel recalled the thrift store manager mentioning his scary temper, but like Curtis had said, they were all works in progress. Or maybe only the woman's preconceived ideas about Evan made his response seem scary.

Lita curled her arm around Evan's waist and rested her head against his shoulder. "And it's their loss too."

"You're right," Curtis agreed. "We hope you can forgive us for thinking the worst about you. The miniatures mean so much to Rachel, we grasped at straws to try to find them."

Evan nodded, and when his gaze shifted to Rachel, his eyes held genuine understanding. "Did you find them?"

The muscle in Rachel's cheek involuntarily flinched. "Not yet. I'm still hoping Sean might confess to taking them and tell the police where he dumped them."

"I'm sorry," Evan said, and it sounded as if he truly was.

Rachel filled her chest with air and held it until the trembling that had begun to overtake her limbs eased. "We did recover Vivien's dollhouse though. And"—she gulped and fixed her gaze on Lita—"and if you'd still like to keep it for your children one day, I want you to have it." Rachel blinked at the sting in her eyes. "Vivien was your family too, no matter what the law says. And I know you'll cherish it as it deserves."

Lita wrinkled her nose. "To be honest, I probably wouldn't. I've never been into dolls. Evan just figured that one day our kids might be, because his sisters were."

Rachel shifted from one foot to the other, emotion welling up so quickly she couldn't speak.

"I can tell the dollhouse is way more important to you."

"Thank you," Rachel blubbered.

"Could I offer a suggestion?" Curtis chimed in. "Perhaps you could choose a piece from the dollhouse?" He looked to Rachel and silently sought her approval.

"That's a wonderful idea," Rachel agreed. "Maybe one of the dolls, or the little dog, to remember your grandmother by?"

Lita's face instantly brightened. "I love that idea. Gran used to have a little dog. A real one, just like her miniature. I adored it as a kid. I would love to keep the carving to remember her by. I know exactly the spot on the shelf above my dresser where I can keep it, right beside a picture of me and Gran the day of the sophomore prom." She smiled at Evan. "It was our first date, remember?"

He dropped a kiss on her lips. "How could I forget?"

The love radiating between them seemed more mature than any Rachel had ever witnessed in her high school days. And it stirred a deep longing in her. Would she and Curtis share a connection like that one day? She thought of the conversation they'd promised to continue later. She pressed a palm to her stomach. Here she'd told him she didn't want to live in fear anymore, and just the thought of continuing the conversation unleashed a cave full of blind bats battering around her belly. She drew in a deep breath. If Mom could do this, so could she. Rachel winged a prayer heavenward. *Lord, help me to walk boldly into the future.*

That evening, after speaking with Officer Scott, Curtis announced, "Sean confessed to everything."

Rachel whirled from where she'd been arranging the dollhouse on a corner curio cabinet in the living room. "Even disabling my car?" she asked.

"Yup. Even breaking into mine. He followed us from our first visit to Happy Haven. He wanted my address so he could spy on us, hoping we'd lead him to the dollhouse."

"So he burgled Evelyn's place too?"

"Yup. He confessed to her break-in and ours and will return Ian's cash. And he gave Officer Scott a general idea of the area where he dumped your miniatures once he realized they weren't Vivien's. Are you up for one more treasure hunt?"

Laughter filled Rachel's eyes. "Sure, why not!"

Two hours later, the air had chilled considerably as dusk slid into night. And they were no closer to finding the elusive bin. "This is where he said," Curtis groused. "Let's try a little farther up the road."

"It's okay," Rachel said.

"We've got to be close," Curtis insisted.

Rachel caught him by the arm and pulled him into a hug. "It's okay. God has already given me more than enough gifts today."

The warmth of her words wrapped around his heart. More than anything, he'd wanted to restore her dad's special gift, but she was right. They had so much to already be thankful for. Still, he'd convince her to try again tomorrow, just in case. He leaned back a fraction so he could look into her face. The moonlight twinkled in her eyes. "Rachel Jones, I'm afraid I've fallen hopelessly in love with you."

Her smile widened. "No need to fear. The feeling is mutual, I assure you."

He grinned and tenderly claimed her lips. They were soft and responsive beneath his, tasting of moonlit walks in pine forests and forever.

Two months later, an official-looking letter from the law firm of Lloyd, Lloyd & McIntosh arrived at the house. "Is this the law firm handling Vivien's estate?" Curtis asked, handing the letter to Rachel.

She glanced at the envelope and handed it back to him. "It's addressed to you."

"What?" Curtis slid his thumb under the flap. "Why would a law firm be writing me? I don't have any long-lost uncles or cousins I don't know about."

"Are you sure?" Rachel teased. "If Mom hadn't given away my miniatures, I might never have discovered mine."

Curtis leaned over and kissed her. "Not to mention fallen in love with a handsome carver who adores you."

"Mmm." Her lips smiled beneath his.

Curtis pulled back reluctantly and scanned the letter. "This is amazing."

They'd resumed their search for the box containing Rachel's miniatures and finally located them, unharmed, not far from where they'd stopped searching that evening. Now the miniatures were reunited in the dollhouse, which sat atop Rachel's dresser, waiting for its next home. A home he knew he and Rachel would someday make together, when the time was right.

"What?"

"Mrs. Bowen left us her ruby ring." The sweet woman had died peacefully in her sleep only two weeks after they'd met. But she had made such an indelible impression on Rachel that they attended her Celebration of Life service at Happy Haven a few days later. Curtis bit his lip, too excited by his sudden idea to wait until he had the ring in hand. "What do you think about having an antique ruby as an engagement ring?"

Rachel sucked in a surprised breath. "You're asking me to marry you?"

Curtis dropped to one knee. "With all of my heart."

Dear Reader,

There is nothing quite so enthralling as sitting in front of a dollhouse, the rooms spread out before you, the tiny pieces of furniture, clocks, dishes, books, and rugs all arranged to your own liking. As a little girl, you dream of one day being mistress of a house like this one. As a grown woman, you disappear into a world of miniature perfection.

Both of us have a connection to dollhouses. Sandra built a dollhouse for her own daughters, and she plays with dollhouses with her grandchildren. Patricia discovered dollhouses as a grown woman, and has several miniature rooms set up that she's always adding to. Dollhouses aren't just for little girls; they can be a passion for a lifetime, or a passion spanning generations, as we explore in our book.

Life is never so easily organized as a dollhouse room though. Real life gets messy and difficult. Real hearts get broken. And that is why we are both so grateful that Jesus came to redeem our real-life messes into something beautiful for Him.

As you read our stories, we hope you dream about a beautiful future with God at the center of your life. Will it be dollhouse perfect? Not a chance! It'll be something even better—redeemed, protected, and made even more beautiful in God's hands.

Patricia and Sandra

About the Authors

Patricia Johns

Patricia Johns is a *Publishers Weekly* bestselling author who writes sweet and inspirational romances. She also has several Amish romances and a cozy mystery. She writes from Alberta, Canada, where the winters are long and snowy—perfect for writing. She lives with her husband, her son, and one rambunctious parrot who only settles down when she is sitting at Patricia's desk. It's a life that suits her perfectly.

Sandra Orchard

Sandra Orchard writes fast-paced, keep-you-guessing stories with a generous dash of sweet romance. Touted by Midwest Book Reviews as "a true master of the [mystery] genre," Sandra is also a bestselling romantic-suspense author. Her novels have garnered numerous Canadian Christian writing awards as well as an RT Reviewers' Choice Award, a National Readers' Choice Award, a Holt Medallion, and a Daphne du Maurier Award of Excellence. When not plotting crimes, Sandra enjoys hiking with her hubby, working in their vegetable gardens, and playing make-believe with their dozen young grandchildren. Sandra hails from Niagara, Canada, and loves to hear from readers.

STORY BEHIND THE NAME

Last Chance, Iowa

Today, Last Chance, Iowa, along the Mormon Trail, hemmed in by farmland and forests, is marked only by a large cemetery. The village was founded in 1851 and acquired a post office in 1865. Many Mormon emigrants and gold seekers passed through the town on their way to lands farther west. Before the railroad bypassed the small village, condemning it to obsolescence, it boasted a general store, a post office, a church, a blacksmith shop, a deep well with a windmill, a brick kiln, a school three-quarters of a mile northeast of the village, about ten houses, and the first doctor of Union township. Although the post office closed in 1888, the church survived well into the second half of the twentieth century. There are several stories about how the village came by its name. A newspaper article from 1871 claims it came about as a joke. The owner of the general store, when asked the name of the town by a traveler, realized it didn't have a name, and so he called it Last Chance. Another story is that all the other names proposed for the town to the postal service were rejected, and they had one last chance to come up with a name.

Gran's Chili Sauce

Ingredients:

12 large tomatoes
2 large onions, chopped
4 green peppers, chopped
1 stalk celery, chopped
4 apples, chopped
4½ cups brown sugar
2 tablespoons salt

1 teaspoon dry mustard
½ teaspoon black pepper
½ teaspoon cayenne pepper
1 tablespoon cinnamon
1 teaspoon ground allspice
1 pint apple cider vinegar

Directions:

Skin tomatoes by briefly dunking them in boiling water. Mash tomatoes in large pot then add onions, green peppers, celery, apples, brown sugar, spices, and vinegar. Stir well. Simmer for one to two hours. Hot pack in hot sterilized jars to preserve for future use.

Make sweet chili con carne by combining one jar chili sauce with browned ground beef and onions, chili powder, spaghetti sauce, and beans of your choice. The grandkids prefer tinned baked beans, navy beans, or pinto beans.

Read on for a sneak peek of another exciting book in the Love's a Mystery series!

Love's a Mystery *in*
Panic, Pennsylvania
by Elizabeth Ludwig &
Barbara Early

A Heart Divided
By Elizabeth Ludwig

Panic, Pennsylvania
July 1917

"There he is…that *Mueller* boy."

The derisive words rasped like sandpaper on Hannah Walker's skin, as irritating and abrasive as the murmurings of treason and spies that poisoned every corner of their small town. Daily, Hannah told herself she would have no part of them. In fact, if she had any sense, she'd ignore the whispers and march right out of Smith's General Store…but she didn't, because with curiosity prickling the nape of her neck, she couldn't help but look.

A few feet away, Niklas Mueller browsed an assortment of pots and pans hanging from hooks in the window. Outlined against the hot July sun streaming through the glass, his shoulders looked even broader, the tilt of his head prouder than when she'd last seen him.

Lifting his hand, Niklas snagged one of the pots and then turned. Hair dark as pitch feathered out from beneath the brim of a battered brown hat. Eyes and eyebrows to match filled a face bronzed by the sun.

For a second, their eyes met. Held. Slowing time. Until a breathless whisper at Hannah's elbow broke her trance.

"Did you hear that? I *told* you people didn't trust the Muellers."

Sucking in a breath, Hannah dragged her gaze away to scowl at her friend. "Edith Davis, you've known Niklas your whole life. You know the rumors about him and his father are nothing more than gossip spurred by the war. And if you haven't noticed, he's hardly a *boy*."

Edith's eyebrows rose an inch to meet the flowers dripping from her linen cloche hat. "Does that mean you *have* noticed?"

Hannah pursed her lips and reached around Edith for a bolt of plain cotton fabric. "I was merely making an observation."

"As was I," Edith whispered. Then she drew up short and straightened, her brown eyes widening. "Oh."

"Good afternoon, Miss Davis."

Hannah immediately recognized the voice rumbling over her shoulder. She blew out a breath and turned.

Niklas touched his finger to the brim of his hat, his sooty brown gaze coming to rest on her. "Miss Walker."

Hearing her surname on his lips was quite different than when they were all growing up and attending the schoolhouse at the edge of town. Then, they'd thought nothing of calling each other by their Christian names. Now, hearing him sound so formal left her feeling a bit flustered.

She inclined her head and reciprocated in kind. "Mr. Mueller."

A smile twitched his lips, as though he alone were privy to her secret thoughts. But of course, that couldn't be. She ignored the urge to press her fingers to her warm cheeks and instead motioned to the pot in his hand. "I didn't realize you cook."

Niklas's grin grew. "It's only Papa and me, so I suppose one of us has to. Either that or starve."

"Yes, well, true enough, I suppose." A second heat wave burned across Hannah's skin.

Niklas nodded to the fabric clutched in her arms. "I didn't realize you could sew."

She couldn't. She despised the chore and complained about it regularly, which explained the grin that was even now widening his full lips. Depositing the bolt of fabric back on the table, Hannah shook her head and smoothed her hands over the folds of her blue skirt. "Edith and I were just browsing."

The mention of Edith's name was like a bucket of water dousing Niklas's smile. "Right. Forgive me for interrupting." He pulled back a step and hitched his thumb toward the register. "I should go. Papa will be waiting."

"Of course. Please tell Mr. Mueller hello for us." At her side, Edith remained silent, so Hannah prompted her with a sharp nudge of her elbow.

"Ow…um…yes, please." Rubbing her ribs, Edith speared Hannah with a dark glare.

"I will tell him. Good day." Giving a nod to each, Niklas spun and wound past rows of barrels brimming with food goods toward the counter.

"Hannah, why did you say that?" Edith punctuated the question with a stomp of her foot. "Now people will think we like the Muellers."

"We do like the Muellers," Hannah said, loud enough for a couple of curious onlookers lingering nearby to hear. "They have always been good and faithful neighbors, and I challenge anyone to say otherwise."

Both eavesdropping women sniffed at her words and continued meandering down the aisle, away from them.

With them gone, Hannah rounded on Edith. "You've been listening to that Sally Bradshaw again, haven't you? We can't let what she or any other gossips say influence how we feel about the Muellers."

"Why not? They're German, and we *are* at war with Germany." Edith narrowed her eyes and pressed her lips tight.

Hannah inhaled sharply through her nose. "Have you forgotten how Karl Mueller helped your father the day his ox landed in the ditch? What do you think would have happened if it hadn't been for Mr. Mueller and his team of horses?"

Edith's gaze fell. "No, I haven't forgotten."

Hannah leaned closer. "And what about when Mr. Mueller loaded his wagon with vegetables for the Sampsons after those wild boars rooted through their garden? Or when Niklas helped the Van Pelts rebuild their barn after it burned down? Those aren't the only instances, surely. There are plenty of people who can attest to all that the Muellers have done for our community."

Edith's face flushed bright red. "You're…you're right. I shouldn't have said anything. I'm sorry."

Hannah relaxed a bit, but the knot in the pit of her stomach remained. The country had only been at war for a short while. What would happen if it dragged on for months—or years—the way her father feared? What would people like Sally Bradshaw say about the Muellers then? Suddenly, she no longer felt like shopping.

Hannah motioned to the elderly proprietor hovering like a gaunt scarecrow behind the counter. "Likely Mr. Smith has my order ready by now. I should get home."

"Me too." Edith grasped her arm. "Oh, but Hannah, you never said if you're planning on going to the church picnic." Her eyes brightened. "All of our friends will be there."

Their friends? Did that include Sally and her two bullish brothers? But why should they stop Hannah from enjoying herself?

She lifted her chin. "We'll be there. I'll bring one of those chess pies you like so much," she added, before Edith could ask.

"Good. I'll see you later." Edith gave a wave, the curls she took such pains to pin each night bouncing prettily against her cheeks as she flounced to the door.

Hannah frowned and fingered a lock of her own hair. How she wished for waves like Edith's, so pretty and thick and blond. She always looked like a ray of sunshine even on the gloomiest of days. Instead, Hannah's hair stayed stubbornly straight, no matter how much Liquid Silmerine she applied. And brown—not a pretty russet brown like Sally Bradshaw's. Hers was mousy and plain.

"Hannah? Is everything all right?" She startled at the voice at her shoulder and turned to see Mr. Smith with his hands on his hips, thin elbows jutting from his sleeve garters like two knobby twigs. "I called your name several times, but it was like you couldn't hear me." He pointed to the counter. "Your order is ready."

"I'm so sorry. I was just…" Hannah shook her head. No sense explaining. He already thought her a ninny. "Thank you, Mr. Smith."

He bobbed his grizzled head and turned to lead her back to the counter. "How are things out at your place? I noticed an extra sack of flour in your order. Your wheat crop looking all right?"

"Oh yes, it's fine. Pa says the wind laid some wheat down a few days ago, but it should recover by harvest time."

"That's good to hear," Mr. Smith said. "Harvest is still a couple of weeks off." He patted the list Hannah had given him. "Let me know if there's anything else you folks need."

Hannah thanked him and, after paying him, slipped outside to where one of Mr. Smith's store hands had her wagon loaded and ready. She frowned, seeing it was Ernest Bradshaw. At seventeen years old, Ernest was lazy and tended to load the wagon sloppily. Still, it was better that she rearrange the supplies herself than to ask him to help and have to contend with another of his sly glances. And, more often than not, when he helped with their order, Hannah found items were missing when she put everything away.

Catching sight of her, Ernest brushed his hands across his trousers and circled to meet her. "Hiya, Hannah. I thought I recognized your wagon. Loaded it up myself."

"Hello, Ernest." Hannah stifled a grimace at the bag of flour that threatened to topple a basket of apples. Pa would be angry if they arrived bruised. She shifted closer to the wagon. "I'm afraid I don't have a tip for you today."

The expectant smile slipped a bit, quickly replaced by the arrogant smirk Hannah found so irritating.

"That's all right. You can make it up another time." Stepping closer, he offered her a hand up onto the seat.

Another time? She wasn't sure she liked the sound of that. Instead of agreeing, she merely smiled, accepted his help into the wagon, and gathered up the reins. "Thanks again. Goodbye, Ernest."

"Bye, Hannah."

He moved to give room to the wagon as Hannah chirped to the mare, but she could feel his gaze lingering on her as she swung onto the street and rounded the corner to head out of town.

Shuddering, Hannah urged the mare into a faster clip. The apples and flour could wait, because the last thing she wanted was to spend one second longer than necessary under Ernest Bradshaw's uncomfortable stare. If that meant bruised apples, so be it.

Of course, eventually, she'd have to deal with him. The length of his glances was becoming increasingly improper. If she wasn't careful, she'd be the next topic for the gossips, a problem her father and Uncle Titus surely didn't need—not with business being so poor. The war made many afraid to spend what little savings they had—and who could blame them? It wasn't like anyone could know how long this troubling season would last or how bad it would get.

That last thought settled like a shroud over Hannah's shoulders and stayed firmly in place all the way home. No matter how hard she tried to shake it—she couldn't help but wonder.

How bad *would* it get? How long before the townsfolk of Panic let panic overtake them?

A NOTE FROM THE EDITORS

We hope you enjoyed another volume in the Love's a Mystery series, created by Guideposts. For over seventy-five years, Guideposts, a nonprofit organization, has been driven by a vision of a world filled with hope. We aspire to be the voice of a trusted friend, a friend who makes you feel more hopeful and connected.

By making a purchase from Guideposts, you join our community in touching millions of lives, inspiring them to believe that all things are possible through faith, hope, and prayer. Your continued support allows us to provide uplifting resources to those in need. Whether through our communities, websites, apps, or publications, we inspire our audiences, bring them together, and comfort, uplift, entertain, and guide them. Visit us at guideposts.org to learn more.

We would love to hear from you. Write us at Guideposts, P.O. Box 5815, Harlan, Iowa 51593 or call us at (800) 932-2145. Did you love *Love's a Mystery in Last Chance, Iowa*? Leave a review for this product on guideposts.org/shop. Your feedback helps others in our community find relevant products.

Find inspiration, find faith, find Guideposts.

Shop our best sellers and favorites at
guideposts.org/shop
Or scan the QR code to go directly to our Shop

**While you are waiting for the next fascinating story
in the *Love's a Mystery* series, check out
some other Guideposts mystery series!**

SAVANNAH SECRETS

Welcome to Savannah, Georgia, a picture-perfect Southern city known for its manicured parks, moss-covered oaks, and antebellum architecture. Walk down one of the cobblestone streets, and you'll come upon Magnolia Investigations. It is here where two friends have joined forces to unravel some of Savannah's deepest secrets. Tag along as clues are exposed, red herrings discarded, and thrilling surprises revealed. Find inspiration in the special bond between Meredith Bellefontaine and Julia Foley. Cheer the friends on as they listen to their hearts and rely on their faith to solve each new case that comes their way.

The Hidden Gate
A Fallen Petal
Double Trouble
Whispering Bells

Where Time Stood Still
The Weight of Years
Willful Transgressions
Season's Meetings
Southern Fried Secrets
The Greatest of These
Patterns of Deception
The Waving Girl
Beneath a Dragon Moon
Garden Variety Crimes
Meant for Good
A Bone to Pick
Honeybees & Legacies
True Grits
Sapphire Secret
Jingle Bell Heist
Buried Secrets
A Puzzle of Pearls
Facing the Facts
Resurrecting Trouble
Forever and a Day

Mysteries of Martha's Vineyard

Priscilla Latham Grant has inherited a lighthouse! So with not much more than a strong will and a sore heart, the recent widow says goodbye to her lifelong Kansas home and heads to the quaint and historic island of Martha's Vineyard, Massachusetts. There, she comes face-to-face with adventures, which include her trusty canine friend, Jake, three delightful cousins she didn't know she had, and Gerald O'Bannon, a handsome Coast Guard captain—plus head-scratching mysteries that crop up with surprising regularity.

A Light in the Darkness
Like a Fish Out of Water
Adrift
Maiden of the Mist
Making Waves
Don't Rock the Boat
A Port in the Storm
Thicker Than Water
Swept Away
Bridge Over Troubled Waters

Smoke on the Water
Shifting Sands
Shark Bait
Seascape in Shadows
Storm Tide
Water Flows Uphill
Catch of the Day
Beyond the Sea
Wider Than an Ocean
Sheeps Passing in the Night
Sail Away Home
Waves of Doubt
Lifeline
Flotsam & Jetsam
Just Over the Horizon

MIRACLES & MYSTERIES OF MERCY HOSPITAL

～⚬ ⚬～

Four talented women from very different walks of life witness the miracles happening around them at Mercy Hospital and soon become fast friends. Join Joy Atkins, Evelyn Perry, Anne Mabry, and Shirley Bashore as, together, they solve the puzzling mysteries that arise at this Charleston, South Carolina, historic hospital—rumored to be under the protection of a guardian angel. Come along as our quartet of faithful friends solve mysteries, stumble upon a few of the hospital's hidden and forgotten passageways, and discover historical treasures along the way! This fast-paced series is filled with inspiration, adventure, mystery, delightful humor, and loads of Southern charm!

Where Mercy Begins
Prescription for Mystery
Angels Watching Over Me
A Change of Art
Conscious Decisions
Surrounded by Mercy
Broken Bonds

Mercy's Healing

To Heal a Heart

A Cross to Bear

Merciful Secrecy

Sunken Hopes

Hair Today, Gone Tomorrow

Pain Relief

Redeemed by Mercy

A Genius Solution

A Hard Pill to Swallow

Ill at Ease

'Twas the Clue Before Christmas

Find more inspiring stories in these best-loved Guideposts fiction series!

Mysteries of Lancaster County

Follow the Classen sisters as they unravel clues and uncover hidden secrets in Mysteries of Lancaster County. As you get to know these women and their friends, you'll see how God brings each of them together for a fresh start in life.

Secrets of Wayfarers Inn

Retired schoolteachers find themselves owners of an old warehouse-turned-inn that is filled with hidden passages, buried secrets, and stunning surprises that will set them on a course to puzzling mysteries from the Underground Railroad.

Tearoom Mysteries Series

Mix one stately Victorian home, a charming lakeside town in Maine, and two adventurous cousins with a passion for tea and hospitality. Add a large scoop of intriguing mystery, and sprinkle generously with faith, family, and friends, and you have the recipe for *Tearoom Mysteries.*

Ordinary Women of the Bible

Richly imagined stories—based on facts from the Bible—have all the plot twists and suspense of a great mystery, while bringing you fascinating insights on what it was like to be a woman living in the ancient world.

To learn more about these books, visit Guideposts.org/Shop